THE
CULTIST'S
WIFE

BJ SIKES

The Cultist's Wife
Copyright © 2024 by BJ Sikes.

All rights reserved. Printed in the United States of America. No part of this book may be used or reproduced in any manner whatsoever without written permission except in the case of brief quotations embodied in critical articles or reviews.

This book is a work of fiction. Names, characters, businesses, organizations, places, events and incidents either are the product of the author's imagination or are used fictitiously. Any resemblance to actual persons, living or dead, events, or locales is entirely coincidental.

For information contact :
bjsikesauthor@gmail.com
www.bjsikesauthor.com

Cover design by Sleepy Fox Studio
Book Formatting by Derek Murphy @Creativindie
ISBN: 979-8-9898010-1-5

First Edition: May 2024

Dedicated to all of the children who follow their parents away from the safety of their homes and into the wilderness.

CHAPTER ONE

Near Bath, England, 1908

Fragrant smoke swirled around Clara, its spicy, musky scent relaxing her. She breathed deeply, released from her corset's constraints. She was free for at least an hour or two this morning before her obligations descended again. Clara's heavy silk robe caressed her body and she shivered with pleasure. She settled more comfortably onto the large cushion on the floor of her darkened sitting room and focused on the single candle flame in front of her.

A childish voice shrieked outside her sitting room. Clara sighed and glanced at the door.

Can't Nanny manage the children for an hour? I just need some time to myself.

The noise faded and her sitting room grew quiet. She took a long steadying breath, trying to regain her inner peace. Her reading into Esoterica and Spiritualism had hinted at possibilities of life beyond the constraints and expectations of society. Her marriage, her home, even having children had all been others' choices. She needed guidance on how to become her own person, to find her own happiness. Her knees ached as she knelt on the cushion, and she shifted. Her feet were numb and tingling. She wiggled her toes and exhaled.

How do the gurus sit like this for hours?

Gathering her focus again, she determined to sit still until her spirit guide manifested and gave her the advice she sought. She had never actually seen her spirit guide or spoken to him, but her references assured her of his presence. She just needed to focus long enough. It had been so much easier to see the spirit world when she was a child. Clara leaned forward and sprinkled more incense on the brazier. A cloud billowed up and she watched as patterns formed in the musky, intoxicating smoke. Coughing a little, Clara squinted in the darkness.

Was that a face in the smoke? Could he be manifesting to her finally?

Clara struggled to sit still. Her body tensed with excitement and her breathing came fast and shallow. The image coalesced further, and the face began to look familiar. She squinted in the gloom.

That face…it's so familiar. Who is it? Oh no…it can't be…

Disappointment fell heavy upon her. The face in the smoke resembled her long-absent husband Theophilus. But why would her spirit guide look like him? Clara scowled at the likeness of her husband's face. This apparition couldn't be her spirit guide. She had somehow conjured up a vision of Theophilus. Her heart thumped hard. Why should he appear to her now when he had been in the Bahamas for five years? Was he dead and his ghost was haunting her? As if in answer to her questioning, the mouth opened in a silent scream and the eyes grew wide in terror. Clara gasped and cringed back from the brazier. Cold crept across her skin. She shivered and reached for her shawl, draping it around her shoulders without shifting her stare from the phantasm. It continued to scream without making a sound, its gaping mouth opening and closing. She pulled the shawl closer, her hands clenching the fabric.

The ghosts I saw as a child never looked like that. I don't think he's dead. Perhaps he's in danger.

The smoke drifted higher, and the phantasm dissipated. Tears filled her eyes. Clara rose off her pillow, wincing at the tingling in her feet. Theophilus's portrait above the mantel, illuminated by the single candle, glared down at her. Life with that cold, brutal man had been joyless. She glowered back at the image, wishing she had the courage to take the painting down.

I wanted insight into becoming happy. Does the road to my happiness lie with helping Theophilus?

She shook her head, remembering all the times when he had laughed at her spiritual explorations. He would find it ludicrous if she told him about having a vision of him being in trouble. But she had been seeking guidance from her spirit guide. Would she have to go to the Bahamas to help Theophilus? She paced across the little sitting room to the window and pulled back the heavy drapes. The misty green countryside stretched away into the distance.

I don't want to leave England to be with Theophilus. He'll take over my life like he did when he was here.

Tears welled up in her eyes and she gulped, trying to suppress them. They poured hot down her cheeks. Clara pressed her trembling hands against her face, but the tears kept coming. Her sobs shook her body and she moaned, trying to catch her breath.

Stop it, stop it. Control yourself, Clara.

She shoved a fist into her mouth to stifle the undignified sounds and sank to her knees, head resting on the windowsill. She fought the urge to shriek her fury.

I can't go. I hate him. I hate him.

Clara sucked in a harsh breath, shuddering. The anger dissipated as quickly as it had overtaken her, leaving Clara weak and empty, her face wet. She pulled out a handkerchief and wiped her tears away. She'd need to repair her ravaged face before tea. She looked back at the brazier. The manifestation had been so vivid. Was it a true seeing or guilt over her hatred of her husband?

She couldn't give up her quest for happiness to go to Theophilus because of this vision. Could she?

***

The sitting room door clicked shut and behind the bookshelf, Elsie sagged with relief. She thought Mama would never leave. Why had she been crying? Elsie clambered out from her hiding place. She pushed her long hair off her face and smoothed down the ruffles of her party dress. The incense smoke still swirled around the darkened room, and she stifled a cough. How could Mama stand to sit here for hours with that stinky smoke? It was so dark. She could barely see anything. Embers in the brazier on the floor flared for a moment, brightening the room. Elsie peered at the swirling smoke. Shapes formed in the air, eerie faces that smiled and frowned at her. Curious, she moved closer. She could almost hear them talking to her. She eyed the shapes in the smoke, trying to make out what they were saying.

The door opened and Elsie started. Her mother stood framed in the doorway, a silhouette tense and still. "Elsinoe, what are you doing in here?"

Elsie blinked and gestured at the brazier. "There's people, Mama. In the smoke."

Her mother moved closer, leaning down to peer at the cloud of smoke. "I can't see anything."

The indistinct faces in the smoke wanted something, Elsie was sure. But what? "I don't think they're really here, are they?" Her voice sounded strange in her ears. "Mama, I think they're ghosts."

Mama stood up straight and waved her arms to dissipate the smoke. "No, Elsinoe, there are no ghosts here. There's no such thing." She didn't sound convinced.

Elsie examined her mother, pale and distant, staring at the smouldering brazier. "But Mama, I saw something. What do they want? Is the house haunted?"

Her mother wrapped her arm around Elsie's shoulders. "Don't be silly, of course the house isn't haunted. You just have a vivid imagination. Back to the nursery now. I'll see you at my party. And Elsinoe, please don't enter my sitting room without permission."

Elsie bit her lip and trudged out. Mama was wrong. There were ghosts. And they wanted to tell Elsie something.

* * *

Clara closed the door behind her daughter and moved through her sitting room. Ghosts. The child had reached the age when the spirit world opened to her. Clara sighed. That ease was lost to her now. She picked up her latest Spiritualist text. She still had some time to herself before the party. Cradling her book, she drifted over to the tall window, pulled back the heavy brocade curtains, and let the misty grey daylight of an English spring trickle into the room. Clara slumped against the window frame and peered down into the garden. Far below, Elsie raced out of the house towards her brother. Laughter reached Clara's high lookout, the laughter of children playing. Her children. They rolled down the grassy hill, clad in their party clothes. Clara placed her hand against the cool glass.

It seems so long ago that I felt that unbound.

She let the curtain drop and the room darkened again, illuminated only by flickers of light from a Moroccan pierced brass lamp. Madame Zavorsky's new book weighed heavily in her arms. Perhaps it held the secret of true happiness that she yearned for. Or perhaps it was too late for her.

CHAPTER TWO

Elsie sat up on the riverside lawn, giggling, and brushed grass out of her tangled blonde ringlets. Her hairbow had disappeared, lost in the roll down the hill. Her little brother Reggie chortled next to her, flat on his back. His white sailor suit was streaked with mud. They'd rolled perilously close to the grassy bank that time. Elsie peered over the edge into the murky green canal.

That water looks deep. I wish I could swim.

A canal boat floated by in the direction of Bath, pulled along by a massive horse. The boat people waved as they drew near. Elsie waved back, her arm pumping in the air. She overbalanced and her hand sank into the soft, cold ground. Mud squelched between her fingers. The grass grew thick near the water, hiding the mud.

Reggie sprang up, his rosy face split with a grin. "C'mon, Elsie, roll again!"

Elsie laughed and jumped to her feet, then caught sight of the grass stains on her white dress. She rubbed at them, smearing mud across her cotton lawn skirt. "Oh, no. My new frock. Mama will be so cross. Mama's birthday tea with Grandmama and Grandpapa is today." Hot tears filled her eyes. "I've got to change before she sees it. Come on, Reg."

Elsie tore up the hill towards the manor house, leaving her little brother to amble behind her. He would have to catch up. Elsie couldn't wait for him. She needed to get changed before Mama saw the ruined frock. She would be even angrier than usual if Elsie ruined her birthday tea. Elsie's mouth watered at the possibility of strawberry jam and scones but the mud on her hand reminded her of more pressing matters. She scampered across the grass towards the house. At four floors, Pendrake Manor towered from the top of the hill, its tall windows staring down at her. Elsie scanned the windows for signs of faces, maybe those ghosts she saw earlier. She hoped her mother wasn't watching. Mama was probably locked in her sitting room still, studying one of those big, dusty books she wouldn't let Elsie read. They were too grown up for an eight-year-old girl, Mama told her, which made Elsie even more curious about the stories they contained.

Elsie veered around the stone terrace. She stayed close to the high wall to remain hidden. Her grandmother often sat and embroidered in the parlour overlooking the gardens at this time of day. Grandmama shouldn't see her in such a state. She was always tidy. Elsie slowed down and hummed, nearing the house and sure she was safe from trouble. She reached the side door into the kitchen and walked straight into her Nanny. Nanny's soft bosom cushioned Elsie's impact.

The woman held Elsie back and examined her. "Miss Elsie! Your dress! And what have you done to your hair?" Her round, rosy face was a picture of distress, her mouth open and round.

Elsie dropped her eyes and twisted her mouth in contrition. "I'm very sorry, Nanny. We were playing on the grass."

Nanny shook her head and tutted. She crossed her arms. "And where is Master Reggie? Did you leave him to fall into the canal?"

Elsie frowned and twisted around but Reggie was nowhere to be seen. "No! I thought he was following me. Where is he? Little pest! He's always getting himself into trouble."

Nanny pursed her lips and made a shooing motion. "You're the older sister. You're supposed to take care of Master Reggie. Go back and find him."

Elsie ran out of the kitchen door calling her brother's name. She headed back down the hill towards the canal but didn't see Reggie. She circled back through the garden, peeking behind the row of hedges where they had searched for fairies earlier. Elsie bit her lip.

He couldn't really have fallen in the canal, could he? He's not that silly.

Elsie cast a look back down the hill, hesitating. She shook her head.

He's probably on the terrace.

She climbed back up to the lower terrace. He liked to play there sometimes. Rounding the corner of the lichen-encrusted wall, she discovered Reggie sitting on the ledge. Elsie breathed a sigh of relief. He had lined up rows of rocks facing each other, pretend soldiers at war. He didn't respond to Elsie's call until she was next to him.

"Reggie! What are you doing out here? You were supposed to follow me. We need to get tidied up for tea."

"Tea! I want tea! Let's go!" He jumped down from the wall, abandoning his stone soldiers.

They headed back into the house and met Nanny on the upper terrace as she puffed up to them. "Well, that's a relief! I'm glad to see you haven't drowned in the canal, Master Reggie!"

Reggie giggled and put his little hand into hers. Nanny ruffled his blond curls and beamed down at him. Elsie made a face. He never got into trouble.

Nanny turned back to Elsie, the smile gone from her face. "Whatever am I going to do with you, Miss Elsie? We haven't got long before your mother's birthday tea and your hair is ruined...and as for that dress! I don't know if I'll ever be able to get the stains out."

Elsie mumbled an apology and followed Nanny upstairs to their nursery at the top of the house. She braced herself for more hair pulling and Nanny tutting.

***

Clara lowered herself onto one of her mother's uncomfortable parlour chairs, careful not to dislodge the lace antimacassars. The door clicked open and her children entered the chintz-filled parlour, faces scrubbed until they glowed pink. Nanny had done well. They looked charming in their party clothes and there was no sign of grass stains or mud. Nanny followed and moved discreetly into a corner of the room. She settled her bulk into a chair and took out some knitting. Reggie smiled at Clara and scampered over for a kiss. Clara pecked him on the cheek and pushed him back so he wouldn't crease her lawn dress.

"You look well, Reginald. Are you behaving for Nanny?"

"Yes, Mama, I'm your good boy." He grinned. She patted his cheek, still rosy from his playtime.

Elsie moved closer and dipped a tiny curtsy. "Happy birthday, Mama."

When had she got so tall? How could she already be eight? Clara winced. She hated to be reminded of her age. Thirty! She was positively ancient. Elsie stood in front of her, shifting from one foot to another. Clara waved her away. "Thank you, Elsinoe. Do stop fidgeting. Go and sit down."

The child's face fell, and she shuffled away. Why did she look so sad? Was it the ghosts she claimed to have seen? Was she going to be a melancholic? Her mood would improve once she got hold of all the birthday treats. That ought to cheer her up. Reggie was lingering nearby. Clara shooed Reggie away to his own chair, exchanging smiles with him. Her baby was getting so grown up too. Five years old and he already looked like a little man in his jacket and long trousers. She supposed he would be her last child. She was getting too old for babies and with her husband on a distant island, another child seemed unlikely.

Her mother flounced into the room, clad in an overabundance of lilac ruffles, followed more sedately by her father. She beamed at Clara. "My darling! Happy birthday! Can it really be thirty years since you were placed into my arms? It seems like yesterday." She reached down and kissed her daughter on both cheeks, careful not to ruffle Clara's hair.

Clara accepted her mother's kisses with a tight smile. "Thank you, Mother."

Her father swept her up into an embrace, careless of both her gown and her hair. A giggle escaped Clara. Father always made her feel like his adored little girl. It was a shame she had so rarely seen him when she was a child. He'd often been away on overseas assignments in Her Majesty's service.

"My Clara-bel! Why, you barely look twenty! I'm sure your mother has forgotten your age." He kissed her cheek, his greying whiskers tickling her.

Clara's mother pursed her lips at her husband. "Now Albert, you're just teasing. I know exactly how old our daughter is."

"Of course you do, my dear, let's not get into a tiff about it. We're celebrating Clara's birthday, not debating her age." He turned to his grandchildren. "Who's ready for scones and strawberry jam?"

The children squealed in delight and jumped up from their chairs. Clara winced at the commotion over the treat. She had directed Nanny to never let them have jam because it makes them so wild. They only got treacle for nursery teas.

They all settled into their chairs and Clara's mother rang the bell for the maid to bring in the tea trolley. It was loaded with enough food for twenty people. Cook must have made extra so that the servants would have plenty to eat from the leftovers. Cook knew Clara would barely eat a sandwich and perhaps a scone. Clara thought she might be putting on weight here at her parents' house and that wouldn't do. She wanted to keep her girlish figure as long as possible. Her mother had stayed slim and that was Clara's goal too. Clara suppressed a sigh. A sandwich would be a better choice, even though it was her birthday. She nodded to the maid to serve her a cucumber sandwich but looked longingly at the scones. They were buttery and flaky. Cook made a lovely scone. Perhaps a small piece, without the cream and jam. She served herself a scone, ignoring her mother's disapproving look. The cucumber sandwich lay forgotten on her plate as she savoured the scone, lingering over every morsel.

"Clara? Are you listening to me?" Her mother's voice broke into her absorption.

Clara looked over, pasting a polite smile on her face. She swallowed the bite of scone. "Yes, Mother?"

Her mother sniffed, obviously put out that Clara had been ignoring her.

"I was asking if you'd heard from Theo. Did he write to you with birthday greetings?"

Clara took a sip of tea to hide her grimace. "No, I have not had a letter for several months. He gets so wrapped up in his work. And the mail from Andros Island is exceedingly slow."

And if he's dead, I'll never get another of those awful letters again.

Clara squashed the hope that he was dead with a guilty pang.

Father clucked his disapproval. "Work? That's hardly an excuse. Why, I would often send letters home when I was stationed overseas. At least monthly. He ought to at least try to send letters more often. It simply doesn't look good, this inattention to his family. It could seem neglectful. What would people say?"

"Father, there's no need to worry. I don't feel in the slightest bit neglected. More tea?"

He subsided into grumbles and accepted more tea. The tiny rose-patterned china cups that her mother favoured were certainly pretty but barely held three sips of tea. Clara glanced over at the children. They were quietly eating their way through an entire pile of scones smothered in jam. Should she disrupt their clandestine feasting? She didn't want to make a fuss in front of her parents. Best to let the children enjoy their greedy treat. Nanny would have to deal with any indigestion caused by the overindulgence.

A quiet knock interrupted the tea party, followed by a maid peeking around the parlour door. "The post has arrived, mum. There's a letter from overseas for Miss Clara— I mean, Mrs. Cooke."

Clara's mother's face lit up with her smile. "There you are, my darling. I will wager that it is a letter from Theo, timed perfectly to arrive on your birthday. How clever of him!" She beckoned to the maid to bring the letters to her. "Yes, here it is, your birthday letter from Theo." Mary took the letter from the maid and passed it to Clara.

Clara's heart sank. He wasn't dead after all and now she'd have to read one of his cold, condescending letters. This was not a birthday treat. She tore the envelope open, heedless of the stamp that Reggie would have steamed off for his collection. She pulled the single sheet of flimsy paper out. It was almost greasy. Sand scattered across her lap when she unfolded it. Shuddering, she squinted to read the spiky, almost illegible writing. And then again. No, it couldn't be. The scone turned dry in her mouth. Was Theophilus actually demanding that she and the children uproot themselves from their home to travel across the ocean to join him? What on Earth was possessing him to make the demand? They'd been perfectly content for the past five years separated by an ocean. What had changed?

Her mother broke the silence. "Clara? Clara? What does Theo say? Is everything all right, my darling? Is Theo ill?"

Clara looked up, her face hot. "He is summoning us to the Bahamas. He wishes us to leave...immediately." Her voice broke.

Her parents gasped in unison. The room erupted in noise as everyone shot questions at her. Clara dropped her suddenly aching head into her hand. Her mother burst into tears and Father shushed her, murmuring words of comfort. Couldn't they all shut up and leave her in peace? She needed to think about Theophilus's demand and this upheaval. Why did he want them now, after all this time? Elsie approached her and tugged on her sleeve. Clara looked up.

The girl's mouth trembled, and tears filled her eyes. "Mama, do we really have to go to the Bahamas? I don't want to go away! Why can't me and Reggie stay here at home?"

Clara shook her head and turned her face away. She needed a moment of peace. "Not right now, Elsinoe. I must think on the matter."

"But, Mama, please—"

Clara's tone was sharp. "Enough, child!"

Elsinoe sniffled and withdrew to her chair.

"Clara. Will you go?" Her father's voice was quiet. His face was drawn with concern.

Clara shrugged her shoulders helplessly. Her world was shrinking back to that of the dutiful wife. "He's my husband, Papa. Don't I have to obey him? That's what I vowed when I married him. Honour and obey." Her vision of Theo screaming in horror and pain returned. Perhaps she should have expected this summons. It seemed possible that her vision had been a true seeing, not a hallucination. She clasped her trembling hands. Theophilus must be in trouble on those faraway islands. He needed her. He didn't say as much in the letter, but the vision made it clear to her. The spirits had spoken. Her marriage vows were binding, as much as she struggled against them.

Despite their mutual disliking, she was being summoned to save her husband from whatever danger he was facing. She had to go to the Bahamas.

Her mother spoke up. "But the children? Why must they go? They could stay here at home in England with your father and I."

Clara was taken aback. She hadn't realized that her mother enjoyed the children's presence at Pendrake Manor. She toyed with the idea for a moment. Being unshackled from the children was tempting but the letter had been clear. "Theophilus specifically mentioned bringing the children. You know he hasn't seen Reginald since he was a baby. I'm sure we won't be there long. It's not likely that I would ever settle down in a primitive colony."

Clara's mother smiled, her eyes bright with tears. "Of course, dear. As much as we want you to stay, if you feel you must go, we can't stop you. You said he wants you immediately. I'll help you pack. We'll be sure to send along plenty of English comestibles for you. Who knows what sort of odd food they eat in the Bahamas."

She got to her feet and stood waiting for Clara. A wave of nausea filled Clara and her forehead prickled with cold sweat. A voyage to the Bahamas. She couldn't imagine why Theophilus wanted them now.

CHAPTER THREE

Elsie stood on the deck of the Lusitania watching the bustle of departure on the docks below her. So many people. The town of Liverpool was huge compared to her erstwhile home at Pendrake Manor. She didn't remember much from her early childhood in London except for the smoky air and all the people. She wished she'd brought her sketch pad and pencils from the cabin. Men shouted orders to others as huge bundles of goods swung from cranes and into the bowels of the giant ship. The long, slow-moving line of steerage passengers snaked onto the lower deck. She guessed they were steerage passengers because of their dark clothing, shabby even from her vantage point high above them. Their faces were downturned for the most part but every once in a while, she'd spot a yearning face peering up. Mothers gathered their children close by, seeming to be anxious that they would slip into the water. Elsie looked around the deck. She wondered where her own mother was. She was probably enjoying herself on the ship she had insisted on taking, saying it was the biggest and grandest ship on the seas. She was certainly not hovering over Elsie to make sure she wasn't getting up to mischief or in any danger. Elsie sighed. She missed Nanny Rodgers. She wished that her nanny hadn't come down with a fever right before the family was due to leave. Nanny hadn't really wanted to journey with them to the Bahamas though, and Mama had said that her illness had seemed a bit too convenient.

The wind picked up, blowing Elsie's hair into her face and making her nose itch. A few splatters of rain hit her bare head and icy tendrils of wind crept into her wool cloak. The steerage passengers had all boarded, and the dock seemed strangely empty. She pulled her hood up, loath to abandon her lonely spot on the deck. This would be her last view of home for who knew how long. Smoke-darkened factories on the harbour blocked her view of the rolling green and yellow autumnal countryside. Autumn was her favourite season. And today was Guy Fawkes Day. She was going to miss the bonfire at the Home Farm at Dunster Castle. A sudden longing for jacket potatoes smothered in butter pulled hot from the embers of the bonfire overwhelmed her. She wondered if they'd even have potatoes in the Bahamas. She regretted ignoring her geography lessons now. She wasn't even sure where the Bahamas were. South and west of England, she thought? Mama told her that the Lusitania would take them to New York in America on a five-day voyage. Then they would take another steamship down the coast of the United States of America to the Bahamas. She tried to remember her globe. So that would put them near Brazil? Or possibly Mexico?

A blast of the ship's horn startled her out of her musings, and she jumped. Was it time to leave? A sudden panic gripped her. She didn't want to leave home to go to some foreign land. She wanted to stay right here in England where everything was safe and known. She looked wildly about her. Maybe she could convince her mother to get off the ship, and forget about this trip to see her father. But where was Mama? Elsie headed along the deck, towards the doors of the first-class salon. The ship shuddered under her boots. She ran back to the railing and looked down. The ship was moving away from the dock. Too late. She couldn't get off now. Surprising herself, she burst into tears, clinging to the railing. The sea spray chilled her. Her tears turned into ice on her cheeks. The ship lurched through the waves and its horn sounded again. Down below, the pilot boat headed back to the port. The towering buildings of Liverpool looked like tiny dolls' houses now and the sea around her loomed immense, unending. The waves picked up, tossing the gigantic ship like Reggie's toy boat on the pond at the Bath Park. Elsie steadied herself against the railing. Her home shrank into the distance. She sniffled and wiped her tears away.

A tugging on her sleeve proved to be Reggie, looking up at her with concern. "Elsie sad? Here, take Bunny." He presented a floppy, faded toy to her.

Elsie sniffed and whispered her thanks. Taking Bunny, she cuddled it against her chest. It did make her feel a little better. Her tears stopped and she took a breath.

"Thank you, my little chuckaboo." Elsie pulled Reggie close and hugged him against her side. He wasn't all bad, she supposed, even if he was ordinarily irritating. She lifted her face into the wind, sharp rain drops stinging her skin. Elsie breathed in the briny air and felt a surge of excitement, her tears forgotten. She was on an adventure, sailing on a steamship across the Atlantic Ocean.

"Let's explore the ship, Reggie!"

The little boy grinned up at her and scampered off on his little legs along the deck towards the life boats dangling above the deck. "Come catch me!"

The deck was empty of other passengers. The weather was too blustery and cold for the adults, Elsie supposed, and she hadn't seen any other children entering the first class lounge when they had embarked. Reggie disappeared around a tall funnel vent sticking up out of the deck.

Elsie ran across the deck and tore around the vent. Where could the little pest have disappeared to? "Reggie! Come back! Where did you go?"

She heard giggling from inside a tarp-covered lifeboat and peeked under the tarp. Her brother grinned back at her. "You found me! Your turn!"

"I said we should EXPLORE the ship, dummy, not play hide and seek.

We haven't even seen the other decks yet. Oh! And we should try to sneak into the engine room. I bet it's jolly good in there."

Reggie climbed out from under the tarp, looking grubby and wet. He had lost his hat somewhere and his damp blond curls stuck to his head. "Brr, I'm cold!"

"Never mind that. Come on, we can run and warm up. Race you to the end of the deck! Ready, steady, go!"

Elsie laughed as she ran, hearing her brother thudding along behind her. He was rubbish at running so she always won the races. She slowed down a little to let him catch up. It would be nice to let him win this once. Reggie pulled ahead of her and reached the end of the first class deck with a yell of triumph.

"I won!" He jumped up and down in his excitement.

Elsie reached his side, thumping against the metal wall to stop herself. The main funnel towered over them, and the engine noise thrummed under her feet. She regarded the funnels thoughtfully as they belched black smoke into the air above their heads. "I wish I knew how to get to the engine room. I want to see how it all works."

"Bet it's loud." Reggie's voice was thin and ragged, worn out from their race. He wheezed each breath. Elsie frowned. He didn't look very good either. He probably needed to rest.

"We'd best go back to the salon. I bet tea will be ready soon."

Reggie's face brightened. "Scones and strawberry jam?"

"Oh, I hope so! Let's go and find out."

The dishevelled children walked sedately back along the deck to the salon for their tea.

CHAPTER FOUR

Andros Island, the Bahamas

Palm trees rustled above the tall, dark woman as she walked down a sandy path towards the white people's yard. Irene carried the month's supply of the burlup they paid such good money for. It had taken her days of stirring, mixing, heating, and adding the right things in the right amounts to create the burlup. Her people called it 'Ogologo-ndu', but the white people called it their Eternal Life potion. Irene was pretty sure it wasn't going to keep someone alive forever, but it did good at making sure folks had a long life. Drinkers of the burlup looked and acted young too. That would have been pretty bad if all it did was keep alive ancient people tottering around and complaining about their aches and pains. Irene chuckled to herself. She was sure the white folk wouldn't be paying her good money if that was the case.

She looked out at the shining blue water of the ocean. The sponge she needed to make the burlup that lengthened both life and youth grew deep in the blue holes off the coast of Andros. Diving that deep was hard and the water movement through the blue holes was unpredictable. Irene worried for weeks on end when her men were at sea, praying for their safe return. Without the sponge, the burlup was useless. It needed to be combined with other ingredients in a specific order. The formula was a family secret, passed from one healer to another. Her sisters knew parts of the recipe and helped with preparing the roots and seeds but only Irene knew the right order to add the ingredients and how to prepare the sponge. Irene hoped that one day, her nephew Johnny would be ready to learn the secret. If she kept him close by, he'd be safe from the dangers of sponge-diving.

The elders of the island all received their share, but every year, as they grew older and new elders were appointed, they wanted more from her. She knew she should give them all she could, but the Order paid in gold for this little flagon. The elders paid her in respect. That was all well and good, but it wouldn't buy her land or build her a new house with a real kitchen.

The breeze felt good on her face. It cooled the air a bit. The sun sure was scorching today. She was pretty glad that she was done with stirring that burlup over a hot stove. Birds cawed overhead, beautiful, colourful ones. She saw them every day of her life but that didn't stop her from admiring them. She suddenly felt lazy, and her footsteps slowed. A guinep tree, full of ripe fruit, beckoned. She paused to pluck one from a bunch hanging over the path and tore off the rind with her teeth. She popped it into her mouth, the sweet-tart pulp bringing a smile to her face. She hoped whoever owned that tree wouldn't mind too much but if it was one of her people, she knew they wouldn't. She scanned the area, trying to see whose yard the tree fronted. Ah, she had travelled further than she realised. She was already at the expansive yard of the white people, the biggity ones who called themselves the Order or some fool name like that. They wouldn't mind. They didn't know half of what they needed to know to farm on Andros. They probably didn't even know when the guineps were ripe, judging from the fallen fruit rotting on the ground below the tree.

She considered another fruit, its enticing aroma tempting her. She was hungry. Food was scarce right now with Alec and the boys gone on a sponge fishing voyage and not able to help her grow food. She wondered if she should try to collect some conch for a stew. Her belly rumbled at the thought of conch stew and that settled it. She snatched another guinep from the tree and ate it. She glanced around. The path and the yard beyond the guinep tree were empty. Chewing slowly, she savoured the guinep. Irene smiled and hummed a song, swaying her hips to the rhythm. The day seemed a little brighter when she sang and danced. Her mama and papa had always had music around them. Just humming one of those old songs from Africa was enough to bring them back to life. They had been so brave yet their hearts were full of joy. Irene still missed them, years gone now. Dead of a fever all her herbs couldn't cure. Irene shook herself.

No sense dwelling on old sadness. They gone from this world now, living with de ancestors and feasting every day. I's not gonna feel sorry for myself. I got t'ings to do.

The path circled the Order's yard to the front gate. Irene took her time. She was in no rush in this heat and besides, it would do those white folk some good to wait for her. They needed to give her respect. Those old white folk would probably shrivel up and die without her burlup. She grinned to herself.

That's right. Irene owns you, white folk. I give you favour by selling you my burlup.

She heard a voice on the other side of the bushes. One of them English gentlemen. He sounded kinda upset so Irene stilled herself and waited. She liked having secret knowledge about the white folk. It could be useful.

"But, Lydia, are you sure it's a good idea ordering Clara to come here? We've done so well without her presence interfering with us. We're happy, aren't we?" Irene heard the Englishman say.

A woman's voice answered, that Lydia. Irene sneered. She detested Lydia. So full of herself. Bossing people around like she was the Queen of Sheba.

"Yes, dear, of course. Nothing will change when Clara arrives. You and I will continue as we have, rest assured of that, my darling."

"Ah! But why does she have to come? Can't we get the money out of her without her coming?" His voice had a whine to it. Irene had to stifle a snort. A grown man like that sounding like a puny little boy begging for sweeties.

"We've tried that, Theo. She sends a pittance when she feels like it. There's no incentive for her to send more. Her parents will no doubt send their precious daughter an allowance when she is here. And the children will be...very useful."

"Yes, you're right, of course, m'dear. The Belvederes will send her an allowance and I'll go to Nassau to pick it up at the bank for her."

"And then the First will be pleased with us and we can buy more of the Eternal Life potion."

Irene raised her eyebrows. It sounded like the Order was running short of cash, but they wanted even more of the burlup. How interesting. She wondered how she could use the knowledge to her benefit. Maybe she could raise the price and get a real house even sooner than she hoped. Someday she would need to cut off the supply all together. She was tired of sending her menfolk out to dive for sponge so often. She was afraid that one of them wouldn't come home one day, like her sister's husband. The voices over the hedge were still talking but she had missed part of the conversation, while engrossed in her thoughts.

"I wish the children weren't coming. Aren't children loud? And nosey?"

Lydia laughed at the man's complaint. "Theo, you're their father! Surely you would know?"

"It's been a long time since I saw them. Five years? The girl, Elsinoe, was three or four. The boy was an infant. I don't really remember what they're like. But why do we need them to come? Wouldn't it be easier to send Clara back to England if the children were there?"

Irene shook her head. She'd whop Alec in the head if he talked about their boys like that. What was wrong with this Englishman? How could he not love his own babies?

"We need the children, remember? They're very useful for our activities. And we need Clara to stay for a while so we can get as much money out of her parents as we can. We don't want her turning and running back home as soon as she gets here."

"I suppose you're right, but they're going to be nuisances, I assure you," Theo murmured. Their voices seemed to grow quiet.

They must be heading off. Time for Irene to appear on de scene to sell these white folk their magic elixir.

Irene began humming again and this time let her voice rise into song, sweet notes soaring into the air attached to sad words of loss. She sashayed down to the gate of the Order's yard, her tall, slim figure catching the eye of a few cult members weeding their vegetable patch.

She waved to catch their attention. "Hey there, I's looking for Ward! You go tell him Irene is here with his magic potion. Hurry now. I's not gonna be kept waiting."

One of the men stretched up and winked at her. "Of course, Irene. I'll go and fetch him now."

Irene snorted. "You best be respectful to me, Horace, or I's gonna put a hurt on you."

He grinned. "Yes, ma'am, I know it."

She suppressed her own grin. Horace never took anyone seriously. She sometimes forgot he was one of them uptight Englishmen. She waited while he sauntered off to the big house. Time to get this batch sold. She needed the money, or she'd never sell to the Order so often. She wasn't so sure that it was such a great idea to let these crazy white folk have longer lives but they didn't seem to be doing much harm. Except maybe to each other. She wondered how that poor Clara woman would fare here on Andros. There wasn't much here for an Englishwoman and Irene didn't think the woman would find much comfort from her cheating husband.

Quit your worrying about folks that have not'ing to do with you and yours.

But still, she worried. Womenfolk weren't treated right a lot of the time and Irene hated to see it. And what did they mean about the children being useful? Were they planning on working those kids like dogs? Kids on the island usually ran around free until they were twelve or so. She spotted a few small figures hoeing the field next to the path. Children working in the hot sun. She clicked her tongue at the sight. Maybe she should mention it to the settlement's elders. She had some pull with them. They didn't like interfering with the white folk but she could push them a little.

Ward came scuttling up to her, all fakey-fake smiles, like he thought she was a low fence. She bared her teeth at him in a ferocious grin. She knew who was being taken and who was on top and it wasn't this smirking white man.

"Ah, there you are, my good woman. I was expecting you a few days ago to be honest but here you are finally. You've got our potion?"

"Yep. Got as much as I could make. It's gonna cost you."

The man's face, red and sweating from the heat, seemed to turn pale. "Um, cost me? Has there been an increase in the price? We hadn't negotiated a price increase."

Irene shrugged. She was enjoying watching Ward squirm, but she knew she couldn't go too far. She needed their money, so she named an amount a little bit higher than the last sale.

His face sagged with relief. "Ah yes, of course, not a problem. And why don't you take a basket of these guinep fruit as thanks? We never seem to eat them before they fall off the plant."

Irene struggled to hide her pleasure at the gift. She merely nodded in response.

Horace popped into view, that mischievous grin on his face again. "Would you like me to help you carry it home, Irene?"

"Why do I need the help of a scrawny white boy like you? You t'ink I can't carry that puny little basket?" Her words were harsher than her tone and she smiled at Horace.

Ward's face was a mask of confusion. He looked from Irene to Horace, obviously trying to figure out if she was serious or teasing. He must've decided to put his oar in. "That's a fine idea. Please, allow Horace to carry home your guineps. No need to strain yourself, Irene."

Irene nodded and handed over the flagon. She weighed the bag Ward handed her, satisfied at the heft. Horace lifted the basket of guineps from the base of the tree. Irene caught a look of distress from a woman in the line of hoeing workers. Someone didn't like her taking part of their harvest.

Irene waved a hand at Horace. "Come on, then."

She strolled away, trailed by Horace, grinning under the weight of the laden basket.

CHAPTER FIVE

Elsie looked over at Reggie. He was still sleeping. How could he sleep when there was so much to see on the ship? It was finally morning and Mother couldn't possibly object to them exploring now. She jumped out of her bunk and scampered over to him. "Reggie! Wake up! It's time to explore the ship!"

He groaned in reply. Exasperated, Elsie shook his shoulder. She could feel heat rising from his skin. "Are you ill or something?"

He turned over and squinted up at her, eyes bleary and crusted. He looked terrible, flushed and sweaty, his blond hair stuck to his forehead. "Um, maybe. I don't feel good," he croaked.

Elsie rolled her eyes. Only her idiotic little brother would be so idiotic as to get sick when they could be having a grand adventure. "Fine, I'm going to have to explore without you then."

"No, Elsie, don't go. I feel yukky. Can I have water?"

Grumbling under her breath, she scanned the cabin for a carafe of water. It was bare except for a pile of her mother's books and a couple of unpacked portmanteaux. She ventured into the compact washroom and found a cup on a shelf tucked behind the sink. The tap trickled out cool water and she filled the cup. Entering the cabin again, she found Reggie asleep and snoring softly.

"Hey. Here's your water." She poked his arm. Snuffling and groaning, he cracked open his eyes and took the cup. He murmured his thanks and slurped down the water. Elsie took the cup before he could drop it. He fell back asleep.

She dressed herself, struggling with the fastenings.

I wish Nanny hadn't got ill. She's so good at these things.

Reggie was still sleeping, gasping a little, when she finally managed to get her bootlaces tied in something like a bow. With a quick look back at her brother, she slipped out of the cabin, only to come face to face with her mother, immaculately dressed in a black and white travelling gown and matching hat.

"Elsinoe. I believe I instructed you to remain in the cabin." She frowned down at her daughter.

Elsie's face flushed and she dropped her gaze to her boots. "Yes, Mama. I thought you meant we were to remain in the cabin at night."

"Don't be impertinent and obtuse. The steward will be bringing your breakfast in shortly. I will be breakfasting with Madame Zavorsky in the dining room."

"Yes, Mama."

Elsie turned and went back into the cabin. She sighed. So much for adventure. At least Mama hadn't assigned any schoolwork. She flopped down onto her bunk to wait for the steward. Reggie was moaning in his sleep.

Their breakfast arrived soon after her mother's departure and Elsie eyed the covered dishes with interest.

The steward revealed the food with a flourish and smiled at her. "Will there be anything further, miss?"

"Oh no, thanks awfully. This looks scrumptious." She dived in, suddenly starving. Never had porridge and kippers tasted so good. "Reg, you should wake up and have some of this. They even sent a little pot of chocolate instead of hot milk. Want some?"

There was no response. Elsie scowled. Was her brother so ill that he didn't want chocolate? She got up from her chair and went to his side. "Hey, didn't you hear me, there's a pot of chocolate. Don't you want some? Mama isn't here to stop us from drinking it. Oh, come on, Reggie, you love chocolate."

The little boy woke up, his eyes bloodshot. "Chocolate? No, my throat hurts." He started crying.

Aghast, Elsie stared at him. He really was sick. Their grand adventure had lost its lustre before it even started. She had a sudden longing for home and her nanny. Nanny fixed everything, from bootlaces to sore throats.

I want to go home. Why did Mama drag us along on this expedition to see Papa? Why couldn't we stay home with Grandmama and Grandpapa?

She gulped back tears and returned to her breakfast, but her appetite was gone. Reggie's breathing was ragged and harsh. It didn't sound right.

I need to find Mama and let her know that Reggie is ill.

She left the cabin again, calling back to her brother. "Don't worry, Reggie, I'm going to get Mama to help you."

Elsie wandered into a long corridor, closed cabin doors on both sides. She had no idea where the dining room was from here. The cabin steward who had delivered breakfast appeared from one of the closed cabins and stopped short. His eyebrows rose in surprise, but he still smiled. "Miss Cooke? Can I be of assistance?"

Elsie exhaled with relief. "Hurrah, I was quite lost! Can you help me find my mother? My brother is ill and needs her."

The steward's face grew pale. "The little master is ill? By all means, let us search for your mother."

Elsie was led from one part of the ship to another, from dining room to reception room to more decks than she could count. Their search for Elsie's mother was fruitless.

"She must be visiting in another passenger's cabin," the steward guessed. Elsie bit her lip, trying not to cry. She took a deep breath. If Mama wasn't around to help, Elsie would have to sort things out by herself.

"Perhaps...would you mind helping me find a doctor for my brother?"

The steward nodded in assent and led her to the ship's infirmary. She scanned the faces of the fellow passengers as they walked but saw no sign of her mother. They entered the quiet infirmary, the air pungent with the medicinal smell of disinfectant. The doctor sat at a desk scribbling in a book. He glanced at Elsie over his glasses with a look of impatience that she was all too familiar with. "Young lady, what appears to be the trouble? Have you grazed your knee scampering about the ship?" His tone was stern.

Elsie shook her head. "No, sir. No, I haven't."

"Well, then, what is it, child?" He stood up, tucking his hands into his waistcoat pockets, and glared down at her. She cowered under his stare, her voice locked in her throat.

The steward cleared his throat and spoke up. "It's her little brother, Doctor. She says he's very ill."

"Very ill? I see. And why am I not speaking to the ill child's parents?"

Elsie burst out, "We can't find her, sir, my mother, I mean! And my brother is very ill; he won't even drink his chocolate!"

The doctor harrumphed. "I see. Well then, I had better attend to your brother." He picked up a large leather bag and placed some items into it. Elsie shuddered at the sight, remembering doctors' visits in the past. The doctor strode out of the infirmary, Elsie and the steward trailing in his wake. Elsie breathed a little easier. Reggie would be better once the doctor saw him. And then maybe she could find where Mama was hiding.

* * *

Clara shifted on her stool in the middle of Madame Zavorsky's, trying not to cough from the incense smoke swirling around her, and looked up. "This was so much easier when I was a child."

Madame Zavorsky's face gleamed in the dimness of her cabin, her dark eyes intent. Her voice was low and husky. "Yes, the young access the spirit world more easily. But you can still see them. Relax, my dear, and inhale the smoke. It will release your mind from its mortal bonds and open your mind's eye."

Clara took a deep breath. The musky, heady scent of the incense tickled her nose. She stifled a sneeze.

Madame Zavorsky continued, a droning rhythm to her words. "Close your eyes. And begin breathing deeply and slowly…"

Clara drifted into a waking dream, lulled by the sound of her mentor's voice and the drugged smoke filling the cabin. Her body grew heavy with her breathing. Waves lifted and dropped the ship, rocking it like a cradle.

"You are letting go and examining your mind, aware now of feelings, sensations, secrets…"

The cabin seemed to disappear, and Clara found herself standing on the deck of the Lusitania. An afternoon sun shone into her eyes. It had been mid-morning when she and Madame Zavorsky began their work. How had she lost so many hours of the day? Fellow passengers strolled by. Clara noticed that the women's skirts were much too short. She could see their ankles.

The deck jolted, sending people to their knees, Clara, distant in her trance, watched but couldn't feel the shaking. She seemed to be floating above the deck. A woman screamed behind her, then a plume of smoke gushed out from near the bridge. Without warning, the ship began listing and people slid towards the deck rail, arms flailing. Crewmembers ran along the slanted deck, their faces grim. Passengers and crew alike tumbled off the ship into the water far below, screaming. Clara gasped and her sight turned black.

With a start, she found herself back in Madame Zavorsky's cabin. Tears streamed down Clara's cheeks. Her body shuddered and she wrapped her arms around herself to still herself. The ship was rocking through the waves, as it had before she had gone into the trance.

"It's sinking. No. It's going to sink."

Madame Zavorsky leaned forward, concern etched across her features. "What is sinking, my dear?"

Clara shuddered and she gasped for air against the constraint of her corset. The porthole shone bright with the morning sun. Not afternoon. The shade was pulled back to reveal a clear, blue sky.

"I had a vision. I was on the deck of the Lusitania. There was an explosion. Smoke. People falling off into the water. The ship was sinking. Do you think what I saw was real?"

Madame Zavorsky scratched her chin and hummed under her breath. "Tell me more about your vision."

Clara described the strange clothing of the passengers, the smoke, and the listing ship.

Madame Zavorsky nodded. "Clara, I believe you saw a vision of the future. Your psychic powers are increasing now that you have been released from the shackles of society."

Clara dabbed at her tears with a delicate handkerchief and sniffed. Release? After five years of independence, the shackles of her marriage were closing back in on her. Her body felt leaden. "No, Madame, my freedom is ending. Perhaps the ship really will sink while I am on board. Then I won't have to be obliged to my husband ever again."

Madame Zavorsky tutted. "Don't say such things, my dear. You have so much still ahead of you. You must be strong in order to complete your spiritual journey. Your husband is a pebble in the road."

The image of kicking the pebble that was Theophilus out of her way made Clara smile. Her teacher returned the smile, a mischievous glint in her eyes. Her presence on this voyage had been an unexpected pleasure and her willingness to tutor her was more than Clara could have asked for.

Someone knocked on the cabin door, a tentative tapping, as if the person didn't want to be knocking. Clara rose from her stool and moved towards the door. She cracked the door and peeked out. Her daughter stood there, her face pinched tight with worry.

Clara opened the cabin door the rest of the way and stared down at Elsie, a frown creasing her forehead. "Elsinoe, why on Earth are you here? You're supposed to be in the cabin, not wandering about the ship."

Elsie gnawed at her trembling lip. Clara exhaled with frustration and motioned for her daughter to enter. Elsie shuffled inside.

"I don't understand why you can't leave me alone for a morning. Why are you bothering me here in Madame Zavorsky's cabin rather than staying in the cabin like I ordered you to? Explain yourself, child."

The girl dropped her gaze to the floor and mumbled a reply.

"What? Oh, for Heaven's sake, speak up."

Elsie spoke in a fast flood of words. "I'm sorry to bother you, Mama, but

Reggie was sick and I couldn't find you and the doctor came and said he has a fever and Reggie was crying and I think you should come..."

Clara's irritation boiled over into anger. "You are being overly dramatic, Elsinoe. It's an unbecoming fault of yours. The doctor would've come to me if Reggie was in danger."

Elsie cringed at Clara's words and blubbered her reply, tears rolling down her cheeks. "I'm sorry, Mama, but no one could find you, and I was so scared, and Reggie is ill, and I want to go home."

Clara rolled her eyes but spotted Madame Zavorsky gesturing for Clara to embrace the sobbing child. She placed a hand on Elsie's shoulder. At her touch, the child launched herself at Clara, wrapped her arms around her and wailing. Clara patted her daughter's back, wincing as the child's tears soaked through her bodice.

"There, there, don't fuss so, dear. You know Reginald will be all better in the morning. He always is. This is just one of his little episodes. There's no need to worry."

Elsie pulled back, her red face swollen and soaked with tears and snot. Her mouth twisted in a small smile. "Really?"

Clara patted her again. "Yes, of course. He'll be fine. You can stop worrying. Now go on back to the cabin and keep him company, that's my good girl."

Clara ushered her out of the cabin, then leaned against the closed door. She cast a wry look at Madame Zavorsky. "I fear I'm just not the maternal type. I've no idea how to manage these children. And look at my dress. Ruined. I should have hired a new nanny to come on this trip. What will happen when we reach Nassau? They'll run wild."

Madame Zavorsky shrugged and settled back into her chair. "They seem old enough to sort themselves out. It's not good to coddle children."

Clara put a hand to her aching forehead. "Yes, I suppose you're right. This trip seems so ill-fated. It feels wrong. I'm out of my element. I don't know what I'm supposed to do once I get there. Why did the spirits tell me to go? What am I supposed to accomplish?"

"All will become clear when it's the right time."

Clara's despair deepened, despite her mentor's reassurance. She was trapped on this voyage with no way home. She couldn't see past the darkness encompassing her.

CHAPTER SIX

Elsie watched the port of New Providence draw closer as the little steamship ploughed through the water. This ship was much smaller than the Lusitania. The waves had tossed them about as they made their way down the coast from New York City. Elsie stood steady on her feet now that the water had calmed. She leaned over the rail, awed by the colours of the ocean. They passed over deep, clear water the colour of Mama's sapphire necklace. The sea lightened to aquamarine. Patches of brilliant amethyst and even emerald sparkled in the water below.

How lovely. It's a sea of jewels.

There were even fish, silver schools shining in the sunlight. Elsie turned her head to look down the length of the ship. Was that a dolphin leaping in the wake of the ship? She breathed in the warm air, tingles of excitement dancing across her skin. They were almost to the Bahamas! It already felt like a magical place. She would have so much to draw. The warm air caressed her skin. She wouldn't need her heavy wool cloak here. The multiple layers of undergarments and dress stifled her but Mama insisted that she wear it all since that was how proper little English girls dressed. Elsie wrinkled her nose at the thought of having to be proper all the time now that Mama was in charge of taking care of them. She missed Nanny's gentle nudges to do what was needed. Mama had always ignored her unless she did something wrong. That would be followed by a cold, quiet scolding that never failed to scare Elsie. Mama never scolded Reggie, her perfect little boy. She didn't even seem to notice when he was naughty, or she blamed it on Elsie. Elsie shook her head. That didn't matter now, she was on an adventure. They drew closer and details of the wharf came into view. Crowds of people stood there, waiting for the ship.

I wonder if my Papa is there? I think he's supposed to meet us.

Elsie strolled along the deck, smiling politely as she walked by the other passengers also waiting for the ship to dock. They were a mix of people, some light-skinned like she was and some with darker shades. She wondered where they were from and where they were going. Elsie had only seen people with dark skin in London, not in the countryside. Maybe it was different here.

A little dark-skinned boy standing on a pile of boxes on the shore hollered to the approaching ship. Elsie couldn't quite make out what he was saying but someone on board must have. One of the sailors flung a shining coin in a soaring arc towards the shore. It fell into the water near the wharf and tumbled through the clear water to the sea bottom. The boy threw off his shirt and dove into the water after the coin, cheered on by his friends. Elsie was thunderstruck.

Is he really going after that coin? He's such a little boy. Is he going to be alright?

She watched intently as the boy reached the sea bottom, snatched up the coin and returned to the surface. He held the coin triumphantly in the air and yelled to his friends.

He did it. Oh my goodness. What a swimmer he is. I wish I could swim like that. As if Mama would ever let me swim in the ocean wearing next to nothing.

Elsie longed to join him in the clear water. It was probably warm like a bath but without all the soap and steam and Nanny trying to scrub behind your ears. The diver boy grinned like mad.

What a life he must lead, so free.

And with the ship's horn blaring out its signal, they arrived. Elsie realised with a start that her mother was probably wondering where she was, impatient to disembark. Scanning the crowd heading to the gangplank, Elsie couldn't see her mother, so she climbed onto metal stairs leading up to the navigation deck. From her vantage point, she spotted her immediately, standing next to the gangplank looking cross. She had Reggie in a firm grip but was craning her head this way and that. Her eyes locked on Elsie standing on the stairs. She beckoned to her, looking even more cross.

Elsie jumped down and pushed her way through the crowd in her mother's direction. If she was quick, perhaps Mama wouldn't be as annoyed with her. Panting with exertion, Elsie burst out from between two lumbering women, half-suffocated by their voluminous skirts.

Her mother stood at the gangway, tapping her foot. "Elsinoe, where have you been? How could you wander off like that when you knew we'd be getting off the ship momentarily?" Her voice was cold and clipped.

Elsie felt her face flush. "I'm sorry, Mama, I was looking at the ocean, it's so beautiful—"

"Enough, I don't want to hear your excuses. Look at your dress. You've got a smudge down it." Her mother reached forward and brushed ineffectively at the offending dirt, then inspected her white glove with a frown. "Now look what you've done, I've got my glove dirty."

Elsie dropped her gaze.

You didn't have to touch my grubby dress with your clean glove.

Her mother shook her head and sighed. "Never mind, your father won't notice, he never did care much for appearances. Let us go, children." She shooed the children ahead of her down the gangplank.

Elsie sniffed the air. The smell of fish, mixed with goats and sea spray assailed her nose. And was that pineapple? Maybe she would get to taste it finally. Mama had always said the fruit was too expensive for children to eat when she served it to the grown-ups at her fancy dinner parties. Elsie scanned the waiting crowds on the wharf, trying to pick out her father but couldn't quite remember his face well enough to know him in the crowd. Her mother seemed to have difficulties too. Elsie saw her searching, a short-sighted squint on her face.

Why won't she wear spectacles? However will we figure out who Papa is?

She didn't need to worry. A man dressed in a beige linen suit and a straw hat was waving at the family as they descended the gangplank. He called out to them. "Clara! Over here! Elsie! Reggie! Here I am!"

Elsie and Reggie ran the rest of the way down the gangplank towards their father, their mother following more sedately behind. When they reached their father, they stopped, suddenly shy. Elsie mumbled her greeting, her face downturned. Reggie stared at the strange man towering over them.

Mama caught up with them, her pace unhurried. "Hello, Theophilus. You're looking...brown. Why, you're almost native." She tittered.

"Clara. Welcome to Nassau." He leaned down as if to kiss her cheek, but she interjected her hand between them for him to take. With a slight smile, he raised her hand to his lips and kissed it. Elsie looked up at him and shivered. His eyes looked hard and glittered like the ocean, belying the smile on his face. He looked like her father, but this wasn't her loving Papa. Elsie didn't know this man and from Mama's face, neither did she. Five years was a long time. Papa had changed. He turned from a wordless exchange with Mama to face Elsie.

He smiled again, a smile that didn't reach those unnerving, glittering eyes. "Hello, Elsie. What a big girl you are. I'm sure you've been a big help for your mother with Reggie on this voyage."

Elsie smiled and nodded. "Yes, Papa."

How did he know that I had to take care of Reggie on the way over? Did he know that Nanny couldn't come along?

"She's quite the little miss, Theophilus. Don't take your eyes off her for a second."

Elsie stiffened at her mother's words.

"Oh, really? We'll see about that. And here's my big boy. Reggie, how are you?" He held his hand out for Reggie to shake. Reggie looked confused but shook hands obediently. Elsie couldn't take her eyes off this stiff facsimile of her father. Granted, she had been little when Papa had left for the Bahamas, but in her memories, he laughed when he played with her, threw her into the air, tickled her. She couldn't imagine this man doing that.

Mama unfurled her lacy parasol and placed it across her shoulder. "I'm sorry, but we can't stand around in the sun all day, Theophilus. Surely it's time for luncheon? Or is it called something else here in the tropics? The porter should be coming with our luggage. I expect we'll need some way to transport it." Her mother looked around the docks. "Perhaps one of those donkey cart things? Are they for hire?"

Father passed a hand across his forehead, looking weary. "A cart? Yes, we can hire a cart, but Clara, how much luggage did you bring?"

Mama bit her lip, darting a look up at Father. "I didn't know how long we'd be here, so I brought enough for a few months. Clothing, linens, and good English comestibles. School books for the children. And my books, of course."

Father looked aghast at the inventory. Mama's face fell. "Did I do something wrong? I assure you, Theophilus, I brought everything I thought you'd want."

"Everything? Where were you intending on putting these household accoutrements?" He looked annoyed now, his mouth thinned into a hard line.

"Are we not to live in a house? I didn't assume the house would be fully furnished so brought a few comforts of home. I'm sorry, Theophilus, I did what I thought right." Mama's eyes looked suspiciously shiny, her face a picture of contrition. Elsie shifted from foot to foot; she'd never seen her mother so uncertain.

He waved a hand in dismissal. "I have you booked into a suite at the Colonial. We won't be on New Providence long. I must get back to Andros Island as soon as possible."

Mama chewed her bottom lip and nodded. "Perhaps we can find somewhere to store our extraneous luggage before moving on to Andros Island?"

Father shrugged and turned to the approaching porter. He and the dark-skinned man had a brief conversation, then Father handed the other man some coins and shook his hand.

"I've sorted out the cart. Come on, let's talk to the Revenue Officer, then we can go and get some luncheon. Yes, Clara, we do have luncheon here. We're not uncivilised."

Mama winced at the rebuke and grabbed the children's hands. The little procession made its way along the dusty white road up from the wharf to the immense hotel dominating the harbour. The breeze off the ocean lent some coolness as they trudged along. Elsie sniffed again at the myriad of scents filling the humid air. They were really in the Bahamas. She smiled.

※ ※ ※

Later that evening, Clara strained to open the heavy wood door of her hotel suite, but it resisted, the wood swollen from the humidity. Theo sighed and pushed past her. He shouldered the door and it opened, creaking with a noise that sent a shiver down Clara's back. She stepped across the threshold. A bouquet of white plumeria in a vase near the door wafted its sweet tropical scent into the room.

"What lovely flowers. How thoughtful of you, Theophilus."

He shot her a dark look. "Not from me. The hotel must have provided them."

Clara squashed down the hurt and drifted towards the flowers. She reached out a finger to stroke a petal. "They're very fragrant. Do they grow on the islands?"

"Plumeria? Yes, there is a native species. They grow abundantly in the coppice."

She creased her forehead and looked over her shoulder at him. "Coppice?"

Theo paced across the room to a window and stared into the dusk. "One of the Bahamian ecosystems. The coppice is a dense hardwood forest. The islanders call it the coppet and claim all sorts of strange creatures live there. These children need to get to bed. They look exhausted."

Luncheon and all the formalities of arrival had taken hours. Reggie and Elsie huddled in the doorway, wide eyes taking in the darkening room full of exotic plants and wicker furniture.

Clara pursed her lips. She waved them in. "Children, come inside and shut the door. Off to bed with you. Your bedroom is that one." She pointed.

"You'll have to share a room tonight but our house on Andros Island will certainly have plenty of bedrooms."

Theo snorted but didn't look away from the window. "Plenty of bedrooms," he muttered.

Clara bit her lip. His tone was mocking, but she had no idea why. He had barely looked at her since her arrival. Could his distance be explained by the long absence or was something else lurking below the surface?

The children ambled towards their bedroom and Elsie stopped at the threshold. "Mama, are you going to bathe us?"

Clara exhaled an exasperated breath. "Elsinoe, you and your brother have been bathing yourselves since we left England, haven't you? Why do you need my help?"

Elsie exchanged a look with Reggie. "There was no bath on the ships, Mama. We only washed our hands and faces."

"No bath? Of course there was. I used it myself. You haven't bathed in ten days?" Clara's lip curled in revulsion. At least they'd changed their clothing regularly. At least she hoped they had changed.

Theo turned from the window and crossed his arms. He stared coldly at his wife. "Clara, why didn't you bring the children's nanny? Your child-rearing skills have not improved since I saw you last. Or is it your powers of observation that are at fault?"

Tears sprang into Clara's eyes. Her throat grew tight. She swallowed. "Nanny fell ill right before we left. I'm sorry; I had no time to find a replacement."

He shrugged. "Just as well. A nanny would get in the way. I don't know where we'd put a nanny at the compound. You'll have to learn how to be a real mother now that you're here."

His rebuke hit her like a slap across the face. She had never thought of herself as a bad mother. All the women in her social circle used nannies. She and Theophilus were still living on different continents, despite standing in the same room. Nothing he said was making sense. No room for a nanny? What compound?

"I beg your pardon for all the questions, Theophilus, but why did you ask us to come to the Bahamas? What kind of establishment will we be staying in that has no room for a nanny?"

Theophilus's face appeared carved from stone. His hard, expressionless eyes bored into her. "Your curiosity is unseemly, Clara. You are my wife. I don't need to explain my reasoning to you. All will be revealed in time."

Clara nodded, her eyes downcast. Theophilus hadn't changed much despite his native attire. Her voice came out almost as a whisper. "I'll run the children a bath. Would you mind terribly ringing the maid for tea? Or would you prefer port?"

"I'm not staying."

She looked back up, trying to read the look on his face. "Not staying? What do you mean? You have a room elsewhere? But...I thought..."

His stone-like expression clashed with his words. "I thought to leave you in peace tonight so that you can acclimate yourself. We've been apart for many years. I'm sure you're accustomed to being alone in your bed."

Was that sarcasm? Clara swallowed. What would make him think she could be adulterous? She let a meagre smile cross her lips. "Yes, I have become accustomed to being alone. I don't allow the children into my bed like more indulgent mothers."

Theo sneered. "I have no doubt that you don't allow children into your bed."

What was he hinting at? Best to ignore it. She knew she had stayed faithful even if he implied otherwise. She scanned the room to avoid his gaze and caught sight of the small trunk containing her books on Spiritualism. Unpacking would give her something to do rather than continuing this unsettling conversation with Theophilus. She moved towards the trunk and clicked open the latches. Smiling to herself, she spotted the book she had purchased right before she had left. Clara lifted it out and placed it tenderly on a side table.

"I thought you were going to bathe the children?" Theo spoke in her ear, looming over her.

Clara startled with a gasp. She hadn't heard his approach. The children. She'd already forgotten about the children and their bath. Elsie and Reggie still lingered at the doorway of their bedroom. "Oh, of course."

Theo reached across her and picked up her book, glancing at the title. "Spurious bosh. Why you have this in your possession is beyond me." He dropped it to the floor.

She stared at the book, pages crumpled from the impact, then at him, wide-eyed. "That's my book." She crouched to retrieve it, then cradled it to her chest.

He splayed the books across the table, scanning the titles. "It seems you've become immersed in all that Spiritualism nonsense. I suppose you needed something to do to fill your time since you had no husband to occupy your time and you obviously weren't paying much attention to my children."

"You've been absent from my life for five years, Theophilus. Yes, I needed an interest, something to fill my time since my husband wasn't available."

Theo laughed. "I think my absence was an excuse for you to squander your money on these ridiculous books. You probably sponsored some charlatan calling herself a medium too, didn't you?"

Clara fought back tears, holding the book as if it were a lifeline. She wouldn't give him the satisfaction of seeing her upset. "I've learned a lot from these books and yes, I am a patron of a few Spiritualists, including Madame Zavorsky. My studies have been enlightening. Worthwhile. I feel that I've grown spiritually under Madame Zavorksky's guidance."

He gave her a withering look. "Clara, your naivete was somewhat charming when you were young but it's ridiculous in a woman of your age."

He knew how to wound her still. She pressed her lips together, resisting the urge to fight back. Arguments were undignified. Theo shrugged and moved towards the door. He glanced back at her. "Good night, children, Clara."

He departed with a bang of the door and Clara sank into a chair. She'd been in the Bahamas for less than a day and her spiritual advancement had been mocked and her independence swept away. She longed to be home.

CHAPTER SEVEN

The sun was still below the horizon when the children crept out of the hotel and into the verdant gardens. The air, still warm, caressed their faces, and heavy dew dripped on them from the overhanging foliage. Neither could sleep from the excitement of being in a foreign land. The spicy food their father ordered for them at dinner last night hadn't help them rest either. He watched them until they choked down every morsel of the native cuisine. Elsie felt like her throat was still burning and dry from the food and she swallowed, trying to moisten it. She hadn't thought to stop for a drink of water before slipping out of the suite where her mother still lay sleeping. Elsie didn't want to wake her. Mama had seemed so lost last night and besides, she would have forbidden the exploration this morning if she knew. Elsie wondered where her father had disappeared to last night after dinner. He had merely said goodnight and left them in their suite.

Reggie tugged Elsie's sleeve. She glanced down at his excited face. He pointed towards what Elsie thought was a palm tree.

"Elsie, look. A monster." His voice was hushed, whether in fear or awe, Elsie couldn't tell. She followed his finger and saw it. Crawling up the slender trunk of the tree and silhouetted in the growing light of dawn was a gigantic lizard.

Elsie gasped. "It's huge. But I think it's a lizard, not a monster."

Reggie shook his head and leaned close to her ear. "No horns on lizards."

Elsie scowled at him. "How do you know that? It's not like you're some lizard expert."

"I got books." His face was mulish. "Not a lizard. It's a monster."

The daylight grew brighter and, as if that were a signal, the lizard, monster, or whatever it was started moving up the trunk, its body moving sinuously as it climbed. Elsie squinted. She couldn't quite make out the horns Reggie claimed to see until the creature looked at her fully. It did have horns. Then it hissed at her, showing a mouth full of sharp teeth.

The children gasped in unison. Elsie didn't know much about lizards, but those teeth didn't look right. The creature scampered higher into the tree and vanished into the fronds high up at the top of the tree.

"You scared it." Reggie's voice held a familiar whine.

She scoffed at him. "Don't be silly. I don't think a lizard that big is going to be scared of a little girl like me. It probably went hunting for its breakfast."

As if on command, the fronds at the top of the palm tree began to rustle and bits of debris fell to the ground. The movement intensified, then stopped. The children waited, fascinated. Something dropped out of the tree and thumped to the ground. It was a very large, very dead rat. Elsie could tell it was dead because it was missing its head. She scowled her disgust. "Ick. Even the rats are bigger here."

"Yeah. It ate the head. Weird."

"Uh huh. Let's go and explore more of the garden. I don't think we should be here when that lizard comes back down."

"Awww, Elsie. I wanna see it again." More whining.

She restrained herself from hitting him across the back of the head. "Reggie, let's go. I mean it. That lizard looked vicious. All those teeth."

She grabbed her brother's arm and tugged him away from the palm tree. He stared up, not seeming to notice Elsie.

"Re-ggie. Come on. Let's gooo…" She tugged harder.

"Oh, okay. Big monster lizard. Maybe Papa knows it. Let's ask him."

At the mention of their father, Elsie felt a rekindled sense of unease. She still didn't feel comfortable around this transformed Papa of theirs.

"I suppose," she mumbled.

"Look, a pond!" Reggie pointed at something glinting through the thick bushes. "D'you think there's fish?"

"Maybe. Let's hope there are no sharks."

"No sharks. They live in the ocean."

Elsie rolled her eyes. "I know that. I was just kidding. Let's go see this pond. Then we'd better get back to the suite. Mama might wake up and wonder where we are."

Elsie spotted a bush overflowing with white flowers. They smelled wonderful.

I'll pick one for Mama. She loves scented flowers.

Pleased with herself for her forethought, she plucked one of the blossoms and followed her brother to explore the pond.

※ ※ ※

Elsie tiptoed into the hotel suite with Reggie hard on her heels. The sitting room was still dimly lit. No one had bothered to open the curtains. She glanced over at her mother's bedroom door. It was open and light streamed out of the room. Mama was already awake. Elsie winced.

"Elsinoe? Reginald? Kindly show yourselves."

The children exchanged looks of dismay. She sounded cross. Elsie took a breath, raised her chin, and marched to the open door. Her mother sat up in her bed, surrounded by books and a breakfast tray. Elsie's stomach grumbled, ready for her own breakfast. Was there toast over on that tray? Her mother's mouth pursed in disapproval when she spotted Elsie at the door.

"Where have you two been? Wandering through the hotel and making nuisances of yourselves, I suppose?"

Elsie shook her head in response and stepped into the room. She raised her cupped hands. An exotic white blossom nestled there. Its rich fragrance wafted into the room.

"Good morning, Mama. We were in the gardens. Look, I brought you a flower. Isn't it pretty?" She sniffed the blossom. "And it smells nice."

She beamed at her mother, but her heart sank at her mother's pinched, tired face.

"You stole a flower from the hotel garden? Elsinoe, you know better than that. What would Grandmama have said if you took a flower from her garden?"

Elsie choked back a sob. She hadn't thought of it as stealing. There were so many plants covered with blooms in the garden. "I'm sorry, Mama. I didn't think."

Her mother closed her eyes for a moment and rubbed her hand across her forehead. She raised the book from her lap and began reading. "Never mind. I'm sure no one will notice. Your father will be here soon. Go and ring for a tray. He'll want tea, I expect."

"Yes, Mama." Elsie's voice felt small and weak. She scurried back into the parlour to do as her mother ordered, dropping the offending flower on an end table. Reggie stood at the threshold to their mother's room looking from Elsie to their mother.

"The monster?" he hissed at Elsie. She shook her head at him.

"Never mind that," she whispered back. His face took on the usual mulish expression when he was thwarted. Elsie glared at him but as always, he ignored her.

"Mama?" he called to her from the door.

Their mother glanced up and raised an eyebrow. "Yes, Reginald? What is it?"

"Mama, saw a big lizard. In the garden. It was a monster."

She shuddered and grimaced. "How perfectly dreadful. I hope you stayed well away from it. Who knows what horrid disease you could get if one of the native fauna bit you."

"It had lots of teeth. And horns."

Their mother dropped her gaze back to her book. "Really. I'm awfully glad you weren't attacked by the beast. Do be careful, darling."

Reggie huffed and turned from the doorway, catching Elsie's sympathetic eye across the room. She smiled ruefully at him. "What did you expect, silly? You know she doesn't care for wild animals." Her tone was hushed, pitched so that her mother wouldn't hear.

"Don't tease me." Reggie stuck his tongue out at her. Elsie returned the gesture, then turned her back on him to ring for the maid. She heard his growl a second before he slammed into her back, pushing her against the wall. She banged her forehead on the wood.

"Ow! You little pest! That hurt!" She turned and shoved him. He tripped over the edge of the rug and fell onto his bottom with a wail. Elsie shushed him but his cries grew shrill and loud.

"MAMA!" he bellowed before scrambling to his feet and running into his mother's room.

Oh no, that's done it. Now I'll be blamed for this.

She could hear his sobs quieting down as he blubbed his grievances to their mother. Wearily, Elsie pulled the bell cord and waited to be summoned to her mother's room. It didn't take long.

"Elsinoe. Kindly come in here." Her mother's voice, quiet and cold, was scarier than if she had shouted. Elsie shuffled into her mother's presence and darted a glance at Reggie, comfortably ensconced on their mother's bed, sniffling.

"As the eldest, I expect your behaviour to be a model for Reginald. Shoving him to the ground is simply not acceptable, Elsinoe. I am quite at a loss. I do not know how to remediate this dreadful conduct you've displayed since we began this journey."

"But, Mama, he started it! He—"

"No excuses, madam. You will go to your room and consider your behaviour. I expect five hundred words on proper conduct before you will be allowed breakfast."

Elsie opened her mouth and closed it again, feeling like a fish.

Five hundred words? Before breakfast?

Her belly growled in response. "Yes, ma'am." Elsie crept away to her room but halfway across the sitting room, she heard a knock. It must be the maid, although it hadn't been long since Elsie had rung. She went to the door and opened it.

Her father was standing there, a stiff smile plastered on his tanned face. "Good morning, young lady. Am I in time to join you all for breakfast?"

Mutely, Elsie nodded and stepped to the side to let her father enter the room. "Where's your mother? Not still in bed?"

"Theophilus? Is that you out there? I wasn't expecting to see you this early. I'm not dressed."

Elsie's father strode across the room to the doorway of his wife's bedroom. "No matter, Clara. I think it's all right for your husband to see you in your dressing gown. I've come to have breakfast with my family although I see you've already had yours. Well, I can have breakfast with the children. What do you two say to griddle cakes with maple syrup? I'll take them down to the dining room, Clara. You can take your time dressing without worrying about the children."

Elsie caught her breath. He strode back, beckoning to the children.

Would Mama say no? Would she mention my punishment?

There was silence from the other room. Elsie's father didn't seem to notice. He ushered them out of the hotel suite and shut the door firmly behind them. Elsie grinned triumphantly at Reggie. So much for the punishment. Instead, she was going to have syrup with griddle cakes, whatever that was.

The plush carpet under her feet on the stairs down to the dining room reminded Elsie of her grandparents' house. She felt a pang of homesickness. Everything was so strange here, and Mama was distant and angry all the time. And she still didn't know what to think of Papa. He was completely different from her memories of him. She examined him as he preceded her down the stairs. He didn't dress like anyone she knew. Her grandpapa always wore dark suits, whether it was summer or winter. The light-coloured jacket and pants Papa wore seemed baggy, like they didn't fit him. He wasn't even wearing a necktie. People in the Bahamas must dress differently than at home.

Maybe Mama will let me leave off my pantaloons now that we're here. I'm so hot, I feel like I'm going to roast.

Her shoes clattered across the marble floor at the bottom of the staircase. The dining room doors stood open, welcoming early breakfasters. The clock in the foyer read seven o'clock. Elsie realised that she had been awake for hours. It was no wonder she was famished. The family entered the dining room and a slim, handsome man greeted them. His stylish scarlet uniform adorned with shiny brass buttons down the front contrasted dramatically with his dark skin.

"May I assist you, sir?" The man spoke with a British accent.

"Good morning, Arthur! How have you been faring?"

Her father knew this man too? Did he know everyone in Nassau?

"I beg your pardon, sir?" The man looked puzzled and a bit put-out.

"I'm Theo. Theo Cooke. With the Governor's Delegation for Agricultural Improvement."

The confusion cleared from the man's face. "Oh yes, Mr. Cooke. We haven't seen you in quite a long time, sir. And these must be your charming children visiting from England." He smiled kindly down at the children. "Welcome to Nassau."

Reggie and Elsie shook the man's hand and murmured polite greetings.

"How long will you children be staying in the Bahamas?" the man named Arthur asked.

The children looked at their father for an answer. Their mother had been vague about the duration of their visit.

Father cleared his throat and muttered, "Not quite sure."

"Ah. Well, I do hope you enjoy your visit. Let's get you seated for breakfast. It's quite early but the kitchen is open."

Elsie caught sight of the garden through the tall windows at the other side of the room. She tugged Reggie's sleeve and pointed. He bounced up onto his toes. "Oh, the garden! I want to sit there."

"No! Not the garden!" Elsie contradicted. Everyone looked at her. "It might be too cold near the windows. I mean too warm." She felt herself colour and lapsed into silence, face hot. She wasn't going to admit to being afraid of what might be lurking out there.

"Elsie, what on Earth are you talking about? I'm sure the temperature by the windows is perfectly fine. And since Reggie is so eager, let's sit there."

Their father waved a hand towards a table up against the windows. The foliage outside pressed up against the glass. Elsie peered out but saw nothing but plants. No giant lizards. She glanced at Reggie. He was also staring out of the window. She knew he was searching for the same thing as she was.

Their father looked from one child to the other, a look of befuddlement across his face. "What are you two so fascinated with out there?"

Elsie turned to her father. "We went exploring in the garden this morning before the sun was up. We saw an odd animal."

Reggie nodded, his face solemn.

Papa frowned and leaned forward. His face had a strange expression, afraid and excited at once. "An odd animal? What did it look like?"

"I don't know…" Elsie bit her lip. She felt stupid for even bringing it up. So they saw a strange-looking lizard. Maybe they were common in the Bahamas.

Reggie bounced in his chair. "A monster, Papa, a big lizard. With horns and lots of teeth." Reggie had no fear of appearing stupid, apparently. Elsie groaned inwardly, waiting for her father's laughter. It didn't come.

He sat there, pale-faced, staring at Reggie. "Are you sure that's what you saw? It was dark. Perhaps you couldn't see clearly."

"No, I saw it. A monster. It climbed up a coconut tree."

Their father turned to Elsie. "Did you see this … monster also?"

She nodded, unable to speak further. He was taking this seriously. He sat back, exhaling. He examined the ceiling for a few moments before returning his gaze to them. "Children, what you saw was more than likely one of the iguanas that live on the islands. They can grow quite large. Not a monster but they can be vicious. Best to stay away from them. You'll need to be careful here. Many dangerous creatures inhabit these islands." He smiled at them, but his eyes remained serious. "Now, let's have some of those griddle cakes smothered with maple syrup. I think you're going to love them."

He didn't bring the subject up again throughout their breakfast. He barely spoke. As they were finishing their food, a party of gentlemen entered the room.

One called out in their direction. "Cooke! Where have you been hiding? Not on Andros all this time, surely?"

Their father winced. The men came over to their table and the children's father stood, shaking hands all around.

"I'm still waiting for that report on the sisal fungus you promised me last year, Cooke."

"Yes, Governor, I know. The...um...the data has yet to be compiled. We need more... field work."

The Governor snorted. He tucked his thumbs in his waistcoat and rocked back on his heels. He didn't look like he believed Papa. "You've been telling me that for months. What have you been getting up to on Andros? Native women?"

Their father flushed and seemed to remember his children sitting and listening. "May I present my children, Elsie and Reggie? Children, this is the Royal Governor of the Bahama Islands, Sir William Gray-Wilson."

Elsie stood up and curtsied. "Pleased to meet you, Sir William."

Reggie sat, licking the syrup off his plate with a finger.

The Governor beamed and patted Elsie on the head. Elsie hated that. "What a delightful child. Well done, Cooke. Must be off. Get that report to me, y'hear? Look slippery about it."

"Yes, sir, of course. Good to see you, sir."

The Governor and his party sauntered off to their table. Elsie's father sighed with relief.

The family finished their meal in silence. Elsie watched Theo glance out the window between bites. She wondered if she'd find out the truth about that strange animal they'd spotted. How dangerous was it? How many more were out there?

CHAPTER EIGHT

The murmur of cultured voices in conversation lulled Clara into a calm she hadn't felt since leaving England. She smiled, letting her gaze drift around the long table shining with silver and lit with candelabra. Clara had been delighted to receive an invitation to Government House for a party to welcome her to the Bahamas. The prospect of socialising with her peers at an elegant event pleased her to no end. Theophilus had not shared her pleasure. He seemed to have become quite the native living out on that island of his, miles from civilization. Happily, the Governor had not allowed refusal, and the couple had ventured from the Colonial Hotel, leaving their children in the care of the hotel's nanny for the evening.

To Clara's surprise, the dinner party was not inside the formal dining room but out in the garden of the mansion. Delicate lanterns festooned the overhanging trees. The glimmering lights gave a fairyland aspect to the garden. A profusion of scented, white plumeria blossoms perfumed the warm air. Clara winced to herself when she spotted them. The flowers seemed to be quite common on the islands. They were the same kind that decorated their hotel room and that Elsinoe had brought her that morning. She shouldn't have been so short with her daughter but when Elsinoe had entered the room, Clara's head was aching abominably from a poor night's sleep.

Her neighbour at the table, the Governor's secretary Mr. Northcroft she thought, leaned closer, his tone low and intimate. "Mrs. Cooke, it is a wonderful treat to have you here and I'm certain your husband is even more thrilled. We rarely have visitors of such distinction. I have heard much of your spiritual gifts from our mutual friend Lady Agatha."

Clara felt the heat rise to her cheeks. She hoped he wouldn't be able to see in the dim light. "You are too kind, Mr. Northcroft. I am merely a student."

"Your modesty is becoming in a lady, but in her last letter, Lady Agatha told me all about the horoscope you created for her. She was most impressed."

Clara could hardly believe her ears. She hadn't known that Lady Agatha liked her horoscope so well. She hadn't heard a thing from the noblewoman since dropping off the packet during a social call months ago. She smiled at her neighbour. "That's so nice to hear. Oh. What's this?"

The server presented a large platter holding what looked like an entire turtle, turned bottom up, its shell filled with a ring of meatballs and an ornate crust of scrolls and ribbons arching where its breastbone had once been. Clara smiled up at the servant who dished some of the turtle meat and crust onto her plate, trying not to show her confusion at the strange dish. Clara looked at Mr. Northcroft with a quirked eyebrow.

"It's baked turtle, Mrs. Cooke. Quite a delicacy."

"I don't believe I've ever been served an entire turtle, only turtle soup."

Mr. Northcroft raised his wineglass to her. "It's a local delicacy, ma'am. Quite a treat."

Clara turned to her food and took a tiny nibble. It was surprisingly flavorful. She glanced at Mr. Northcroft from under her eyelashes. He nodded his encouragement and she took a larger bite. The Bahamas was certainly an adventure. Clara sipped her wine. It was fruity and cool. Not the type of wine served at home. She supposed the wine needed to be more refreshing in this climate. She took another sip, then dared more of the turtle.

"That's it, eat it up. What a trooper you are, Mrs. Cooke." His admiring tone filled her with pleasure, and she raised her glass to him, smiling into his eyes, which she noted were a lovely shade of hazel. "You seem knowledgeable of the local cuisine. Have you been in the Bahamas long?"

"About five years now. I am finding it hard to imagine leaving the Summerlands."

Clara raised her eyebrows. "The Summerlands? What a delightful sobriquet. So you don't mind the heat year-round?"

Mr. Northcroft shook his head, his face gone distant and dreamy. "Not at all. I shall be rather loath to leave the islands, truthfully. I'm writing a book about the Bahamas, y'know. Perhaps my words will sustain me when the Governor moves to a different post and I with him."

Clara's curiosity was piqued. She loved to read but the idea of writing a book seemed insurmountable, an alien idea. "You're writing a book? How marvellous. Will it be a terribly intellectual discourse on the state of the economy of the British Crown Colony of the Bahamas?"

Mr. Northcroft laughed aloud, drawing stares from other people at the table, including her husband, Clara noted. "An intellectual discourse? Not at all! It will be more of a love letter to the Bahamas. An amalgam of memoir and travelogue is my intent. I will more than likely be the only person to actually read it but that doesn't matter to me. I will have put my memories on paper so that I will never forget all the glorious details."

Clara's food sat untouched as she listened. She finished her wine, and a comfortable glow filled her. She relaxed, feeling the tensions of travel to a foreign land fall from her body. "I would read it." Her voice was quiet, pitched low for his ears alone.

He beamed back at her. "A true reader, what? I suppose my scribbles will be light reading for you. After all, you can make sense of those astrological tomes..." His voice trailed off and he looked ill at ease, as if he were afraid of offending her.

Clara laughed. "No, no, you're right, they are tomes, and I must admit, quite a chore to comprehend."

She remembered her manners and with a rueful parting grin at Mr. Northcroft, turned to her other dining partner. She recognized the red-haired man at once as the Governor's aide-de-camp, Lieutenant MacLachlan. He looked quite dashing in his dress uniform. He must have caught her movement out of the corner of his eye for he immediately turned and greeted her with a smile. "Mrs. Cooke, it's a pleasure to meet you at last. I hope you and the children are settling into your suite at the Colonial. Och, but it seems a short time ago that I saw your own husband to his rooms there when he arrived from England. How long has he been here now? Five years? And gone from you all that time. You must have had quite a reunion. I'm sure he was pleased as punch to see you and the little ones."

Having spoken his piece, the lieutenant went back to his food without awaiting a response from Clara. The servants had discretely removed the turtle and replaced it with the next course. From the looks of it, they were serving Rib of Beef au Jus with mashed potatoes and string beans. Clara breathed a sigh of relief. Good, solid English food. Thank Heavens.

The lieutenant must have heard her little exhalation. He chuckled. "Lady Gray-Wilson likes to have a bit of local flavour in her dinners, but she is always sure to have familiar food to follow. Of course, beef is hard to come by here and we don't get choice cuts. They have to ship it over from Florida, you see."

"Everything is so different here. The food, the flowers, even the native fauna are wildly different. Do you know, my children saw a giant lizard in the hotel garden this morning? They claimed it was five feet long with horns and huge teeth."

The lieutenant gave her an odd look. "That sounds quite large for an iguana, but they can get big. We generally don't see the very large specimens right here in Nassau. I wonder how it got to the hotel garden."

"Well, they are English children who've never seen a lizard larger than a few inches long. I didn't put much stock in their estimate of its size. An iguana is a large Bahamian lizard with horns and fangs?"

The lieutenant shrugged. "Yes, iguanas live on the islands, but I don't know that I've seen fangs or horns on an iguana. Children imagine interesting things. Still, there are strange things on the Out Islands. I'd advise caution if you are to join your husband on Andros Island."

Clara paused, her fork hovering above her dinner. "Strange things? Whatever do you mean, Lieutenant?"

He cut into a piece of rare beef and speared it with his fork, then cast a look at her. "We've heard rumours of dangerous creatures inhabiting the coppice. And the Governor is a bit concerned about certain activities concerning British subjects on Andros Island. I shouldn't say more. But please, Mrs. Cooke, be careful."

Clara nodded to be agreeable and tucked into her dinner. She had no idea what he was talking about. She and the lieutenant exchanged pleasantries about the food, but he seemed to have run out of interesting discussion topics and Clara was too tired to try. She barely made it through the rhubarb pie and a cheese board before signalling to her husband that it was time to leave. They exchanged pleasantries with their hosts and left Government House.

Theophilus was silent until they were a distance from the house. He stopped, grabbed Clara's arm, and whirled her to face him. "What do you think you were doing at dinner? Your behaviour was shocking. Were you trying to embarrass me?"

Clara gasped. It was as if he had slapped her across the face. Her eyes filled with tears.

"I beg your pardon?" Her voice came out as a whisper.

"You flirted all evening long with Mr. Northcroft and Lieutenant MacLachlan. Your manner may pass as appropriate in London society, but you will be labelled as a hussy here in Nassau with that sort of behaviour."

She shook her head, uncomprehending. She had tried to be charming and entertaining, as she always did at social events. Clearly the norm here was different. "I beg your pardon, Theophilus. I didn't realise that I was behaving inappropriately."

"Perhaps if you drank less wine, you would be able to tell."

Clara's face grew warm. Had she really drunk that much wine? She didn't think so. She dropped her gaze to the ground. "I beg your pardon," she repeated.

"Forget it. You need to return to your hotel to rest before our voyage to Andros tomorrow."

"Tomorrow? But...why so soon? I thought we'd get our bearings here first and recover from our trip from England before going on to Andros. I'm—I'm not ready to go out there yet." She looked up at his face, but his impassive expression told her nothing.

"We're leaving in the morning. I don't want to be in Nassau any longer. The Governor is sure to badger me again if I stay."

Despite her reluctance to leave, it sounded like Theophilus was determined. There was nothing she could do about it. She would have to go to that remote island with her husband who wouldn't even stay in the same hotel as she did, let alone the same room. She didn't actually mind his distance, but she didn't know what he expected. How would it be when they were staying on a practically deserted island together? Swallowing her disappointment, she nodded. "How long will we be staying on Andros?"

His eyes dropped and he looked shifty suddenly. "Let's not decide that right now. We'll get over there and see how it goes."

Clara still didn't know why he had summoned her and the children to the Bahamas so precipitously. Perhaps he was waiting to tell her when they got to Andros. Clara had no inkling of the danger he might be in. Her vision had been so vague. And now with the mention of dangerous creatures on Andros Island? "Well. All right. Do I need to withdraw funds from the bank here before we depart?"

Theophilus cleared his throat. "Yes. Draw the entirety of your quarterly allowance. We may not get back to Nassau for a while. It's a bit of a trek to the settlement on Andros."

Clara laughed, an attempt at levity. "The entirety of my allowance? My goodness, is living over on Andros Island very expensive then?"

Theo did not laugh in return. "Just get it all, Clara. And no bank notes. We want English sovereigns."

Rebuffed, she fell silent. He was her husband so she couldn't very well deny him her funds, but she would have liked some indication about what the money would be needed for. And why the insistence on coins? They would be much heavier to carry on their sea voyage over to Andros Island. Perhaps he was worried about the effect of salt water on the paper money. She'd get him the money, but since he didn't know that her parents had raised her allowance for her trip, she decided to keep that amount back. Who knew what could happen to the money on their way to Andros? Were there still pirates? A wave of tiredness hit her and she almost staggered. The wine, the argument, and her poor sleep since leaving England all compounded her fatigue.

"Ah, here we are. I'll bid you goodnight here. The boat leaves at 1pm. I trust that will be enough time for you to take care of your banking and packing. There isn't much room on the boat. No more than three trunks. You might ask at Government House to see if you can leave your excess baggage there."

Clara nodded her acquiescence, stifling a sigh. He left her in the lobby of the hotel.

CHAPTER NINE

Clara tried not to look over the side of the boat as it bobbed through the waves. The clear water below them was deep, deep blue. After one peek into the seemingly bottomless depths, Clara withdrew from the railing, dizzy with vertigo. The children were still clinging to the railing, pointing and jabbering at every fish and frond of seaweed they spotted. She unfurled her parasol for a little relief from the sun beating down on the deck. Her wide hat didn't protect her from the penetrating tropical sun. Despite the intense sunlight, the warm air did feel pleasant, and the heat penetrated her bones, melting and relaxing her. She didn't miss the cold, damp English weather. She didn't even miss her family at the moment. Perhaps this deserted island holiday Theophilus seemed intent on would be nice. Perhaps the name of the ship, Cheer Up, was a good omen. She was still uncertain that this little boat was the best choice to make a 55-mile journey across the sea from Nassau to Andros Island, but the captain, a Captain E. Manuel Edgecombe, assured her that he made the journey twice a month. They were sailing in what looked like the middle of the ocean, although Nassau was only an hour behind them.

They would be arriving at the settlement soon after suppertime, the captain had told them. It would be dark by then. Clara had asked the hotel to pack a picnic basket since she didn't know when they would be able to eat. Theo still hadn't told her where they would be staying but Clara was guessing there would be no luxurious hotel on Andros Island. Perhaps a little boarding house was to be their final destination.

Summoning up her courage, she spoke to Theophilus for the first time since boarding. "Pardon me, Theophilus. Where will we be staying when we arrive at this Driggs Hill settlement? I can't imagine there's anything like the Colonial Hotel there."

She smiled to show him that she was making a little joke.

He turned from his vigil at the bow and growled in response. "No, there is no grand hotel there. You will be staying in a little house."

"Have the servants been informed that we'll be arriving late this evening?"

Theo raised his eyebrows and smirked. "No. No one knows when we'll be getting to Driggs Hill, but they'll know soon enough. It's a very small place and they'll be waiting for the mailboat."

Clara was nonplussed. How very odd. "So they won't have supper held for us?"

Theo shook his head, his incomprehensible smirk still stretched across his lips.

She tried to smile despite the obvious lack of welcome planned for them. "I'm glad that I ordered a picnic basket for us. Shall I save it for later or are you hungry now?"

"I ate before we boarded. Give something to the children. They're looking a bit ragged."

Glancing quickly over to her children, she saw that they sat on the deck, leaning against the railing. They looked flushed. Their excited energy had been expended. Clara called them over and handed them each a sandwich and bottle of milk.

"Sit down in the shade and eat something, children. Reginald, where is your hat?"

The boy pulled his cap out of his jacket pocket. "Here, Mama."

"Put it on your head or you'll burn to a crisp." She frowned at her son with his damp curls plastered to his head.

"Clara, why didn't you buy straw hats for the children at the Straw Market in Nassau? They would be much more practical than that cap."

Clara twisted her mouth in disdain. "Straw hats? They look so...native. I really didn't think the children would look appropriate in straw hats. I mean, you can get away with the straw hat because you've lived here for a long time and your clothing suits it..."

She trailed off, wondering if she'd offended Theo by referring to his attire as "native." He didn't seem to notice.

"The straw hat is a practical defence against the sunlight. You should all wear them here. That filmy white thing on your head will be ruined within a week."

As if to lend credence to his words, a wind whipped up, tearing at the veiling and ribbons on Clara's hat. She clutched at her hat and pushed the veil away from her eyes and mouth. The wind continued to pull at the fripperies on her hat and succeeded in loosening a feather. The white plume went flying away to land in the ocean.

"Oh! My feather!" Tears sprang to her eyes at the loss. She loved the hat, and the feathers, real ostrich, had been quite dear.

"There, what did I tell you? That hat is completely impractical."

Clara looked down at the worn deck. Why did he always have to be right? "I'm going to sit in the cabin out of the wind."

The wind buffeted her as she minced towards the cabin door. Was it getting windier? She glanced over her shoulder and saw a huge bank of puffy rain clouds on the horizon. She hoped that they weren't heading into a storm. Clara shuddered to think of the little boat being tossed about on a rough sea.

The cabin was quiet but stuffy and hot. There was a dirty wooden bench along one wall and stacks of wooden boxes and canvas bags crowding the rest of the room. She looked at the mess in despair, not daring to sit. The grime would ruin her white gown. It had seemed like a good wardrobe choice in the tropical heat, but she hadn't anticipated how filthy this boat would be. What was Theophilus thinking to drag her onto this vessel? Was he trying to make her suffer? She wondered again why he had summoned her to the Bahamas when he plainly didn't want her here.

The deck under her shuddered and leapt. She stumbled, then put out a hand to brace herself on the wall. Clara peeked out through the round window in the door and saw tall waves racing by the side of the boat, making it pitch up and down. The cumulus clouds were closer now and the sky above was darkening.

Oh, no. We're riding into that storm. What was that stupid captain thinking?

The little vessel dipped down into the trough of a wave and back up again. Clara placed both hands against the wall to brace herself, trying not to mourn the certain ruin of her gloves. Thankfully, she had never been seasick so the violent movement as they plunged through the waves didn't bother her. She peered through the window again and spotted the children clinging to the railing. Else was holding onto Reggie, trying to prevent him from being plunged overboard. Clara gasped. There was no sign of Theophilus.

Clara opened the cabin door, and a gust of wind knocked her back a step. She gripped the frame of the door and called out. "Elsinoe! Reginald! Come away from there!"

The children looked at her, their eyes wide with fear.

"I can't let go, Mama. We'll fall in." Elsie's voice was full of tears.

Clara tottered across the deck to them, trying to keep her feet under her. She reached the children and, in a moment of stillness as they traversed the top of a wave, grabbed them both. She dragged them towards the cabin door. All three reached the cabin as the boat began another descent down a wave. Clara pushed them inside before stepping in herself. She slammed the door shut. "Sit down and catch your breath. What were you doing standing next to the railing? You could have been swept overboard."

Reggie was crying. Elsie looked close to tears herself. "We were watching the waves and then didn't know where to go. Papa is up at the front of the boat and the captain is busy."

"Bow. The front of the boat is the bow," Clara corrected her absently.

The girl nodded in response.

"We'll remain here until the sea calms down."

Reggie sobbed and clung to Clara. "Mama, we going to sink? Big waves."

Clara shushed him, caressing his hair. He'd lost his cap again. "No, we're not going to sink. It's merely a storm." She hoped. Clara had no idea how seaworthy this boat was, despite the captain's reassurances. How often did he pilot through this kind of tempest?

They waited in the cabin, watching rain lash down across the deck. The wind howled through cracks in the cabin walls but thankfully, the rain did not penetrate their refuge. The storm continued for what seemed like hours and hours but when the sky lightened and the wind died down, Clara checked her pocket watch. It had been barely an hour. The storms in the tropics were intense but brief. The sun reappeared and steam rose from the wooden deck.

"Come children, we can go back outside now."

The temperature climbed back up instantly once the clouds passed. Clara went looking for something to quench her thirst. She found the picnic basket shoved in between two canvas-wrapped bundles. It must have slid there during the storm. She opened the lid and gasped in dismay. The rain had drenched the contents of the wicker basket through. The bottles of fruit juice and the jars of potted meats were unscathed but everything else was a soggy mess. Her stomach grumbled but she was no stranger to starving herself, so she plucked a bottle of juice out of the basket. She heard heavy footsteps behind her and turned.

Theo stood there, his clothing dripping onto the deck. "I see you weathered the storm a bit better than I. The food does not seem to have been so fortunate."

"Theophilus! You're soaking. Did you stand on the deck for the entirety of the storm?"

"Yes, it was quite invigorating. I'll dry off soon enough in the sun." He smiled, a genuine smile of pleasure. It was as if he truly enjoyed being tossed about in the storm. Clara hadn't remembered this sense of adventure. He must have developed it here.

"The children are still in the cabin. I had to drag them off the railing during the storm. They could have fallen overboard." She eyed him accusingly.

Theo stiffened, she hoped at the implied criticism. He had been very distant with the children and seemed to be shunning all parental responsibilities. "I told you to keep a closer eye on them. The Bahamas are not safe like England."

Was he blaming her for the children's peril? Would he take no responsibility for them? Feeling on the verge of an argument she didn't want to have, Clara took a steadying breath. She swallowed her angry retort, then stooped and picked up two more bottles of juice for the children. She clutched them to her chest and walked off without a word. Now that it was light again, Clara could see that they were sailing along close to land. The water was a light aquamarine here and when she glanced over the side of the boat, the bottom of the ocean appeared close through the transparent water. With the coast so close by, they would be safe from more inclement weather and would be at Driggs Hill on time.

CHAPTER TEN

A single light burned at the end of the dock where the Cheer Up pulled to. It had been dark for hours and Clara had wondered how Captain Edgecombe was able to navigate through the reef next to the island. She had only the foggiest notion of nautical navigation. They were finally here and safe, so her ignorance didn't matter in the slightest. She squinted at the dock, picking out two shadowy figures standing there. The moon was dark that night and only starlight brightened the sky. The captain cut the engine and threw the mooring line around the bollard on the wooden pier. The little boat shuddered to a halt. Clara breathed in and released the breath, relaxing a little of the tension she'd gathered since the storm.

A voice called out of the gloom, no doubt from one of the people on the pier. "Ahoy there, Cheer Up. Welcome back to Andros!"

The captain called back a terse response.

Theo spoke up. "Ward, is that you? It's Theo. I'm back from Nassau with Clara and the children."

Another lantern flared to life, held by one of the people on the dock. Clara could see a man standing there, tall and slim, with a pale face. The light was too poor for her to discern more.

"Theo! Welcome back!" Another voice, this time it was a woman's voice, warm and husky. Clara felt a pang of jealousy at the welcome in the strange woman's voice.

Theo climbed onto the pier, not stopping to wait for Clara and the children and shook hands with the people on the dock. Clara stood, feeling awkward and uncomfortable, unsure what to do. Was she supposed to join Theo on the dock? Wait for the captain to bring their luggage onto the deck of the boat? Theo was talking to the people in a low voice, and it seemed an eternity before he turned back, beckoning her. She stepped onto rickety planking, thankful that she was unable to see more of the dubious pier. She approached the trio with her society smile firmly in place. Theo introduced her to the couple, Ward and Lydia. She assumed they were married since they were out at night together, but Theo didn't provide a last name for either.

"And the children? Where are they?"

Ward looked around eagerly, unusually interested in a pair of strange children. Clara flinched. The children? Where were they? She had last seen them curled up sleeping in the cabin of the boat. She turned back to the boat and saw them standing on the deck, rubbing sleep out of their eyes. They looked lost and frightened. Clara felt a pang of guilt for forgetting them, if only for a moment. There was so much going on that she lost track of things, including her children apparently. Not for the first time, she regretted the fever that had kept Nanny Rodgers from accompanying them. This would all be so much easier if Clara had assistance with the children.

Theo's tone was jovial, unusual for him. "Oh, there they are. Come, children, you must meet Lydia and Ward."

Elsie and Reggie shuffled down the gangplank towards the adults, clinging to each other. Clara watched them approach. Their clothing was rumpled and dirty from the trip, certainly not making a great first impression on these new people. Not that she looked fresh either. She winced to think of how her white linen gown looked after the trip from Nassau.

The children shook hands wordlessly with Ward and Lydia. Clara closed her eyes, exhausted. She imagined the children felt the same. "We're all very hungry and tired. Perhaps you could walk with us to our guesthouse?"

Lydia and Ward exchanged looks, smirking at each other. What a strange couple. Clara couldn't make out what the smirks meant but at that point, didn't care. The captain deposited their luggage with a thump on the dock behind her. Clara glanced down at the bags then up at the captain. "Can we pay you to carry the luggage up to our lodgings, Captain Edgecombe?"

Clara put her hand into her reticule, clasping one of the sovereigns that Theo had insisted she bring. A sovereign seemed an extravagant amount of money to pay but since there were no porters on the deserted pier, she didn't feel that she had much choice.

The captain harrumphed and spat into the water. "I ain't no stevedore, missus."

Clara withdrew her hand and cast a beseeching look at Theo.

He shrugged. "I told you not to bring much luggage. We're not in a tourist-friendly port."

Clara looked around at the group. "Perhaps...perhaps we can all lend a hand?" Ward shrugged and grabbed the handles on one side of her large steamer trunk and gestured to Theo to take the other side. Lydia glared at the offending bags before reaching down and picking one up. Clara hoisted what she could, leaving the children to struggle under the weight of another trunk, fortunately much smaller. The little procession made its way along the seemingly endless pier to the beach. The rickety wooden pier was easy going compared to the sand she found herself wading through, tripping and stumbling, her shoes filling with sand. She heard Reggie whimpering softly behind her and Elsie murmuring words of comfort to him. From the sounds behind Clara, the children dropped the trunk several times as they followed the adults up to a sparse row of trees. Clara was too tired to check. Her arms and shoulders were burning with the unaccustomed exertion, but she stifled her own moans. The ground was firmer through the trees. They were following some kind of rough sand track. Clara could see very little in the gloom but there was light from lanterns hanging on dim structures between the trees. They stumbled along without speaking and she thought the walk would never end. Eventually they arrived at a fork in the trail and took a path that followed along a high hedge of plants. She could see glimmers of light through the dense foliage and when they reached a break in the hedge, the lights inside dazzled her after the long, dim walk. The hedge bordered a large compound of small huts with a big house in the centre. Lanterns glowed at the doorway of each hut and along the paths leading to them. The light streaming from all the windows of the three-storey, sprawling building eclipsed the meagre lantern light. Silhouettes of people moved in the windows and voices murmured all around her, but she couldn't see anyone clearly.

Her stomach growled and she turned to Ward. "At last! I'm absolutely famished. Do you suppose the kitchen could be convinced to feed us?"

Ward and Lydia again exchanged a peculiar look.

He spoke first. "Mealtimes are strictly enforced but since this is your first night, I suppose we could make an exception."

At that, Clara was confused. Was he the proprietor of this establishment? She thought he was a friend of Theo's. He certainly didn't seem like an innkeeper. She decided to squash her curiosity for now.

"That would be lovely. We'll happily pay extra, Mr...." she trailed off. He had been introduced to her as simply Ward, but she didn't feel that would be appropriate.

He laughed, a short, sharp laugh. "Don't worry about that, Clara. Let's see what we can get you to eat before we show you to your... house."

At that remark, Lydia snickered. Clara couldn't make out what was so funny. And Ward seemed to think they were on first name terms. Social norms appeared to be vastly different here. She would need to adapt. They all walked up the steps to the veranda of the big house and the men dropped the trunk to one side of the door. Clara let her burden go with relief, rubbing her aching arms. She gestured to the exhausted children to do the same. The foyer of the house was expansive, but the ceiling was low. Their shoes clattered across the uncarpeted, wooden floor. People greeted them with brusque nods as they walked by. The dining room seemed more like a school's dining hall than a proper hotel dining room. Long trestle tables and benches filled the sparsely decorated room. The furniture looked well-worn and not entirely clean. Bread crusts and fruit cores littered the ground.

Ward gestured towards a table. "Sit down. I'll ask about dinner. Everyone else ate a few hours ago. There is no eating after 8pm, but I'll make an exception for you this once. Please remember that in the future, dinner is at 7pm and you will be expected to be here on time."

Ward's tone seemed a bit more dictatorial than your average innkeeper, but Clara again decided that things were different here. She didn't care at this point, she only wanted to eat. The children slumped onto a bench and Elsie laid her head onto her arms on the table.

Reggie scrunched up his face and started to whine. "I'm hungry, Mama, hungry, Mama—"

Clara shushed him with a frown. "Be a good boy, Reginald, no grizzling. You'll get something to eat soon."

She glanced around the room and noticed Theo sitting at the other end of the table, talking in a low voice to Lydia. They both had their backs to Clara and the children. Clara fought the surge of jealousy that rose in her.

Who is this Lydia person? Why is she having an intimate conversation with my husband?

She tried to draw in a calming breath but was too exhausted to settle herself easily. Fortunately, a man entered the dining room bearing a tray of food and a pitcher of fruit juice. Steam rose from bowls of spicy rice and some kind of legume. The dish was not familiar to Clara, but she was beyond caring. The man, a stranger who didn't introduce himself, placed the bowls in front of them without speaking. They thanked him but he didn't respond, merely took the empty tray and left the room. The food was spicier than she was accustomed to, but she gobbled it down with unseemly haste. Even the children wolfed down their portions, then gulped down the fruit juice the man had brought.

They ate every morsel of the unfamiliar food, then Reggie tugged on Clara's sleeve. "I'm still hungry, Mama."

Clara shook her head. The servant with the food had left and it seemed that everyone else had gone to bed. Lydia left the room without a word, although Clara caught Theo watching her leave.

He approached Clara and the children. "Time to show you to your quarters. I'm sure you're ready for your beds."

He led them out of the dining hall towards the front door, surprising Clara. She had assumed their room would be in the larger house. They moved back through the garden, along a lantern-lit pathway to one of the small straw-roofed huts.

"How quaint." Her tone, dripping with sarcasm, belied her words. She was exhausted and her manners suffered because of it. Theo didn't respond. He opened the wooden door. It screeched as he shoved it open. Stepping inside, he lit an oil lamp on the wall. Clara almost wished he hadn't. The dark floor seemed to move then cleared, revealing the light sand of the surrounding ground. Clara suppressed a shriek. Theo snorted in response.

"Don't mind the cockroaches. They clear out as soon as people start moving around in these huts. They're reclusive insects."

Clara gaped at him, but he didn't seem to notice. He pointed out the paltry furniture: a single raised bed, a chest for clothes, a rickety chair, and a pile of straw mats.

"And where will the children sleep?" Clara's voice was faint.

"Oh, I'm sure they can curl up together on those mats. There are extra blankets on the bed and it's so warm, I doubt you'll need much."

She nodded, feeling like a marionette. "And a sink? The facilities?"

"You'll have to fetch water in that bucket to wash and I'm sure there's a chamber pot under the bed. Dump it in the pit on the edge of the yard. You'll know where by the smell."

Clara's fog started to clear, and anger built in her belly. Controlling her voice, she continued with her questions. "And where do you sleep, Theo?" Her tone was deceptively calm, sweet.

"I have a room assigned to me in the Order House. The big house where we had dinner. Good night, all."

And with that, he was gone, leaving them alone. Clara gaped after him. The children looked at her with huge eyes. Fury blazed up in her.

How dare he treat me this way? As if I were something to be tucked away when I'm not needed? And to bring me to stay in this squalor? The Order House? That didn't sound like an inn.

"Mama?" Elsie's pleading voice broke into her thoughts.

"What?" she snapped in return.

"We're very tired. Can we please lie down?"

Clara gritted her teeth, holding back a screech of rage. This wasn't the children's fault, and they did need to sleep. "Yes, of course, dear. Help me move these mats to make a bed for you."

She held her breath as they adjusted the mats, hoping insects wouldn't scurry out. They created makeshift beds on the floor. Reggie and Elsie took off their shoes and laid down in their clothing, falling asleep in moments.

Clara slumped onto the bed, watching them sleep. She didn't know what tomorrow would bring but she knew she'd have to confront Theo over the squalid living conditions. She needed answers about his expectations. Why had he brought them here?

CHAPTER ELEVEN

The wind rustled through the palm trees, warm and soft. Irene and her sisters sat in their yard, shelling pigeon peas in a companionable silence. Mae finished her pile of pods and brushed her hands off. She stared off into the distance. "When do you suppose the men will be back from sponging? Storm yesterday was a fierce one."

A shadow passed across Alice's face. Her husband had died a few years back while out sponging. A storm blew up from behind an island, then a wave had washed him overboard.

Irene saw her sister's expression and patted her hand. "Alec and the boys were heading down south, away from the Tongue. Plenty of bights down that way to shelter in. Henry's been gone a while longer though. Where he say they were going?" She looked across at Mae, trying to catch her eye.

Mae grimaced an attempt at a smile. "I think they going to the other side of the island. Storms powerful fierce over there, he says. I shouldn't worry though. That ship master, he not dumb, he knows to take shelter when storm's coming."

Alice must have had enough of this talk. "Irene, where's Mary this morning? She still got de morning sick?"

Irene nodded. Her son's wife was expecting their first baby and spent most of every morning chucking up her insides. "I'd best go and check on her. See if I can get her to take some tea. She stubborn. Says she don't need no medicine."

Mae shook her head, clicking her tongue. She didn't care much for young Mary. The girl had come down from North Andros and had snagged Daniel's interest with her teasing wiles. "Fool chile. I remember when I had de morning sick, and your teas fixed me up right."

Irene nodded, handing her bowl of peas to Alice. "I got some ready in my house. I'll go and see if I can get her to drink it up."

"That girl oughta listen up to you, Irene. You got de medicine knowledge."

"She don't think so. She says I's doing witchdoctoring on her. Her family don't use bush medicine like we do."

Mae pushed herself off the ground, huffing with exertion. She loved food and it showed in her voluptuous figure. She brushed the dust from her skirt and stretched. "'Bout time for me to get lunch on."

Alice stirred the peas with one finger, staring into the bowl. Irene's heart sank at the sight. Alice had always been prone to the blues, but it seemed worse these days.

Irene touched Alice's shoulder. "I's thinking to go crabbing tonight. Wouldn't mind company." Irene smiled down at her sister, hoping to pique her interest. Alice loved crabbing and it was a sure way to snap her out of her funk.

"Sure thing. That sounds good. See you at dusk. You coming too, Mae?"

"I think I'll stay home and keep an eye on things here. I'll let you two fetch me crabs."

Irene and Alice exchanged smiles. Mae had always been lazy, but no one minded.

Irene strode out away, heading to her son's house, trying to hide her relief at Alice's assent to the crabbing expedition. When she was out of earshot, she exhaled heavily. Taking care of her family's health in their minds and bodies was burdensome at times, especially when she was worried herself about her husband and sons. For all her brave words, she wasn't sure if they had been able to find shelter from the storm. She simply had to hope and pray that they were all right.

* * *

Elsie woke, groggy and disoriented, lying on a sandy floor. She blinked against the sunlight streaming in through the cracks between the logs in the wall next to her head. Focusing her eyes, she saw a roof made of straw, and a bare, shabby room that comprised the entire inside of the wooden shack she was lying in. Her blankets were twisted around her legs, and she kicked free, one foot striking a lump under the covers. The lump groaned, revealing itself to be Reggie. He sat up, his face screwed up in annoyance. "Why'd you kick me? I was sleeping."

Elsie yawned and shrugged. "Sorry, Reg. Didn't know it was you."

She looked around, wondering where her mother was. Not in the tiny hut. She and Reggie were its only inhabitants now. Her tummy grumbled loudly, and her brother giggled.

"Be quiet, pest. It's my tummy wanting food."

"Me too. What's for breakfast? Where's Mama? I'm hungry."

"Oh, Reggie, do shut up. We'll have to go and find her."

Elsie got to her feet and smoothed her dress, but it was a wrinkled mess. She couldn't imagine what her hair looked like but was sure her mother would let her know. As if summoned, Mama entered the hut, looking fresh and tidy, her hair plaited down her back. Elsie thought that she looked too young to be their mother with her hair like that.

"Finally! You two have slept an age. Now get yourselves cleaned up and wear something you can play in. You'll have to do something with your hair,

Elsie, it looks like a rat's nest. I can't imagine why you wore it down on the boat ride here. The wind tangled it horribly."

Elsie resisted the urge to roll her eyes. Her mother had told her to wear her hair loose yesterday, because she thought it looked prettier. She stood looking around for her brush and clothes, feeling lost. Their luggage was piled in the corner of the room, and she didn't know where anything was. She didn't even know where her art case was. It hadn't got left behind in Nassau, had it? Mama must have found her possessions since she was wearing clean clothes. Elsie rummaged around in the bags and found her hairbrush. Her hair was snarled, and the hairbrush tugged at it.

"Mama, I can't do it. Will you brush my hair, please?"

Her mother sighed deeply before taking the brush. She pulled hard on the knots. Elsie gritted her teeth against the pain, but tears sprang to her eyes. Mama wasn't very good at gentle brushing like Nanny. Nanny never pulled her hair this hard.

"Mama, it hurts."

Her voice was soft but the note of accusation in it must have angered her mother and she yanked hard. "I can't help it. Your hair is matted. I can't get the brush through it. We'll have to cut it off."

Elsie gasped. Cut her hair? She'd always had waist-length hair, as long as she could remember. "No, Mama, please don't cut it off. I'll be good, I won't complain, I promise."

Her mother exhaled a loud breath and continued brushing. Reggie watched in silence from their nest of blankets on the floor. No doubt he was relieved that his hair was short and didn't tangle easily. Elsie resisted the urge to stick her tongue out at him.

Papa walked into the hut without warning as Mama was finishing Elsie's hair. "Good morning, everyone. I trust you slept well."

Elsie murmured a greeting. Reggie sat without speaking, seeming to still be in awe of his father.

Mama nudged Elsie out of the way and faced Papa. "Good morning, Theophilus. We need to discuss our accommodations. I was expecting something rustic, but this is beyond the pale. What kind of establishment is this?"

"Ah yes. It is rather rustic. Clara, Ward has asked me to bring you to see him this morning. This isn't an inn. It's the compound of a community of acolytes, the Order of Andronicus. We think it's time you understood what we are doing here. Ward wants to speak to you about it."

"The Order of—and this isn't an inn. Not surprising, I must say. Are you part of this order?"

"Yes. I've been a member for five years."

"I see. Since you arrived here from England. And what does that mean exactly?"

"Go and talk to Ward. He'll explain."

Elsie sat silently, drinking in every word. How very strange. What were they talking about? What were acolytes?

Mama pursed her lips. "I think that would be wise. He's expecting me this morning?"

Papa nodded and escorted Mama out. They left without explaining what was going on or where breakfast was going to be. Elsie sat and braided her hair. She supposed she'd better get dressed and be ready to go when Mama returned. She didn't want to keep her mother waiting. Elsie buttoned up her dress. Despite leaving off her petticoat, she still felt stifled in the little hut. She ventured outside, hoping for a cool breeze. She sensed Reggie following behind her. He shadowed her everywhere at home, so that wasn't a surprise.

The gardens, or yard as Papa had called it, stretched in all directions around her. Sandy paths meandered through scrub and rows of leafy plants. Tall palm trees swayed high above her head, the ground below them littered with fronds and what looked like giant wooden balls but were probably seeds or fruit. Short bushes bore fruit in yellow, green, and red. Elsie didn't know what kind of fruit hung on the bushes, but she was hungry enough to try eating them. Before she could approach one of the fruit-laden bushes, a man appeared, sauntering around a corner. He seemed small for an adult, but his beard marked him as such.

He must have caught sight of the children hovering in front of the hut because he called out to them. "Hullo there! You're new. Are you Theo's little ones?" His wide smile drew a similar response from Elsie, and she nodded, feeling shy. The man drew closer, and his kindly face made Elsie feel a little better. "I'm Horace. What's your name?"

Elsie held out her hand to shake his. "My name is Elsie. This is my brother Reggie. Pleased to meet you, Mr. Horace."

Horace shook her hand, laughing. He showed all his teeth when he laughed. "Just Horace. And it's good to meet you too. What are you planning to do with your first day here on Andros? Has your mother set you to studying?" He winked and made a mock grimace.

Elsie giggled at his funny faces. "No, she didn't. I don't know what we're supposed to do. Perhaps explore the island?"

Horace frowned and shook his head. "I don't think you ought to go wandering around alone. There are lots of dangers on the island…sink holes, quicksand, venomous creatures, scary monsters, bugs so large they'll carry you away…" He broke off his listing of the dangers to slap at his arm, leaving a smear of blood. "And mosquitoes. Blood-sucking parasites. They're everywhere, but especially out in the wilderness."

The wilderness didn't sound like a place Elsie wanted to explore.

Reggie stepped forward to examine the remains of the insect, finally breaking his silence. "It sucks your blood? Ewwww."

Horace brushed the dead insect off his arm. "Yep, they suck the blood right out of you. Better come with me to our little farm. You don't want to go out into the forest and mangrove swamps, they're full of these nasty things."

Elsie was curious about Horace and what he was doing, and she couldn't think of a good reason why not to accompany the funny little man. He didn't act like the other adults she knew. They strolled along the sandy trail, turning this way and that. Horace seemed to have a destination in mind, so she followed along. She stared longingly at the fruit she spotted growing next to the path.

Finally, she couldn't hold her tongue one more second. "Horace? Do you think it would be alright if we ate some of this fruit?"

He stopped and glanced back at her, a bemused look on his face. "Fruit? You want to eat fruit? I don't see why not. Eat whatever you like. Make sure it's ripe or you'll give yourselves a tummy ache." With those words of advice, he resumed his saunter. Elsie reached out and grabbed a round, pinkish red plum and popped it into her mouth. It was vaguely sweet but made her mouth pucker. She gulped it down, wrinkling her nose.

Maybe that one wasn't ripe.

It did nothing to quell her complaining, empty stomach so she tried another. This one was darker, more purple than red. It was a little sweeter than the first and didn't dry out her mouth like the first one.

Emboldened by his sister, Reggie plucked a yellow berry. He nibbled a bit off and pulled a face. "Sour."

Elsie nodded in response. The tropics had some weird fruit, that was certain. "Horace? Is any of this fruit good to eat?"

Her plaintive tone must have penetrated. He stopped fully and faced them. "You're awfully adventurous eaters for little English children. Not many would eat raw gooseberries and unripe coco plums. Have you had your breakfast today?" The children shook their heads in unison. Horace tutted and surveyed the area. "I'm sorry, but it's far too late for breakfast at the Order House and you won't find anything but water when we get to the bean plot. We're going to weed today. Let me see, what's around that might provide a bit more sustenance? Oh, here's some sapodilla. You'll like these." He gave them each a handful of fuzzy, brown fruit. Elsie quirked an eyebrow at him and Horace laughed. "No, really, try them. They're quite delicious and they'll keep you going until luncheon."

Elsie took a tentative bite. It was delicious, like brown sugar or caramel. "Ooo, it is good. Go ahead, Reggie, they're scrumptious."

They continued their way to the bean plot, devouring handfuls of fruit, and arrived with sticky hands and faces. A group of adults and children scraped at the reddish soil with hoes. None of them looked up. They moved slowly and Elsie didn't think they were particularly clever at weeding, if that's what they were doing. They worked without speaking, even the children.

Horace waved at one of the men and called out in a cheerful voice, "Good morning, Stephen!"

The man straightened up and scowled in their direction. "It's about time you appeared. The morning is half-gone. And who is this trailing in your wake?" He eyed the children suspiciously from under bushy black eyebrows.

Horace gestured towards Elsie and Reggie. "This is Elsie and Reggie. They're Theo's children, arrived only last night."

Stephen's scowl didn't shift. He seemed not to care who they were. "Everyone works around here. You don't work, you don't eat. Understand?"

Elsie and Reggie nodded and moved closer, grabbing hoes. Their grandmother had let them weed the perennial beds in her garden, a task they had always enjoyed. They'd show these people how to properly weed a garden. Reggie leaned close to Elsie and whispered, "This is lots more fun than schoolwork! I hope Mama keeps forgetting it."

Elsie giggled. "Just don't remind her and we'll be safe from grammar and maths for ages."

The children chattered as they worked, pointing out to each other colourful twittering birds flying from bush to bush and little lizards darting among the rocky ground next to the cultivated plot. They didn't spot the sharp-toothed lizards that climbed trees and ate rat heads. The air was sweet with the smell of crushed leaves and ripe fruit. Everything was so different here. No one told her what to do or what to say, like at home. What a lovely holiday they were having. She couldn't wait to tell Grandmama and Grandpapa about the delicious fruit hanging off bushes everywhere and the lovely birds, so unlike England. The people were a little odd and she wasn't sure why the children were so quiet, but Horace was nice.

CHAPTER TWELVE

The Order House bustled with activity when Clara arrived that morning, escorted by Theo. He took her bag of sovereigns and disappeared as soon as they entered the building. Clara carried a satchel full of her favourite texts on astronomy and Spiritualism. She knew nothing about the Order of Andronicus and the teachings it espoused but she felt hopeful that she would share in meaningful discussions with its members. Ward in particular had seemed interested in Clara's thoughts. That Lydia woman had not. Pushing away the unpleasant thought, Clara mounted the steps and entered the grand foyer. Ward had summoned her here this morning to talk. She wondered how she would find him.

A slight woman, pale and dishevelled, knelt on the floor, scrubbing. She glanced up at Clara, scowled, then dropped her gaze back to her work. Clara frowned.

The servants here are very unfriendly. Almost surly.

"Ah, Clara, you have arrived at last. I expect you were exhausted from your journey." Ward looked older in the daylight. At night, his hair had looked blond, but she could see the grey in it now. His face was more lined, drawn. "In the future, do make sure you are here no later than seven o'clock. Now, let us talk in my office."

She was taken aback by his presumption, telling her when she needed to be at the Order House, not to mention using her given name. Seven o'clock was very early in her social circle, although she supposed an early start to the day was a necessity in this hot climate. The brief walk over from that squalid excuse for a house had been sweltering. Ah yes, she must discuss her accommodations with Ward. Her sordid accommodations must have been some mistake. She walked by Ward's side, careful not to brush against him. She had chosen simpler clothing today, a narrow skirt and shirtwaist. They entered a room, sparsely furnished with a desk and two chairs. The blinds were drawn but the light was still bright. Ward waved her into a seat, taking the one on the other side of the desk. He smiled at her with that same hard, glittering stare that Theo had. Something about his eyes made her want to look away.

"We should talk about expectations and a little about the Order."

Clara dropped her satchel to the floor and gave him a careful smile. "Yes. I must apologise for my misunderstanding. I was under the impression that Theo was bringing me here on a holiday, so I assumed you were an innkeeper last night. Frightfully sorry."

Ward laughed, a short, humourless bark. "No, indeed, this is not an inn. We are a reclusive community of people gathered for a spiritual purpose."

"Theo alluded to that but gave me no details. While this may not be the holiday I was expecting, I am most curious about the Order's belief system and studies in esoterica. Do you follow the teachings of Madame B? I have read her work—"

Ward held up his hand, stopping her from continuing. It trembled with a palsy, as if he were much older than he appeared. "We do not discuss our philosophies with outsiders, I'm afraid. If you want to study with us, you will have to join the Order, like your husband did. He has found much satisfaction in our teachings." He gestured at her bag. "You will not need those books. Ours is an oral tradition. It is easier to retain secrecy, you understand, if nothing is written down."

Clara was nonplussed and more than a little intrigued. Secret, unwritten teachings? And the idea that Theo had joined this mysterious spiritualist order? He had never been one for the immaterial world. She remembered her vision. Was there something going on here that placed Theo in danger? "How very mysterious. And are you the leader of this order?" Her tone came out more flirtatious than she had intended. His gaze grew warm. She squirmed a little in her seat. She certainly wasn't interested in a flirtation with this man.

"No, I am the—Deputy. Our leader is not present at the moment but we expect The First to appear at any moment."

Curious. It sounded like they were expecting some sort of apparition. "Oh. Has he been gone for a long time?"

"The comings and goings of The First are not something we discuss. The First will be present when it is time."

Clara wetted her lips. She was used to Spiritualists spouting bizarre nonsense at times, but that was usually during a seance or some other trance. Perhaps this man was the danger facing Theo. "How fascinating. Well, I think I'd better be going. I'm not sure what the children are doing. They've been unattended this whole time. I wasn't able to bring their nanny along."

She snatched up her satchel and got to her feet. Ward also stood. "No, I don't think you should go. The children are fine. I sent Horace over to keep them busy."

"Did you? That was very kind of you."

"Please be seated, Clara. We have so much to talk about."

She felt the weight of social obligation. Walking out would be rude and she couldn't be rude. She returned to her seat, clutching the bag of books to her stomach like a life preserver. "Very well. I'm certain we could discuss a great deal, but you told me you couldn't divulge the teachings of the Order unless I became a member."

She watched a predatory smile spread across his face and into his overly bright eyes. "But you are going to become a member, Clara, are you not?" It didn't sound like a question to her.

She suppressed a shiver, not wanting him to see weakness. "I think that decision would have to be made carefully, deliberately. I'm not even certain what it would entail."

"As a member of the Order, you would receive daily training in our teachings. You would stay here with us and partake in meals and our shared experiences. You would take part in the community work."

The memory of the woman scrubbing the foyer flashed into her mind. Community work? Were the people she took to be servants actually members of the Order? "It sounds very—isolated."

He gazed at her, his expression unreadable. He got up from his chair and walked around the desk. She tilted her head up to look at him. "We find the isolation to be most conducive to our spiritual practice. I think you will too. Imagine, no social obligations to interfere with your studies. Everyone around you sharing your knowledge and beliefs. You long for this, Clara. You want to be part of this community."

He stared deep into her eyes. She sat transfixed, feeling like a rabbit trapped in the gaze of a fox. She swallowed. "I—I don't know."

He nodded. "Yes, you do, Clara. You want to be part of this. Every fibre of your being is craving to be with us. Let go of those societal restraints. Be the person you want to be, not the person you've been told to be."

She struggled, and thoughts of her parents, her friends, her teachers held her back from agreeing. She creased her forehead, trying to resist Ward's persuasion. "But—no, I can't, I can't do that. I have obligations."

She surged to her feet. He clamped his hands down on her shoulders, never breaking eye contact. "Yes, you can. Clara, I can feel that you want to join us. You want to grasp true happiness, freedom, mental stimulation. You will get all of that here with us."

She tried to break away but couldn't look away from his glittering eyes.

"Stay here with us, Clara. Become one with the Order. It's everything you've dreamed of."

She felt herself soften. What was the point of resisting? This was what she'd been striving for, hadn't it? Her search for happiness? "I have to talk to

Theophilus. He's my husband. I can't make this sort of commitment without him."

Ward smiled, confident. "You must know that Theo wants this. Why do you think he summoned you here? He may not have mentioned it because he wanted to be sure it was your decision. He didn't want you to feel forced into this. You yourself must make the commitment, but rest assured, he will not object."

Clara felt light-headed and detached from her body. She took a slow, shallow breath and nodded. There really were no difficulties. This was something she'd been yearning for. "I see. Theophilus doesn't object. And he brought me here for this. I must join you. How do I do that?"

Ward released her shoulders and moved away, only now looking away from her. "You'll attend our weekly assemblies and come here to the Order House for study. Until you are Exalted, you'll be assigned chores as one of the Mean. I will fetch Lydia. She will find you something to do." He resumed his seat at his desk and rang a small bell. Lydia appeared immediately. She must have been waiting outside the door.

"Lydia, Clara is joining us. Please see that she is assigned a duty rota and a study mentor."

Lydia crooked a finger at Clara and sauntered away, not checking to see if Clara was following. In a daze, Clara joined her in the foyer. What had she got herself into? And what would Theophilus say? Had he really intended this when he summoned her here? She really ought to have a talk with him soon.

"Hurry it up, Mean. You'll be helping in the kitchen today. You probably can't cook so they'll have you cleaning, I'm sure. If you can do that." Lydia stared pointedly at Clara's soft, white hands. Clara didn't respond to the woman's taunts. She was too busy wondering what the future held in store for her as a member of the Order of Andronicus.

CHAPTER THIRTEEN

Steam rose from the pot of conch stew, fragrant and spicy. Irene stirred, moving slowly in the heat of her tiny kitchen. She dropped her gaze to the charcoal bin. She'd have to fetch more charcoal for the stove before the stew was done. A shadow fell across her, interrupting her musings. She looked back and spied her husband silhouetted in the bright doorway, flanked by her son Joe.

Irene beamed at them. "Alec! Joe! You home early."

The men didn't respond. Alec moved into the little hut and Irene got a better look at his face. It was drawn, and there was a greyish pallor to his rich brown skin. Her stomach clenched and she caught a quick breath. She glanced at Joe, hovering in the doorway, then past him, seeking her other son.

"Where's Daniel?" she asked, dreading the answer.

Alec finally spoke, his voice cracking. "De sea—de sea took him."

"No!" The cry escaped Irene's lips then rose into a wail. A rushing sound filled her ears and she sank to her knees, arms wrapped around her middle, trying to hold back the pain. Alec started speaking again, a low murmur of words. Something about Daniel going down too far, too far into a blue hole, diving for the rare sponge she needed for the ogologo-ndu potion, diving and not coming up. She wept as he spoke, not responding to his quiet monologue. Her boy, her sweet, sweet boy taken from her by the sea. Grief all but overwhelmed Irene. She looked up and stared into Alec's eyes. Her torment was echoed in his face. Her sobs quieted. Alec's face was wet with tears. Feeling ancient, she slowly held out her hand to him and he grasped it painfully hard. Joe crept closer and put his hand on her shoulder. Irene grabbed at his hand.

The family remained silent, holding hands, gazes locked while the forgotten stew bubbled and spat on the stove. The smell of burnt conch roused Irene to her senses and she stood, stiff and silent, to attend to the pot.

"I can't do it no more, Reenie." Alec's voice was quiet in her ear. He approached her from behind and wrapped his arms around her waist, leaning his head against hers. He murmured into her hair. "De sea, she took my boy. I can't do it, Reenie, I can't go back out there."

Irene stiffened in his embrace. She turned and pushed him away from her. "Y'mean, give up fishing? How do you suppose we'll eat? And without de ogologo-ndu, we're never gonna make enough money to buy us a real house with some land."

Alec gulped. He didn't meet her eyes. "I could, I could farm someone else's land. We'd get by alright, Reenie."

"I's tired of getting by, Alec. That big-eyed sea took our boy but she's not gonna drag us down too. The white folk want my potion bad and they pay good money for it. They're big-eyed for more years, with no thought for what's gonna happen de longer they take that stuff. But they pay and pay and soon we'll be able to buy our own place."

Alec's face sagged in defeat but he made another attempt to convince her. "You wanna risk me or Joe getting took next time? How much longer, Reenie? I's feeling old, getting slow."

Irene took his hands, running her fingers across his scarred knuckles. "I know, honey, I know. Just a little longer. I got enough sponge for just one batch but then I'll need more. We're so close to buying that land. Just a little longer. Just one more trip."

He nodded and sagged against her, his head heavy on her shoulder. Irene swallowed down bitter guilt. Just a little longer and pray she wouldn't lose another to the sea.

CHAPTER FOURTEEN

Clara scurried into the assembly room, earning scowls from those already gathered there. She hadn't known where the assembly room was or exactly what time the event started so she was late. Ward stood at the front of the room, speaking.

"...this matter thus animated responds very readily to the influence of human thought, and every impulse sent out, either from the mental body or from the astral body of man, immediately clothes itself in a temporary vehicle of this vitalised matter."

She looked for a seat but they were all filled so she stood at the back of the room. Other members were there, their clothing faded and dirty. They must be members of the Mean. She studied their faces. They were enrapt at Ward's words, yearning. Clara wasn't sure why they were so taken with the speech. It sounded like something taken from Madame B's book on Spiritualism. It was interesting but certainly not earth-shattering. She turned her attention back to Ward. His voice was smooth and deep. He was a handsome man if you didn't notice the hardness in his eyes.

A man next to her passed her a cup. She scrutinised the cloudy liquid inside and glanced back at the man. He was watching her expectantly and nodded at her. He must be intending for her to drink. She stole a glance around and saw other members of the Mean sipping from cups. Perhaps it was some sacramental offering. She took a cautious sip and twisted her mouth in disgust. It was bitter and almost rancid. She made as if to pass the beverage along but the man grasped her arm, shaking his head. She was supposed to drink more of the wretched stuff? Clara brought the cup to her lips and pretended to take a long swallow. She grimaced and successfully got rid of the cup this time.

Ward's voice took on a droning quality. What was he saying? Something about a man-fish?

"...Dagon divides his Cosmogeny and Genesis into two portions...dogs with tails of fishes...the water-men terrible and bad she herself created..."

His words sounded nonsensical but she felt calmer, relaxed and wondered what was in the cup. The Mean around her seemed to sigh in unison and their faces slackened in a sort of rapture.

Was the Order giving its members some sort of euphoric drug?

She knew that to be a common practice, intended to open the mind to new concepts, and release mental inhibitions. Not wanting to be seen as out of place, she pretended to the same rapture, stealing glances at the other members. Those seated didn't seem to be drinking from the passing cups. She spotted Theo and Lydia sitting together near the front. The Order members called the Exalted must be allowed to sit during Assembly. Ward stopped talking and raised his arms in a benediction. The Exalted arose as one and filed towards him. He grasped a small flagon from the podium and flourished it. The Exalted knelt in front of him and he walked down the line, dribbling liquid from the flagon into their open mouths. A dark-haired woman that Clara had not seen before started trembling violently. She fell to the ground, thrashing from side to side. Her fellow Exalted ignored her. Clara frowned, her forehead creasing.

Isn't anyone going to help her?

The others of the Mean stood silently, still caught up in the rapture of their own drug. Clara could see Ward scowling down at the afflicted woman. The woman's moans filled the room but no one moved. Her heels banged against the wooden floor. Clara squirmed, not wanting to break ranks but filled with anxiety. With a final moan, the woman sank into unconsciousness. Ward resumed his talking, ignoring the unconscious woman on the floor in front of him. He called the meeting to an end. As people began moving out of the room, he gestured to the nearby Mean to carry the woman out. Clara remained where she was, still taken aback by the strange situation. The Mean crossed in front of her with their limp burden. Clara caught sight of the woman's blueish face. Her eyes were wide-open and staring. Was she dead? Clara couldn't tell but she shuddered and backed away. What was in that flagon?

As she pondered, Lydia approached her, a sneer on her lovely face. "Why are you lingering here? Have you already forgotten your assigned task?"

Clara tried not to scowl. Lydia was obviously high ranking in the Order and not to be offended. "No, I was about to leave."

"Oh? Were you? It looked more like you were loitering about, taking interest in things that don't concern you."

"What do you mean? I was—"

Lydia's eyes narrowed. "Did you drink the concoction that you were offered?"

Clara flushed. She nodded. She did drink a little sip but not as much as most of the Mean had.

"I don't believe you. There are consequences for not complying, Mean."

"Yes, ma'am." Clara lowered her eyes, almost whispering. She spotted two men approaching and looked up. It was Theo and Ward.

Theo looked sharply at Lydia. "What's going on?"

Lydia smirked, taking Theo's arm. "This Mean didn't accept all of the offering. Look at how overwrought she is."

Theo didn't look at Clara, nor did he respond. Ward studied Clara thoughtfully. "Clara, my dear. The offering is intended to help you. It will make you more open to possibilities. It's how you become Exalted. I know it's vile-tasting stuff, but next time, be sure to take the entire draught. Do you understand?"

Clara's eyes filled with tears at his kind rebuke. She nodded her assent. He drifted away, accompanied by Theo and other members of the Exalted. Lydia lingered, her poisonous gaze still locked on her. "Do you think you'll somehow become Exalted? That would be nothing short of miraculous."

Lydia twirled away, her long red-gold hair drifting behind her. Clara's stomach lurched with nausea. Her first Assembly and already she was marked as a failure. Why did Lydia hate her so much? What did Theophilus tell her during their cleansing sessions?

CHAPTER FIFTEEN

The next morning, Horace appeared again to accompany the children to the garden. "We'll be digging up sweet potatoes today. You've had breakfast, right?"

Elsie nodded. "Yes, we went with Mama up to the Order House. The food was weird. No toast or bacon. Only eggs and lots of fruit. And some kind of yukky mush. I didn't eat it."

Horace smiled at them. "We grow almost all our own food, you know. That's why it's important that everyone helps in the gardens."

"Oh, I didn't know that. But Mama and Papa weren't in the garden yesterday."

Horace's face darkened. He looked more serious than normal. "Ah, that's different. Your father is one of the Exalted. He is no longer required to do menial work."

"And Mama? Is she Exalted too?" Elsie wondered what people did when they were Exalted.

Horace shook his head, his expression even darker. "No, she's not Exalted. She was assigned duties inside the Order House."

Horace's bad mood was incomprehensible to Elsie. Why would Mama's duties upset him?

They strolled along another path, going in a different direction. The sweet potato plot was not far and the same sullen group were gathered there.

Elsie leaned over to Reggie. "I wonder how long we have to work for? I want to go and explore the woods."

Reggie's face was flushed from the heat. He nodded. "And the beach. Let's go swim in the ocean."

"But we haven't got bathing costumes."

Reggie grinned mischievously. "We can swim in our underclothes."

Elsie gasped. "Reggie! We can't do that!"

"Why not?"

Elsie was silent at that. Why not? It didn't seem like there were a lot of people around on the island. She noticed huge, puffy clouds gathering overhead, moving fast. Big, fat raindrops hit her face, at first only a few but quickly increasing. Shrieking with delighted surprise, she raced towards the shelter of a nearby tree. Its wide, glossy leaves shielded her from most of the sudden downpour. Reggie joined her, his hair plastered to his head, and they clung together laughing. The rain was so much warmer than at home although it did cool the air a little. Raindrops bounced off the ground and she could barely see the other side of the plot through the rain. Elsie spotted Horace also hiding from the rain under a large bush but the rest of the gardeners continued to toil. Within a short time, they were all drenched but didn't seem to notice. They didn't stop their ungainly attempts at weeding nor did they look up. Even the children kept working. Elsie didn't know what to make of these strange, quiet people.

"What's wrong with them?" Reggie had noticed their odd behaviour too.

"Hush, Reg, don't be rude." She tried to keep her voice low but realised that no one would be able to hear them through the din of rain pounding on the ground and plants around them. A large drop of water trickled down the back of her neck and she jumped.

The storm cleared within minutes and the children ventured back out. Puddles of water spotted the ground here and there but soon disappeared. The sun came back out, as bright and hot as before and the birds resumed their song. The gardeners worked on, paying no attention to Elsie and Reggie. Elsie carefully scrutinised them before deciding they didn't seem to care what was going on. "Hey, let's sneak off and explore. I bet they won't notice."

Reggie's face lit up. "Sure!"

They placed their hoes carefully up against a tree and headed for the first path they spotted. Elsie glanced back at the group and caught Horace's eye. He winked at her and she grinned, then scampered out of his view. The path meandered through more lush vegetation until they came to a low stone wall. The stones were rough and provided plenty of footholds so the children were up and over it in an instant. Jumping down, they landed on fallen branches and leaves. They were in a dense, dark pine forest with no clearings or paths. Insects buzzed and birds chittered. Elsie remembered Horace's warning about mosquitoes and looked around uneasily.

"Now what?" Reggie's voice broke into her musings. Elsie looked down at her brother.

"I dunno. You want to climb a tree? We can see more that way." As she suggested climbing, she realised that her dress would get in the way. Reggie was already heading for a likely climbing tree.

"Hang on, Reggie. I need to figure out how to climb in this dress."

"Take it off."

Reggie's lack of modesty really is quite shocking. He does have a good point. If I take off the dress, it won't get torn or dirty.

She looked down at the bodice of her dress and saw smears of reddish dirt.

Well, it won't get dirtier.

With that decided, she stripped down to her pantaloons and chemise. She felt cooler immediately and heaved a sigh of relief. Reggie looked down at her, grinning, from up in the tree. He was already higher up than Papa was tall. "Come on, Elsie. It's easy. There are little berries up here. Can we eat them?"

"Hold on, I'm coming." She dropped her dress over a bush and launched herself up onto a low-hanging branch. The bark felt smooth under her hands. She clambered up to the branch where Reggie sat. He held out a handful of round, purplish berries.

"They look all right. We can try a couple and see." She popped a couple into her mouth. They were sweet and juicy like grapes but a little salty. "Pretty good."

Reggie ate one and must have liked it. He scampered higher into the tree for more. Elsie joined him and between them, they stripped the lower branches bare of the fruit. More grew higher but the branches were thin and didn't look like they'd support their weight.

Her hunger satisfied for now, Elsie surveyed the area. She could see the Order House from her perch. It didn't look very far away so they must not have wandered far. The little plot they had weeded wasn't visible from the tree through the foliage. Reggie was also checking the terrain from another branch. "Elsie, look, the ocean. Over there, the blue line."

Elsie craned her neck to see what he was pointing out. "We should go to the beach. Do you see how to get there? I don't think we can push through the underbrush all the way there."

He shook his head. "Not that way. Maybe another way."

She sighed. She wanted to see the ocean but the land here wasn't easy to move around in like England. No well-worn paths through fields here. It struck her as alien and forbidding. "Maybe we should head back. Mama might be looking for us."

"Awww, Elsie. Do we have to?"

She raised her eyebrows at her brother's whining. It might work with their mother but Elsie always wanted to pinch him when he started whining. "Don't whinge, Reggie. We don't want Mama upset with us, do we? Besides, I want a proper meal and it's probably time for luncheon."

At the mention of food, Reggie perked up and swiftly clambered out of the tree. Elsie jumped down, landing awkwardly on the litter of twigs and branches on the ground. She twisted her ankle and winced. Her boots didn't support her ankles enough for this sort of activity. Elsie grabbed her dress off the bush and drew it over her head. She congratulated herself on keeping her dress relatively clean. All the dirt and grime was on her underclothes and her mother wouldn't see it. The children picked their way back to the stone wall. It seemed to take a lot longer to get back to it than Elsie remembered but eventually, they spotted the light-coloured stones. Heaving herself back over the wall, Elsie jumped down to the other side, wincing as her ankle pained her anew.

"Which way to food?' Reggie grinned at her.

"I think the Order House is that way." They headed along a path in what Elsie thought was the right direction. They saw no one else as they wandered. The path ended back in the sweet potato plot they had left earlier. The same group of people were still there, hoeing but Horace was gone. They didn't seem to have made much progress.

The man called Stephen looked up at their approach. "Where have you two been? You will receive demerits for leaving before work time was done. You will be assigned amends to make up for your failings."

The children gaped at him. What was he talking about? Amends?

"Um, sorry," Reggie mumbled.

"I didn't realise. I'm sorry." Elsie felt her face flush red from the rebuke.

"Can we eat now?" Reggie was always hungry, even after gorging on fruit.

"You missed luncheon while you were delinquent from work." Stephen looked almost satisfied as he made the pronouncement. Elsie's jaw dropped. They had missed luncheon? "You may have some water, then you must get back to work. These weeds will take over the plot and then our crop will suffer."

The children drank long from the round green water jug. Elsie wondered what the globe was originally. It looked like part of a plant. She remained silent, not wishing to draw Stephen's attention. She'd ask Horace later. Her tummy rumbled and she wondered how long she would have to wait for dinner.

CHAPTER SIXTEEN

The smell woke Elsie. Reggie groaned next to her. She opened her eyes to see him sitting on the chamber pot. "Oh, Reggie, that's disgusting. Couldn't you go outside?"

His only response was another groan. She buried her face in the blankets to escape the stench he was making but it didn't seem to help. He staggered back to their pile of bedding on the floor and collapsed.

"Aren't you going to dump the chamber pot in the midden? It smells horrible."

"I'm sorry, Elsie." His voice was faint.

He's ill again. What is it this time? The fruit?

Her mother walked into the hut and wrinkled her nose. She was wearing clean clothes but Elsie noticed that they were looking worn and her shirtwaist was stained around the cuffs. "Elsinoe, take that revolting chamber pot outside."

"But, Mama, it's not mine, it's Reggie's."

Mama looked at Reggie, flushed and groaning. "Reginald is too unwell to do it so you will have to help."

"Yes, Mama," Elsie mumbled. She unwound herself from her covers and lifted up the full chamber pot. She made a disgusted face and hurried outside to dump it. It was filthy so she rinsed it with the bucket of water left next to the midden for that purpose. As Elsie returned to the hut, she met her mother leaving.

"I have to go up to the Order House for my cleansing session. You'll need to take care of Reggie today."

"But, Mama—"

"Hush, I need to go, Elsinoe. You did very well on the ship when he was ill, remember? I have every faith that your nursing skills are more than adequate to care for a little tummy upset."

With that, she was gone, strolling along the path up to the Order House.

"Elsie?" A weak voice from inside beckoned her. "I need the chamber pot again."

Elsie flounced back into the hut. This was not going to be the best of days. "All right, Reggie, here I come. You probably need to something to drink as well."

She brought in the chamber pot and helped Reggie onto it. The little boy nodded miserably as he sat there. "My tummy really hurts."

Elsie nodded sympathetically. Her own stomach wasn't feeling too great either. She guessed it was all that weird fruit yesterday. Sighing, she stood up to fetch a cup of water for her brother.

He shook his head at her approach. "I'm not sure I want to drink anything..."

She should have expected the vomiting but couldn't get out of the way. It splashed on the floor and her bare feet. Fortunately, Reggie missed the bedding.

Elsie swallowed bile. "Oh, ugh. That's not good. Now I need to clean that up too."

Reggie burst into tears, his face red.

"Aw, Reggie, don't cry, it's okay, I'll take care of it."

She bustled around cleaning, trying not to gag herself. By the time she got everything wiped up and Reggie back in bed, she was exhausted. She wanted to collapse into bed herself but knew she needed to find some medicine for Reggie. His face was pale and his skin was clammy to the touch. He'd stopped throwing up for now but she put the water bucket next to his head just in case.

Now what? There's no doctor around here, is there?

She sat in the doorway of the hut and stared out into the woods, racking her brain for a solution. Should she go up to the Order House and ask? Mama had been pretty definite about Elsie taking care of Reggie so maybe that wasn't a good idea. Another of the workers? No, they never spoke to her so she didn't want to ask them for medicine. The idea of asking Horace popped into her mind and as if bidden, he appeared, whistling as he sauntered down the path.

"Horace! I am so glad to see you!"

He smiled, a crooked little grin on his face. "Are you? That's nice to hear. I came by to see if you were ready to go and do some more farming. You seem to enjoy it. And I think Stephen is expecting you."

Elsie grimaced at the mention of Stephen. He was so mean. He didn't even thank them for their help and between she and Reggie, they had done more weeding than the whole rest of the crew. "I can't help today. Reggie's ill and I need to find a doctor for him. Mama told me to take care of him but he needs medicine."

"The little man is ill? What's wrong with him?"

Elsie told Horace about her morning of cleaning up Reggie's messes. "And I don't know what to do. He can't even drink water without throwing it up. Is there a doctor here?"

"Folks on Andros Island don't really go to doctors. They use bush medicine or go to the wise woman."

"Bush medicine?"

Elsie must have looked as confused as she felt. Horace explained, "Bush medicine is when you use the different plants that grow on the island for medicine. I can tell you what plants you need to look for to help Reggie's tummy ache."

"Okay. Will you go with me to find these medicine plants?"

Horace drew his eyebrows together and shook his head. "I need to get to work or Stephen will be annoyed with me and then I'll get demerits. You need to make Reggie tea with calabash leaves. You know what the calabash tree looks like, right? It's the one with the round green fruit we turn into bowls and water pitchers."

"Oh. I wondered what made those water pitchers."

"Yes, you'll need to find a tree growing them. There should be a few growing on the south side of the yard, in the woods. South is that way." He pointed the direction out for her.

"Okay. Do you think I can leave Reggie?"

"Certainly. Leave him a little water and tell him to sip slowly. I'll let Stephen know you're not coming."

Elsie felt a surge of relief. "Thank you very much, Horace. You've been so helpful."

Horace grinned his thanks. He ruffled her hair before calling good wishes to Reggie and wandering off to the garden.

"Reggie, I'm going to find you some medicine. Try to rest, alright?"

Reggie appeared to be sleeping so Elsie left a cup of water near him and tiptoed out.

She headed in the direction Horace had pointed out and walked until she reached the stone boundary of the yard. She didn't see the trees bearing big green balls that Horace described. This was going to be harder than he made it sound.

***

Elsie stumbled through the pine tree forest, trees towering over her head. Thorny bushes grabbed her skirt as she pushed through them. The rocky ground seemed to trip her on purpose. None of the plants here seemed to fit the description of the calabash tree that Horace had given. It had sounded odd enough for her to recognize but she hadn't seen a single tree with giant green balls hanging off it, just a lot of scrubby tall pine trees that weren't even good for climbing. The mosquitoes were bad in this part of the forest, probably from the muddy hollows that she sank into when she wasn't tripping over rocks. How long had she been out here? It felt like hours. Was Reggie alright, alone and sick in the hut? What would happen if he woke up and needed something? There was no one around in their little clump of huts. They were all working in the gardens or up at the big house.

She kept looking for the elusive calabash tree, wishing there was a tree she could climb to make it easier to spot her target. Birds called overhead, their song unfamiliar but still beautiful. She spotted them flittering about. They weren't English birds, that was certain. She saw flashes of yellow and orange, and once, a vivid purple bird, tiny and fast-moving. Was it a hummingbird? She had seen drawings of hummingbirds in her zoology book but never seen one in person.

Elsie sighed. The hot humid air pressed against her and her tummy grumbled. It seemed like she was always hungry. With a start, she remembered that since Reggie had woken up ill before breakfast, Elsie hadn't eaten. She sighed. By now, she was sure to have missed breakfast at the Order House and would have to subsist on whatever she could scrounge out here. Which looked to be precious little. She stopped and put her hands on her hips, breathing hard from the effort of clambering about in the heat. She surveyed the area, trying to decide which direction she should go. Horace had said south. Was she still heading south? The sun was high overhead now and the ground was flat. She couldn't see landmarks and she hoped she could find her way back to the yard. Her frustration boiled over and she stamped her foot.

"Oh, this is stupid!"

She heard a giggle and whirled around, looking for the source. A small dark-skinned boy, dressed in baggy, light-coloured clothes was grinning at her. Where had he come from?

"Who are you? What do you want?"

Her voice was cross and she was sure she looked ferocious but the boy kept grinning. "Name of Johnny. Who're you? You lost? White girl wandering around the barren, sure enough you're gonna get in trouble."

"I'm Elsie and I'm not lost. I'm looking for something."

He chortled at her statement. "Looking for something? What, you lose your baby doll out here? You're never gonna find it. There be creatures out here that steal lost things and you never get them back."

Elsie fumed. Lost dolly, indeed. "I am not looking for a stupid doll, you stupid boy."

She turned and stomped away from him, but the uneven ground made it hard to make a satisfying exit. She stumbled on downed branches and rocks underfoot. A branch cracked right behind her and she jumped. The boy had followed and was right behind her. "So what you looking for?"

Elsie glowered at him. "I'm trying to find something for my brother. He's ill."

"You got a brother? I don't have a brother, just two pesky older sisters. They don't help when I get sick. My aunty does. Why your mama not helping him?"

Elsie snorted, darting a look sideways at him. "She's too busy."

As soon as the words left Elsie's lips, her heart sank. Mama was always too busy. Why hadn't they just waited for Nanny to get well so she could come too? Elsie still didn't understand why Mama had been in such a rush to leave home.

The boy shrugged. "So you gotta help your brother. What ya doing out here then?"

"I need to find some medicine for him. A friend told me to get some leaves from the calabash tree."

"Oh, he got de runs then? Yeah, Aunty Irene says de calabash does help that, but there be no calabash trees near here."

Elsie's heart sank. She'd been wandering around here for nothing. "There aren't? Do you know where they grow?"

The boy puffed himself up. "Sure, I know where some grow. Over by de blue hole. You want me to show you?"

Elsie sighed with relief. "Yes, please! That would be so kind of you."

The boy looked embarrassed. He dropped his gaze and shuffled one foot along the ground. "Aww, it's not'ing. Come on, it's not so far from here."

The children scrambled through the undergrowth, Johnny chattering as they went. He knew a lot about the forest's plants and animals. A small blue lizard scampered up a tree and Johnny darted forward to grab it. He brandished it in Elsie's face. "Hah!"

"Pretty. I've never seen a blue lizard."

His face fell. "You weren't scared."

She smirked and held her hand out for the little reptile. "This one doesn't have big, pointy teeth like the one we saw in Nassau."

Johnny scowled and let the lizard escape into the undergrowth. "They got Mr. Sharp in Nassau too? That a mean lizard. They come out just before sun up. Rest of de time, they live in de palm tops."

Elsie shuddered. "They eat rat heads. Disgusting."

He laughed and they walked on, passing pink and white orchids that Elsie was tempted to pick for her mother. She remembered the last time she brought Mama a flower and decided not to do it again. Best not to make her mother angry. The ground seemed to be rising until they finally came out onto a limestone bluff. Below them was what looked like a small, perfectly round lake. The water was dark and looked very deep.

"That's de blue hole. They call it Lug Hole. It goes all de way under de ground and out to de ocean."

"Oh, it's pretty. It's so hot out here, I'd love to go for a swim."

Johnny's face grew stern. "No way. You don't ever wanna get in a blue hole unless you want Lusca to drag ya down and eat you up."

Elsie giggled. He must be teasing her again. "You're joking, right? What's the Lusca supposed to be?"

"I mean it. Lusca lives down there. She'll grab you and eat you if you swim in de blue holes."

She was taken aback. Johnny sounded like he really believed that there was something dangerous in the water. "All right then. What's a Lusca anyway?"

Johnny shook his head and moved away from the edge. His face was tight with fear. His earlier bravado had disappeared. "That's a calabash tree. Pick some leaves and let's go. I don't wanna be here no more. This place gives me the heebie-jeebies."

Elsie didn't want to upset him. He had been kind to her by guiding her to the right spot. She picked a handful of the leaves and realised she didn't have a spot to put them. She would just have to carry them in her hand and hope she didn't drop them as she traipsed through the woods back to the Order's yard.

Johnny must have noticed her dilemma. "Here, I got a pocket. I'll carry de leaves for you."

She rewarded him with a brilliant smile and passed the leaves to him. She wanted one more peek at the beautiful water so moved back to the edge of the bluff. Bubbles appeared on the surface, near the middle of the blue hole. She pointed them out to Johnny. "Hey, look at those bubbles. That's strange, isn't it?"

Johnny gasped. "It's de Lusca!"

He grabbed her hand and yanked hard, pulling her along as he ran away from the cliff edge. The yank hurt her shoulder but Elsie held on and let Johnny drag her back into the woods. They ran until both were panting and out of breath. Johnny looked distraught and on the verge of tears. She was baffled by his reaction.

"Johnny, why did we have to run away? We weren't in the water so the Lusca couldn't get us, right?"

He shook his head. "Lusca has long, long tentacles. She could've grabbed us right off de ledge."

Elsie shivered. What kind of creature was he talking about? She thought maybe some ferocious fish but tentacles sounded more like a giant squid. "She has tentacles? Tell me, what is this Lusca?"

Johnny took a deep breath and closed his eyes. "The Lusca is a great big octopus but it got a shark head. Her tentacles be so long, my mama and Irene say she can grab people right off de shore."

"Good thing we left, huh? The bubbles were her breathing or something?"

He nodded and started walking again. He didn't seem to want to talk about the monster in the blue hole. After walking for a while, Elsie broke the silence. "Johnny? Can you help me find the Order's yard? I'm a bit turned around."

"De Order? Is that what those white folk call themselves? Sure, I can get you back there."

She wondered how long she had been out in the woods with Johnny. Was Reggie okay? She had been enjoying herself. It would have been fun to stay out exploring with Johnny before the encounter with the Lusca. But now she had to go back and take care of Reggie. Why did she always have to take care of her little brother? He was always getting sick or tagging along and slowing her down. She just wanted to have fun without worrying about him all the time. Her face must have shown her thoughts.

Johnny looked at her with concern.. "What's wrong? We're not lost or not'in. You'll be back with your folks in no time. See that big cocoa-nut palm tree? Dat's right on the edge of your folks' yard."

Elsie shook her head. "Nah, that's not it. I was having fun and now I have to go and take care of my stupid little brother."

Johnny chewed on his lip, obviously thinking. "Well, how 'bout we have fun when he gets better? We can go to de beach. I'll show you how to fish and catch crabs."

Her mood brightened. She hadn't even gone to the beach yet and was dying to swim in the clear blue water. "That would be super! Thanks, Johnny."

They reached the stone boundary wall of the Order's yard and followed it to an opening. Johnny handed her the bundle of leaves. Elsie flashed a smile of thanks and raced up the path, calling goodbyes over her shoulder. She needed to get back to the hut. Reggie was waiting for his medicine. The sooner he got better, the sooner they could have fun exploring the island with Johnny.

CHAPTER SEVENTEEN

Clara's head buzzed with energy yet her body was completely relaxed. The full dose of the concoction was quite potent. She understood why the Mean took it without reserve even though they didn't seem to experience it as she did. She wanted to talk, to share her thoughts but the rest of the Mean stood at the back of the Assembly, listening to Ward with their jaws slack. This lecture again struck Clara as an odd mélange of several different philosophies. She tried to understand his points but he seemed to mostly be extolling the physical form of human existence. It contradicted what he had said earlier about cultivating oneself as intermediary to devas in order to become one with the Divine. No one else seemed to notice that he wasn't making a great deal of sense. Maybe the concoction didn't work well on her. It amplified her critical thinking rather than making her feel open and accepting.

Ward finally wound down and Clara breathed a sigh of relief. Her mind was spinning trying to keep up with his contradictions and convoluted logic. The Exalted moved up to receive their own offering. Clara wondered why they received theirs at the end of the Assembly rather than at the beginning. Perhaps as Exalted, they understood Ward without the need of the euphoric given to the Mean. If that was the case, what were they imbibing?

The crowd started to shift and move out of the room. The Assembly was over. Clara was tired of scrubbing pots and counters in the kitchen. She wanted to have a proper discussion and this seemed to be the best opportunity. She cornered Ward as he left. Smiling widely and she hoped charmingly, Clara launched into her thoughts on esotericism. "Ward, I've been meaning to ask you what you thought about astrology and how we can incorporate its teachings into the Order. It could aid you in fortuitous decisions—"

Ward drew back, his face creased with a frown. "Clara." He looked her up and down. "Whatever are you talking about?"

A small group of Exalted, including Lydia, Clara noticed unhappily, had gathered. Clara drew a settling breath. "I've been thinking and you see, according to esotericism, everything is connected so that as above, so below, which leads to astrology being such a useful tool for us to determine our affairs."

Lydia tittered. Clara shot her a dirty look. "It is so amusing when one of the Mean tries to have an intelligent conversation about the workings of the Order. They really ought to stick to the menial labour that is more suited to their intellects."

The fury rose in Clara's body, obliterating the last shreds of calm left over from the concoction. She shook and opened her mouth to respond. Ward held his hand up to silence her. "Clara, as one of the Mean, it is more fitting for you to be silent and pay attention. Your thoughts are as yet unformed, unenlightened. You will require a great deal more cleansing sessions before you can become Exalted and truly understand our purpose."

She shut her mouth, glaring at Lydia but not daring to show defiance to Ward. He grasped her arm, startling her and she shot a glance at him.

"But you have such enthusiasm. Lydia, it occurs to me that I need a personal servant, one who will serve me with this kind of energy and enthusiasm. Don't you?"

Lydia looked confused and more than a little annoyed. "A personal servant? What do you need that one of the Exalted can't provide you?"

His answering smile made Clara want to flee but his hand still had a firm grip on her arm. He squeezed gently and she looked down at his hand. "There are plenty of lowly tasks that I wouldn't dream of asking an Exalted to perform for me. I think Clara here with her... interesting ideas... can fill that role for me. And I will personally conduct her cleansing sessions."

Lydia bared her teeth in an approximation of a smile. "Of course, Ward. If that is what you desire. I'll inform the kitchen that their scullery maid has been reassigned."

Ward waved a hand as if the detail was insignificant to him. He grasped Clara's wrist. "Come along, Clara. You can get started in my suite. I'll show you what needs to be taken care of up there. Lydia, inform anyone who inquires that I'm not to be disturbed. Clara, after you complete the services I require, I intend to begin right away on your cleansing process. I imagine we have a lot of work ahead of us." He stared at her. "You must learn to accept physical degradation before you can elevate."

Clara was disbelieving. Physical degradation? What on Earth was Ward planning? She looked around wildly for Theo. He wouldn't allow this man to do whatever he wanted with her, would he? Clara caught sight of Theo, staring back at her without expression. He turned away. Clara bit her lip, shoulders tensing. Her husband had abandoned her to whatever her fate might be at the leader's hands. Would it be worth the promised wisdom? Ward strode away, tugging her along in his wake. She stumbled behind him.

CHAPTER EIGHTEEN

Reggie wasn't much better the next morning. Elsie had brewed him cups and cups of the calabash leaf tea but he was still groaning from the pain in his belly. At least he was able to keep down some of the tea. She chewed on a strand of hair, trying to figure out what to do next. Mama had barely spoken this morning before heading up to the Order House. Elsie wasn't even sure if she noticed that Reggie was still sick.

"Reggie, I'll be back soon. I'm going to eat breakfast. I'll bring you back some bread or something."

He shook his head and closed his eyes. Elsie sighed and dragged herself up to the Order House. She was exhausted from tending to her brother and hadn't had much to eat yesterday. She intended to make up for that at breakfast and hopefully get some help with Reggie. Thoughts of food filled her mind and her mouth started watering. She met Horace walking up the steps to the porch of the Order House.

"Good morning, Elsie!" His infectious smile lightened her mood and she smiled back. "And where is young Reggie? Not poorly still, I hope?"

Her smile dropped from her face. "He's not much better. I found those leaves you told me to get. They helped a little." Something told her to keep quiet about her exploration yesterday and her new friend.

Horace's kind eyes looked sad at the news. They walked into the Order House together. "I'm sorry to hear that. Have you spoken to your parents yet about it?"

"No. I hardly ever see Mama and haven't seen Papa since the night we arrived. I'm not sure what to do, Horace. Is there someone here who is a doctor?"

"A doctor? No, there's no doctor here. We don't get ill here, I suppose. Perhaps someone up at Driggs Hill can help. That's where the port is, where you arrived on the boat."

"I guess I'll ask Mama to find out. Have you seen her this morning?"

Horace scanned the full dining room then shook his head. "I'm sorry, I don't see either of your parents. Maybe Reggie will get better all on his own. Just a bit of nursing from his kind and competent sister?"

Elsie sniffed back her tears. "He's not very strong, Horace. He gets ill an awful lot. Nanny said he had a weak constitution. I wish she were here. She was always so good at making him well again."

"You have a nanny? I had a nanny. She was quite cruel. Was yours nice? Why didn't she come with you?"

Elsie explained about her nanny's sudden illness before the family left for the Bahamas. Horace nodded thoughtfully, still scanning the room. They sat down and ate breakfast in a companionable silence.

Elsie stuffed some sort of flat bread into her apron pocket and rose from the table. "I'd better get back to Reggie."

Horace took her hand and squeezed it. "Don't worry, Elsie. I think I know someone who can help you. I'll go and talk to her, okay?

"Thank you, Horace. You're a good friend." She felt a weight lift off her and returned to the hut feeling hopeful.

***

Irene sat on the stoop of her house, pounding roots into a mash. She had enough to finish up another batch of potion for the white folk in the big yard down the road. She'd need to go foraging for herbs again soon though. She didn't want to take that long, hot walk down the Queen's Road to deliver the potion. Maybe this time she'd send her nephew. Then she wouldn't have to look at that Ward man. His pasty face with its fake smile made her want to smack him. He paid well though. Pretty soon, all the gold he'd given her for the potion would buy Irene and her family some more land and better houses. She was tired of living in a one-room shack that let in the rain and wind.

The scent of the mash rose to her nostrils, sweet and acrid. It was ready. With a grunt, Irene got to her feet. Her hips ached from sitting on the flat rock they used as a stoop. She felt all of her forty years. Irene rubbed her lower back to ease the stiffness and watched her nephew climbing a cocoa-nut tree. Darn fool boy was too little to make it all the way up to the cocoa-nuts.

That boy is always looking for food. I don't think his belly is ever full.

She smiled fondly at him. "Johnny! Get down out that tree, boy, right-right now!"

Johnny kept a tight grip on the tree trunk with his arms and legs and hazarded a glance down at his aunt. He didn't move at first but then must have realised she meant business as she stood watching him, hands on hips. Pushing away from the tree with his arms, he jumped to the ground. Johnny faced his aunt, a pout on his lips. "But Aunty Irene, I's thirsty. I wanted some cocoa-nut water."

She tsked at him. "You always wanting something, chile. I think you got a hollow leg. You come on over here and I'll give you some fresh pineapple juice. I know you like that."

"Pineapple juice? You de best Aunty in de world!" The boy came running to her, grinning widely. A thought seemed to occur to him and the grin dropped. "You not gonna medicine me, are you?"

She laughed out loud. "Why? You sick? You need me to medicine you?"

Johnny shook his head vigorously. She reached down and pinched his ear playfully.

A white man sauntered into the yard, interrupting their banter. Irene narrowed her eyes as he approached. He looked familiar but she couldn't tell who he was from across the yard.

"Good day to you, Irene!"

She recognized his voice with its snooty English accent. It was Horace, one of them white folk from the big yard that Ward was boss of.

"Irene, do you remember me? I live down at the Order yard. You helped me with some stomach troubles last rainy season. And I helped you carry home some guineps a while ago."

She recalled the time when this man, Horace, came to her for some of her herbal medicines. She hadn't ever found out how he knew to come to her for help. He had given her some good cloth in exchange for her healing, enough for a whole skirt. He was cheeky too, carrying her guineps home when he knew she didn't need the help.

"Why are you darkening my door again, Horace? You sick again? I told you, you got to quit eating bad food. They give you rotten food down there again?"

He smiled in response, seeming not to notice her gruff tone and shook his head. "I didn't come on my own behalf, Irene. There's a little boy at the yard who's quite ill. His sister has dosed him with calabash leaf tea but he's still poorly. I was hoping to convince you to treat him. You are the most skilled healer on South Andros. I know he'll get better with your help."

Irene considered his request. Why should she care about some little white boy who belonged to those Order people? She'd rather they left her island, not getting healing from her like they were part of the community.

Johnny spoke up as she pondered the situation. "You talking about Elsie's little brother, mister? Is he still sick?"

Horace's eyes opened wide with surprise. "You know Elsie and Reggie?"

Johnny nodded. "Sure. Well, I know Elsie. I helped her find the calabash leaves yesterday. Some fool told her de wrong way to go to find de calabash trees."

Horace's face turned red under his tan and stayed silent.

Irene turned to her nephew, bending from the waist to stare him in the eyes. "You know this white girl? Since when you been hanging around with de children at that yard? You know we don't mix with them."

Johnny appeared to be unperturbed by Irene. "I don't mix with none of those other children, Aunty Irene. Only Elsie. De others are boring. They don't talk at all and they just work, work, work. Elsie is different. She's brave."

Irene snorted. "Only Elsie, huh? And where did you go looking for de calabash tree? They're growing up de road and I didn't see you walking around with a white girl yesterday."

"Nah, I was down below their yard, looking around for crabs and I spotted this girl wandering around. She looked lost. She said she needed calabash leaves for her sick brother so I took her to de trees over by Lug Hole."

He stopped and gulped audibly.

"Lug Hole? You went over near Lug Hole?" She hissed. "You never supposed to go near that place, Johnny. I's gonna give you a cut hip for that." She grabbed a switch broom leaning up against the wall with one hand and her nephew with the other. Johnny howled in anticipation of the pain.

Horace stepped closer, holding a hand up to stop Irene. "Hold on, please. He was merely trying to help Elsie. She's been left to care for her little brother and is quite desperate. Her parents are...too busy to help. She's very young herself. Probably only a little older than your son there."

"He isn't my son, he's my nephew, and he deserves a whipping for disobeying our rules." The fight drained out of her. "Later. You wait til I tell your mama, Johnny. She gonna whip you good. This little girl, this Elsie. You say she trying to nurse her little brother all by herself?"

"Yes, Irene, but she says he's not getting better. I told her to try the calabash leaves like you gave me but she says they're not working. Please come and help. She says he's always been sickly. I'm afraid he may die if this continues."

Irene crossed her arms. "What's that to me? I still don't see why his own mama can't take care of him. You got healers, don't you?"

Horace's mouth drooped and his eyes grew bright with tears. "Please, Irene. We have no healers at the Order. The boy needs you."

She glowered at him. "I take care of my own people, not yours."

Horace dropped his gaze and his shoulders slumped. Irene caught sight of Johnny, shifting from one foot to another.

The child gave her a soulful look, his big brown eyes begging her. "You can't let Reggie die, Aunty Irene. It wouldn't be right."

Johnny knew her well. Irene wasn't one to go letting a child die from a sickness she could cure, and she could cure most childhood sicknesses. She sighed dramatically to let Horace know that she was giving in reluctantly. "All right, I'll come and see to this sickly boy. But a little bitty piece of cloth isn't going to do this time. You're going to owe me cash, Horace. I wasn't planning a walk down to your yard today in this heat. Now you wait here while I collect my things."

Horace thanked her profusely, promising her as much money as he could find.

She gathered her herbal teas and a charm for keeping out the spirits from attacking the boy while he was weak. Johnny and Horace waited for her outside her hut in silence. She straightened her shoulders. "I's ready now. Let's go see about this boy."

The three of them walked out of Irene's yard together. She had a quick word with her sister Alice as they left since Johnny was coming along. Maybe he would learn a bit about healing. It would be good to train another healer. Neither of her own children nor her nieces had shown interest and this place needed all the healers it could get.

***

The sun beat down on them as they trudged along the Queen's Road. Irene was grateful for her straw hat but the sun still baked her out on the white sand road. They passed an old man sitting under a palm tree. He watched them walk by without a word. No one else was fool enough to be out on the road. Everyone waited until the sun dropped behind the trees.

The trail leading to the Order yard was better. It was narrow and protected from the sun on both sides by densely growing plants. The mosquitoes liked it well enough though. She smacked at a couple on her neck.

Johnny tugged her dress. "Aunty Irene, I's thirsty. I never got my juice."

She snorted in return, shaking her head. "You just gonna have to wait til we get to their yard then you can have your fill of water."

He let out a low whine of protest but was otherwise silent.

When they finally made it to the gate of the Order's yard, Irene was also parched and in need of water. Horace led them straight into the hut where a young girl sat on the dirt floor, mopping a boy's forehead with a wet rag.

She looked up with a smile. "Horace! You came back! Oh Horace, Reggie's worse, he's really hot now, and he won't wake up."

At that dire pronouncement, Irene pushed her way past Horace and approached the children. The girl gaped at Irene looming over her.

Irene squinted down. "For true, this boy is plenty sick. Good t'ing you came and got me."

The girl scrambled to her feet. "How do you do, ma'am? My name is Elsie Cooke and this is my brother Reggie. Are you a doctor?"

Irene snickered at that. "First off, chile, you call me Aunty Irene. I's not a ma'am and I's not a doctor. I's just a healer."

"Yes, ma—I mean Aunty Irene."

Elsie darted a look at Horace who nodded encouragingly. "Irene is the finest healer on the island. She cured me of a nasty stomach complaint a while ago. I brought her to help Reggie."

Elsie nodded, a troubled look still pasted across her face. "Thank you. Can you help him, ma—Aunty Irene?"

Irene knelt next to Reggie and placed a hand on his forehead. It felt hot but dry to the touch. She tsked. "Have you been giving this boy anyt'ing to drink? He's parched."

Elsie's voice trembled. "I keep trying but he vomits it right back up. Even the calabash leaf tea. Is he going to die?"

Her voice wobbled even more and she sniffed back tears.

"Now don't fuss, girl, I got plenty of tricks for this sort of t'ing. Go and fetch me a big pitcher of fresh water. Make sure it's clean."

Elsie nodded and dashed out of the hut, Johnny on her heels.

Irene continued her examination, feeling his pulse, listening to his chest. He was poorly, that was sure. She scanned the dingy little room, looking for signs of a hexing. She didn't see anything suspicious but would have to check outside too. She lifted the little boy, checking under him for hexes, but only cockroaches scattered from the blankets.

Ignorant white folks letting their babies sleep on de floor. They don't know that just brings de sickness.

She picked his slight body off the floor and carefully placed him on the only bed in the hut. He shivered in his sleep and she placed covers back over him. She darted a look back at the door and saw Horace hovering there, a look of deep concern on his face. "Will he be all right, Irene?"

The little boy was very ill and her tone came out a little harsher than she had intended. "You go on out of here, don't need you watching me over my shoulder. Send Johnny in here when he gets back."

He dropped his head and backed away, muttering an apology. Irene squashed the niggling voice that wanted to tell him that it would be all right. She didn't lie to people. This child was plenty sick. She hummed a healing song and dug through her herb pouch, choosing carefully. She placed roots and berries into her wooden bowl and rubbed dried leaves over them. Irene brought out a rounded stone and crushed the herbs together. She sniffed the mixture and reached into her pouch for another handful of leaves. Mixing that together, a sharp scent rose into the air. That smelled right. Now she needed the fresh water and some way to heat it. As she expected, there was no stove in the hut so she stepped outside, looking for an outdoor oven or a fire pit. Horace hovered nearby but didn't speak. "Horace, how do you folk heat water? There's no stove in that hut."

He looked around, frowning. "Uh, I'm not sure. We usually eat up at the Order House. Oh, it looks like Elsie made a little fire over here. What a resourceful child she is. I wonder who taught her how to make a fire pit."

Irene huffed. "Don't much care who taught her. You know how to build up a fire?"

Horace nodded and squatted next to the little fire pit, piling up twigs. Satisfied that he looked like he knew what he was doing, Irene looked around for the children with the water. How far was the fresh water? What folks built their houses so far from fresh water? She shook her head in disgust at the incompetence.

The children returned up the path, bearing calabash gourds full of water, splashing out of the tops. They walked carefully, trying not to spill. Johnny presented his overflowing gourd. "Aunty Irene, we didn't know how much water you needed so we brought two."

They were beaming at their own cleverness. Horace had got a small fire going so she directed the children to start boiling water in the can that Elsie had scrounged from somewhere.

"Johnny, tell me when that water is boiling. Don't try to carry it anywhere, you'll just get burnt and then I'll have to fix you up too."

She re-entered the hut to check on Reggie. He looked a little better, less flushed and restless. Irene knelt down next to the bed and started her healing song again, this time with the words. She closed her eyes and rocked with the rhythm, opening up to agwu. She felt healing power flowing through her and placed her hands on the little boy's chest. After a time, she felt the deity move out of her and she drew a deep, shuddering breath. She opened her eyes and placed a hand on the boy's forehead. It felt much cooler.

"Aunty Irene?" A little voice startled her. She darted a look at the doorway. Elsie stood there, eyes wide. "The water is boiling."

Irene dipped her head in response and raised herself to her feet. Her knees complained at her. She'd been kneeling, unmoving, for some time then. Time passed strangely when the deity possessed her. She picked up her bowl of herbs and made her way to the fire. Without speaking or acknowledging the others sitting around the fire pit, she poured the hot water over the herbs. The pungent scent of the herbal tea filled her nostrils and she coughed a little. The tea was good and strong and combined with her healing, the boy would be healed from drinking it.

Reggie was stirring when Irene approached him with the tea. He opened his eyes and blinked up at her. "Are you an angel? Am I dead?" His voice was hoarse and weak.

A laugh burst out of Irene, surprising her. "No, you not dead, little one, and I's no angel. I's just Aunty Irene. I've come to help you get better. You were real sick. Your fren Horace came up to my yard and fetched me."

He mumbled something and his eyes drifted shut. Irene knelt next to him at the bed and gently shook him. "Don't go back to sleep yet, little one. I got medicine for you."

Reggie cracked an eye open. "Don't like medicine."

Irene smiled, remembering her own boys being stubborn about taking medicine. "You don't have to like it. You just gotta drink it." She slipped an arm under the boy's shoulders and lifted him off the mattress. She placed the bowl to his lips. "C'mon now. Drink your medicine."

Reggie didn't open his eyes but she could tell he was awake. "Don't want to, Nanny. No medicine."

Irene tried not to laugh. Who was Nanny? "I's not your Nanny. I's Aunty Irene. Drink up, boy."

Despite his words, Reggie sipped the tea obediently, then pulled a face. He opened his eyes fully, looking up at Irene with an offended expression. "Yuk. That tastes awful."

"Yep, maybe so but it's gonna make your belly feel better."

She sensed someone behind her and glanced over her shoulder. Elsie was standing just outside the hut, peering at them. "Is he going to be all right, Aunty Irene? Oh, Reggie, you're awake. How do you feel?"

Reggie flapped a hand at his sister. "Hi, Elsie. A bit better. The Nanny angel helped me. But she gave me nasty medicine."

Irene harrumphed. "I told you, I's not an angel, and I's not your Nanny. I's Aunty Irene. Come, come, Elsie. I'll show you what you need to do to help your brother."

Elsie moved closer and Irene heard her suck in a breath suddenly. "Oh dear, Aunty Irene, you've put Reggie in Mama's bed. She didn't say he could sleep there. She might be upset."

Irene felt anger smouldering in her gut. Who was this mother that would begrudge her sick son a comfortable bed? She deserved a whipping. "Child, that boy ain't gonna sleep on the floor with all those roaches. That just leads to sickness. Those are filthy bugs, eating on garbage and such. You not doing yourself any good sleeping down there neither. Your mama needs to get more beds in here."

Elsie bit her lip. She looked worried. "Yes, ma'am. I mean Aunty Irene. Maybe I can ask Horace to help us get some more beds."

Irene wondered again about this child's parents. Is that the way things are in the Order? The children taking care of themselves or having to beg an adult for help? It wasn't her business how other folks lived but she didn't like seeing children treated badly. It wasn't her business though. She'd done all she could. It was time for her to get out of the white people's yard. "I go on now. I'll send Johnny down tomorrow with more medicine. Your brother's gonna be alright. You don't have to worry now."

She placed a quick hand on the little girl's hair, trying to reassure her with a touch. The girl smiled bravely back at her and waved. Irene strode away, Johnny trailing behind her.

CHAPTER NINETEEN

Clara cornered Theo after breakfast. She hadn't spoken to her husband in three days. He had left every room as soon as she entered it and Ward kept Clara too busy for her to go looking for Theo. She wanted some answers from Theo and she was tired of being treated like a pariah.

"Theophilus, I must speak to you. I've been here for almost a week and I barely see you. This is a very odd way for us to conduct a marriage."

He stared at her coolly, an inscrutable expression on his face. He looked at her as if she were some sort of talking rodent: somewhat fascinating but mostly repellent.

"Clara. I can't imagine what you want from me. Are you bored? I thought you were busy making sure all of Ward's needs were met." He had a sneer in his voice.

She paused, her self-righteous indignation deflated somewhat. "His needs? I thought...that is, I was doing what I was told. Being obedient. Serving. Isn't that how I learn to be more aware? And then to become Exalted?"

He shrugged. "I suppose if that's what Ward has told you."

He made as if to leave.

"Theophilus, please wait. I would like to discuss our living situation, that is, mine and the children's. That hut we've been assigned is unspeakably sordid. I wouldn't house pigs in it. Why can't we stay here at the house with you? It seems ridiculous to separate a family this way."

Theo sighed. He looked across the room, as if anything was more preferable to look at than his wife. "That's how the Order works. We can't have children running about distracting our studies or cleansing sessions. And you're not Exalted, so you can't stay here. You're lucky that the children have been allowed to remain with you. The other children live together in the children's hut."

She spluttered. Did he actually mean for her to remain in that disgusting little shack indefinitely? Drawing a calming breath, she tried for a rational approach. "Theophilus, that hut is unhealthy. There are insects. Many insects. Reginald has been quite ill and I'm certain it's from staying there. Is there no other option? Something a little less—primitive?"

He was still not looking at her. Clara gazed in the direction he was staring and saw Lydia on the other side of the room. She was leaning close to Ward and talking. It looked like an intimate conversation. Ward's hand rested on her shoulder and his face was close to hers. Clara watched for a moment, wondering about their relationship but shrugged it off. She had more important issues to worry about.

She tried again to get Theo's attention, this time reaching out and touching his arm. "Theophilus? Is there no way you can acquire some better accommodation for us? And aren't you going to spend time with the children? Elsinoe seems to have got a bit wild and above herself. I could use your assistance with disciplining her."

Theo finally dragged his gaze from across the room and scowled at Clara.

"Clara, can you cease your nagging? You're disrupting my quietude. I'll do what I can but I'm not promising anything."

Clara heaved a sigh. He hadn't committed to changing their accommodations. She glimpsed Lydia out of the corner of her eye, striding across the room towards them. Clara tried not to wince visibly. Lydia was obnoxious and bossy, but Theo still seemed to favour her. They certainly spent a lot of time together.

"Good morning, Theo." Lydia gave Theo a doting look, not sparing a glance at Clara. "Are you ready for our cleansing session? I've been waiting for ages to get you alone."

Theo chuckled, his eyes warm as they lingered on her face. "It's been barely a week. We met before I left for Nassau."

Lydia pouted in response. "I suppose you're right. Well, shall we?"

Clara stood fuming at the playful exchange.

How dare this woman flirt with my husband? The hussy. And he plays along with it?

"Theophilus, I don't believe we were finished with our discussion. I must insist that you find us more healthful accommodation."

Lydia insinuated herself between Clara and Theo, her lip curling. "Insist? The Mean do not insist on anything. You take what you are given. The way to enlightenment is not paved with fine living. You must learn to release your ties to your earthly comforts, Clara."

Clara stared at Lydia's contemptuous face. She almost capitulated but a morsel of strength rose in her. "I don't believe I was having a discussion with you, Lydia. This is a private conversation between my husband and I."

Colour rose in Lydia's face and she looked shocked, as if Clara had slapped her. "That sounds like insolence. If you weren't assigned to Ward, I'd have you digging latrines after that remark."

Theo spoke up, frowning at Clara. "Clara, Lydia is correct. That was quite rude. Lydia is my spiritual mentor. I insist that you apologise for your bad manners and poor attitude."

Clara's jaw dropped. What? She was the one supposed to apologise? "I beg your pardon? You want me to apologise? To her?"

"Yes, I do. Lydia is one of the Exalted and as such, you must show the respect that is due her position." Theo's face stiffened and he looked every inch the nobleman.

Lydia narrowed her eyes at Clara and leaned close to her. "You need to learn your place. You're one of the Mean, not some fancy society lady. Unless you want to run home to England and give up the pretence that you can someday become Exalted?"

Clara's eyes filled with tears and her face felt hot. Leave now? After being stifled in England all her life as one of the society ladies that Lydia mocked? She couldn't give up this opportunity for spiritual growth, even if she had to denigrate herself to Lydia. She mumbled an apology.

Lydia sneered. "Not giving up then? You'd better head to Ward's office. He has some special task for you today. I'm sure you'll find it intriguing. Or was that demeaning?" Lydia laughed, a cruel note in her voice. "Come, Theo. We need to get started. I'm not sure how much cleansing I'll need after this."

Theo and Lydia moved off, leaving Clara in a turmoil of frustration and anger. She wouldn't give up. She wouldn't give them that satisfaction.

***

Johnny poked his head in the door of their hut. "Hey, Elsie. Aunty Irene sent me with herbs for Reggie. He better?"

Elsie jumped up from the ground next to Reggie's bed, abandoning her sketch. Horace had managed to scrounge up two little cots for them. They weren't much but it was certainly better than the floor.

"Johnny! You came! It's so good to see you. Reggie's better. But I'm frightfully bored sitting here."

Johnny came into the hut and looked around. He scowled at the walls. "You folk must be real poor to live in this trash house. It's kinda nasty. Look at those great big holes between de wall logs. That ain't gonna keep out de rain come de rainy season."

Elsie flushed with embarrassment even though she hadn't chosen this place. Why had her Papa left them here?

"We're not poor. We live in a big house in England. It has four floors and a beautiful garden. We're just staying here while they get our real house ready."

She bit her lip at her lie. Why had she fibbed to Johnny? He didn't respond, except with just "huh."

Reggie woke up and yawned, looking around the room. He did look much better, more like his old self. His flushed cheeks and the weird glassy-eyed stare were both gone. "Hello, are you Johnny?"

Johnny opened his eyes wide in surprise. "Uh, yeah. How'd you know my name?"

"Elsie told me all about you. She says you had an adventure in the forest and then your Aunty helped me get better. I sort of remember her. She looked like a tall, brown angel."

Johnny sniggered. "Never heard anybody call Aunty Irene an angel. She can be awful fierce. But she fixes up people real well. We're going crabbing later, after dark. You wanna come?"

Elsie's face brightened at the thought of an expedition. "Sure! Mama stays at the Order House very late so I can sneak out. Crab is yummy. But how do you catch them? They have those pinchy claws."

"Oh, don't worry, I'll show you. You just gotta grab 'em by de leg and toss 'em in de sack. Sometimes they turn around and grab you with their claws but you pull 'em right off. It don't hurt much."

Elsie nodded. Something different to eat would be a treat. The sparse meals at the Order House left her hungry. All they seemed to serve were vegetables or some kind of gruel. "Can we go find some fruit or something in the forest now? I'm hungry."

"We could go fishing. There's all kinds of fish swimming around out there in de ocean. We stand in de water on de beach and de fish just swim right by."

"Fishing? I love to go fishing. My grandpapa used to take us fishing on the river. Oh, but I don't have a fishing pole."

Johnny laughed at her ignorance. "You don't need a pole. We just scoop 'em up with a net. I got nets at home."

Elsie wrinkled her forehead. It sounded like fun but it occurred to her that maybe she shouldn't go and leave Reggie. She looked at Reggie uncertainly. "Reggie, you feeling all right? Do you want to come fishing or stay here and rest?"

Reggie looked doubtful and rubbed his stomach. "I want to fish. But my tummy feels kinda bad."

Elsie nodded. He shouldn't go fishing if he was still ill. She felt guilty at leaving Reggie alone but he seemed to be out of danger. "I'll get you some more water and make tea with the herbs Aunty Irene sent you. You stay here and drink it, okay?"

The little boy nodded, looking sleepy again. "Yeah, I will. Maybe Horace will come and see me. He tells me funny stories."

Elsie made the tea quickly. She had a lot of experience now making tea over a fire using an old can to heat the water. She made sure Reggie was comfortable, then skipped out of the hut. "I'm ready! Let's go!"

Johnny grinned at her in return and the children raced down the path towards the gate. Elsie hoped that she wouldn't run into her mother or Stephen. She caught a glimpse down a side path of someone who could have been Stephen. Her heart leapt in fear and she put on a burst of speed to get out of sight. Johnny kept up with her. He ran fast. They raced out of the gate and down the trail towards the Queen's Road, giggling. They reached the road at the same time and stopped, panting. Their impromptu race had winded both of them. Johnny caught his breath first and gestured away from the trail to the Order yard, towards the east. "De beach is that way. It's real close from here. Can you hear de waves?"

Elsie nodded, excited that she was finally going to see the ocean and wade in its water. The road was busy and she stepped out of the way of a horse cart. A dark-skinned man was driving. He called out as he passed the children. "Johnny Lowe! Why you hanging 'bout with that white girl? She gonna bring you not'ing but trouble."

Johnny stared at the man, without saying a word. When the man had passed by, Johnny stuck out his tongue at the man's back. Elsie stared with wide eyes at the departing horse cart. "Who was that? And why does he think I'm going to bring you trouble?"

Johnny scowled in response. "Don't pay him no mind. He just don't like white people. C'mon, we gotta stop by my house to get de nets."

The children tramped along in silence. Elsie gaped at the yellow birds flitting through the trees and the lizards that skittered here and there. There were so many different types of wild animals on the island. And tonight, she was going to catch crabs. She bounced a little with glee.

Elsie spotted Irene sitting on the stoop of a little house when the children walked into Johnny's family yard. The woman looked up and tipped her head in their direction. "Your brother doing okay, Elsie?"

"Yes, thank you, Aunty Irene. He slept a lot and his tummy was still hurting a little this morning so I made him some more of your tea and told him to stay in bed."

"That's good. You a good little healer, chile. What you doing here then?"

Johnny spoke up, an ingratiating grin on his face. "I's taking Elsie beach fishing, Aunty Irene. They don't feed her much down at de big house. I gotta get my nets and bucket. You want me to catch you some?"

Irene scratched her head, appearing to be considering the request. "Sure, I could use a little bonefish for supper. Best ask your mama though if she wants some fish too. Don't forget, we going out crabbing tonight. De crabs are moving."

Johnny beamed. "I didn't forget about de crabs, Aunty Irene. I told Elsie she should come too. She likes crab but she never caught one herself."

Irene frowned at her nephew and shook her head. "Johnny, why'd you tell her that? We can't take her into de coppet at night. Her folks would be wexed if they found out. I don't want to get in trouble with those white folk."

Elsie spoke up in Johnny's defence, concerned that her evening adventure was in danger of cancellation. "It's all right, Aunty Irene. I asked my Mama and she said it would be fine for me to go with you. As long as there were adults present."

Irene squinted at the little girl, her lips pursed. "Why you lying to me, chile? I know your mama never said so. If you were my chile, I would give you a cut hip for lying to me like that." Irene turned to Johnny. "We're not taking this white girl crabbing and that's that."

Elsie felt hot tears of shame and disappointment filling her eyes. She gulped back a sob. She was too old to cry over a missed treat. Johnny tried to intercede. "Aww, c'mon, Aunty Irene. There's no harm in it. Her mama's never around. She won't even know if Elsie's out with us."

Irene's expression grew fierce. "I said no, Johnny, and that's the end of it.

Now get going or I's gonna send this girl home right now and you stay into de home tonight."

Johnny ducked his head and ran to the side of his house to retrieve the fishing equipment. Elsie stayed where she was at the gate of the yard, not meeting Irene's eyes. It seemed to take forever for Johnny to collect his nets and bucket. Irene just sat on her stoop, mashing something in a bowl. Probably more of her medicine. Neither spoke. Johnny came rushing up, loaded with nets and a bucket that banged against his leg as he ran. "Got everything. Let's go before the fish is all gone." He laughed and called a farewell to his aunt. Elsie took a net and skipped down the sandy path towards the beach. The fishing would be fun even if she couldn't go crabbing later.

CHAPTER TWENTY

Clara drifted down the path towards her hut, her mind lost in a fog after her cleansing session with Ward. The afternoon with him had passed by in a blink, leaving a sense of euphoria. He had promised an enlightening activity but she would first have to rise above physical abasement. She wasn't exactly sure what had transpired during the session. She remembered kneeling and his eyes, boring into her from above.

A bright green bird fluttered past, startling her out of her reverie. She realised that she was filthy. Her clothes were covered in mud and rotten fruit juice and she smelled of sweat. What exactly had happened? She would need to wash and change her clothes before dinner. That would mean heating water. Which would mean building a fire. A wave of exhaustion hit her but she couldn't rest while stinking and dirty. Her euphoria evaporated. She looked around the clearing. The children were nowhere to be found. Reginald appeared to have recovered from whatever ailment he had come down with. Elsinoe had been quite truculent the evening before about how she had nursed her brother. Clara had been too tired to rebuke her impertinence.

Clara gathered her wash cloth and towel with some clean clothes, then put them down on her cot with a sigh. The fire needed to be started first and then water. Couldn't Theophilus even get them a house with a stove or some other way to heat water without resorting to an open fire on the ground? At the thought of her husband, the image of him and Lydia walking off together that morning rose in her mind and red-hot anger filled her. Clara slammed her hand against the door jamb of the little hut, making the structure shake. She stamped out to the fire pit and saw wood in it, in preparation for a fire. She sighed with relief. She had no clue how to prepare a fire so that it would burn without smoking. An actual pot sat on one of the rocks surrounding the fire pit. It hadn't been there that morning. It would do well enough to boil water in. There was even one of those round, green gourds full of water on the ground. She picked up the gourd and poured water into the pot but the pot slipped to one side and the water ran on to the ground, sinking into the sand. Clara cursed under her breath. Now she was going to have to fetch water. She cast a longing look at the hut. Her astrology books were piled under her cot but she hadn't had a chance to cast a horoscope since arriving on this wretched island. Perhaps the stars were not favourable for this venture.

"Mars must be opposing the Sun," she muttered.

She picked up the empty gourd and trudged along the path towards the well. The heat oppressed her and mosquitoes buzzed around her face. She slapped at them and pushed tendrils of hair off her sweaty forehead. Children's voices drifted along the path towards her. She heard laughter, then saw her children running towards her, chasing a small dark-skinned boy. They all skidded to a halt when they saw her.

"Mama! Where are you going?"

Clara's anger boiled up without warning. She was hot, exhausted, stinking, and in no mood to even have the children near her. She didn't bother answering Elsie's question. "What are you two doing scampering about with this boy? And who is he exactly?"

Reggie and Elsie exchanged glances, then Reggie piped up. "This is Johnny. He's Irene's nephew."

Clara crossed her arms, the gourd dangling from her fingers. "And who is Irene? Why is this boy in the Order's compound? I'm quite certain he doesn't belong here."

Elsie placed an arm around Reggie's shoulders. "Irene is the healer who helped make Reggie get well. She lives at Driggs Hill."

Clara lifted a lip in a sneer. "One of the islanders with their so-called bush medicine. Superstitious nonsense. I'm sure Reggie would have been just fine without this Irene's help. I don't want you two associating with the islanders. They're not our people."

All three children wore identical expressions of dismay. Elsie spoke up. The girl was definitely becoming far too belligerent. "Mama, she really did help. And Johnny has been taking us fishing and helped us find good fruit to eat in the forest."

"Don't argue with me, Elsinoe. Boy, you need to go home now."

"His name's Johnny." Elsie pitched her voice low but Clara heard her.

"Elsinoe, I'm tired of your insolence. Go back to the hut immediately. Goodbye, Johnny."

Johnny looked stricken and Clara felt a momentary pang of guilt at upsetting the boy. He had done no harm really. Still, her children didn't need him around. She didn't want them going native like Theophilus. Associating with one of the islander children would encourage that.

Johnny ran off without a backwards glance.

Reggie looked up at his mother. "Mama, he helped us. We were really hungry. He showed us how to fish. We cooked yummy fish on the fire."

"If you're hungry, Reginald, you need to be sure to be at the Order House for meals."

The boy whined in response. "But the food there is yucky. And they take it away before I'm done."

Clara growled her impatience. "Reginald, I am in no mood to hear whining. Go back to the hut with your sister and remain there until I get back."

He shuffled his feet in the sand, slowly walking along the path. Clara turned and made her way to the well. The sooner she was clean, the more settled she'd feel. Her nerves were a wreck. She was shaking just from the little spat she'd had with the children. The reality of her experience with physical degradation was more difficult than she had ever imagined. How could it possibly lead to wisdom?

***

Irene sat in the sun, feeling it warm her bones. She sighed, relaxing. The burlup was almost finished and she would be glad to stop mashing and pounding roots and other ingredients. Her sisters sat next to her, cross-legged on the sand. The three women hummed as they worked, a song of magic and inspiration. They didn't look at each other but mashed ingredients and passed the bowls almost in a dance. Irene smiled. It was good to work with her sisters like this. She always felt so close to them when they made the ogologo-ndu potion together. One day, maybe they would be able to give it all to the elders rather than selling so much of it to the Order. But right now they needed the gold so they could buy land and build new houses. The whole family was tired of living on a leasehold yard that could be taken away from them at a moment's notice. And their yard was too close to the ocean. Irene worried about flooding when the big storms came.

Her musings were broken when Alice spoke. "Irene, Johnny been telling me about those white chillun he been hanging about with. He says you gave healing to de boy. Their hut is disgusting, he says, and they don't get proper food."

Irene shot Alice a look. "Yeah, I saw that dirt house of theirs. It's no business of ours, Alice. Those white folk do what they want."

Alice had always been soft-hearted, especially about children. "But they not getting enough to eat, Irene. That not right."

Mae spoke up now. "That shameful, not feeding your chillun. They spending all that gold on burlup but not feeding their chillun? What they thinking?"

Irene scowled. She hadn't thought of it that way. The Order did seem to have plenty of gold but they didn't seem to be using it to take care of their folks. "Yeah. I hear you. That don't sound right."

She resumed her pounding, dropping her gaze down into the bowl.

"What you going to do about it, Irene?" Alice had stopped moving.

Irene looked up to see what Alice was doing and saw that both her sisters were staring at her. "Do? What I going to do? I's not going to do anything. It not my business and not yours." Her sisters frowned at her. Irene shook her head at them. "We need to finish this burlup so we can get paid. We got almost enough to buy that land on the other side of Driggs Hill. C'mon, you two, get mashing." They both complied but Irene could feel the waves of disapproval emanating off them both. "What you want from me? I's trying to make our lives better. We don't want to always be leaseholders, am I right?"

Alice looked at her reproachfully. Her voice was soft in response. "We know that, Irene, and we grateful. It's just those chillun...it makes my heart sad to see them. It like no one loves them." Her deep brown eyes filled with tears.

Irene's chest grew tight with sadness. Alice already had enough suffering in her life, why did she have to take on other people's grief? "You got a good heart, Alice. What you think we should do about it?"

Alice sat looking thoughtful. Her sisters waited. She was a slow thinker but she always had something wise to say. "I was thinking of what I would do if it was Johnny who looked so sad and hungry. I'd sit him down and feed him some good fish stew. Then I'd put my arms around him and tell him some of de ol' storees. You know, like our mama used to tell us when we were little? Huh. You know, I don't think I ever told Johnny de old storees. I told them to my girls but he was born so late, I was too busy to tell stories. Then when de sea took John..."

She fell silent, gazing off into the trees. Mae reached across and patted her on the hand. "I used to tell de ol storees to my chillun. Those were good times. They would laugh or sometime, they stare like de creatures would come right out of de woods after them."

Irene smiled, remembering telling those same stories to her sons. It seemed like forever ago. Memories of Daniel and Joe as little boys overwhelmed her with sadness. Daniel would never see his child. She tried to distract herself with the problem of Reggie and Elsie. Her sisters had the right of it. The children weren't being treated properly. "Alice, you know what I think, I think you want to treat those chillun like they our own."

Alice laughed, a low, soft sound. Her round face softened. "I wouldn't mind a couple more little ones. You know I always loved having them around and now my Johnny's the last one I got."

All their children were growing up. Johnny was the last little one. Alice did have a lot of love to give children but her own were mostly done being mothered. They wanted to be off on their own. Most of the time, Irene didn't see her other nieces or nephews. They were with friends working the fields or out on the sponging boats. "And what you think de parents going to say if you start caring for their chillun? And can we spare de extra food to feed extra mouths? You know de cassava didn't come up this year."

Even as she spoke, Irene knew she'd lost the argument. Alice had that determined look on her face that said she wasn't going to let anyone change her mind. "Irene, I don't think those folks will know different. They all wrapped up in whatever they do at that big house and don't know what their chillun doing. And we got food to share. We not that poor."

Irene laughed. It sounded like Elsie and Reggie were getting themselves a new mama. She wondered how this was going to work.

Johnny slouched into the compound. Alice got up from the ground and went to him. "Where your new friends, love?"

He shrugged. Johnny's shoulders were slumped and his usually cheerful face sad. "Their muma told them they couldn't play with me no more. They got to work in de garden like de other children in that yard."

"Aw, baby, I's sorry. Why she say that?"

The boy shrugged again. "She said something about her kids getting to be natives or something. What that mean, mama?"

Alice's mouth pinched and she wrapped her arm around his shoulder. "She just being a snooty white lady, that's all, honey. It just mean she ignorant. You don't pay it no mind."

Johnny nodded. Irene tried to cheer him up, not wanting to see her favourite nephew sad. "Johnny-boy, I got some cocoa-nut milk fresh in my house. You want a cup?"

She knew how to appeal to her always-ravenous nephew. His face brightened immediately and he grinned. "Yes, please, Aunty Irene. That sound good."

She got up and fetched a cup of the cocoa-nut milk for him. "You hungry too? Ha-ha, of course you are. You always hungry, boy." She grinned at him and scrubbed a hand across his curls. He nodded.

Mae dragged herself to her feet, her bulk slowing her down. "It about time for lunch and I got some conch stew cooking. C'mon in and eat." She swayed into her house, beckoning to them. Irene moved to join her but spotted a couple of figures hovering at the gate. She squinted at them. It was Reggie and Elsie.

Alice must have spotted them at the same time for she gave a cry of joy and strode towards them. "Hello, chillun, we about to have something to eat. How about you come in and eat with us? Mae made some of her conch stew. Come on in now."

The children smiled shyly at her and approached. Alice took their hands and led them into the courtyard. "Johnny, look who came to visit. We going to have lunch together, right?"

Irene looked around at everyone gathered in the courtyard. They all looked happy. She decided not to ask Elsie and Reggie if their mother knew they had come visiting Johnny.

CHAPTER TWENTY-ONE

Irene poured the viscous fluid into a flagon and sealed it with a cork. The little clay flagon full of ogologo-ndu didn't seem like much but it represented weeks of work and scrounging for all the ingredients, including that fatal sponge diving trip by Irene's husband and sons. Daniel's last trip. She glanced across the courtyard towards her house. Alec and Joe slept inside, still exhausted from that trip. They'd only been back for two weeks but she had asked them to go again soon, too soon. Daniel's face haunted her, her darling son, victim of her need for the sponge. She felt a coldness deep inside her. Was it greed that sent her men into danger? Irene sighed and started the walk down to the Order's yard. It was later than she had planned and dusk was falling. She would have to walk home in the dark and there was only a half moon tonight. It was a good thing that the path was white sand and would glow under the moonlight.

The Order yard was quiet and she didn't see a single soul around. They must be all eating their dinner, she thought as she sauntered along. Her thoughts distracted her and she realised that she didn't recognize this part of the yard. Seeing that the path ended at a large hut in front of her, she turned and stood looking around the area, trying to decide which way to go. Angry male voices approached from behind her. She didn't know the other members of the Order besides Ward and didn't want to get on the wrong side of angry white men. She glanced around, then stepped behind a large, full cocoplum bush. They wouldn't notice her there in the growing dusk and once they passed, she could go on her way. She could see the men between the branches of the bush. Just two of them, still arguing. To her dismay, one gestured for the other to halt a few feet from her hiding place. Had they spotted her? She felt idiotic for hiding. Irene, the powerful healer, respected member of her community, cowering from two white men. She gathered her courage in preparation for stepping back onto the path when something one of them said made her pause.

"I tell you, we need a better sacrifice. Our requests are not being heard. The blood is not enough."

"You want to kill one of them outright? I don't think that will be well-received by certain members. They would see blood sacrifice as taking this one step too far."

Irene felt her blood go cold. Blood sacrifice? What were these people up to?

"They need never know. We'll take care of it secretly."

"I don't know. It seems too much, too extreme. And what if we're caught?"

"Are you turning into a coward? You know that our attempts to raise—" The voice broke off. "Did you hear that? I think someone's coming."

Irene held her breath. Had they heard her hiding in the bush next to them?

"They're all at dinner. No one's out here."

"What about the children? Maybe one of them escaped from the hut."

The Cultist's Wife

The children? Were they talking about Reggie and Elsie? Had they been confined to a hut for visiting her yard?

One of the men laughed, a sharp harsh laugh. "The children? They can barely move at night after working in the garden all day and their—treatment."

Irene felt a sinking sensation in her guts. What kind of trouble were Elsie and Reggie in? The men moved off, still arguing. She waited, hidden, until her limbs stopped trembling and she was sure the men were gone. Who were they? Did Ward know that members of his Order were talking of blood sacrifice? Should she tell him? Irene wondered how Ward would react to her telling him that members of his Order were up to no good. Would he even believe her? Or did he condone it? She barely knew the man. All she'd seen were a tendency to anger and the typical white man's arrogance but no hint of actual cruelty. She picked her way along the darkened path carefully, listening for the men she hoped had departed. All she heard was night birds hooting and tweeting in the treetops. Reaching a crossroads, she looked around, trying to decide what direction would lead to the Order House. She couldn't tell in the dark. The Order had constructed a maze of pathways in their yard and plants overgrew the paths. She couldn't even see the lights from the Order House because of the dense foliage. She kept walking, knowing that while large, the Order's yard wasn't the interior wilderness of Andros. She would eventually find the big house. She started to feel angry at herself for getting lost like a little child wandering in the coppet. Why had she even ventured out here when it was growing dark? She could have made Ward wait for the burlup. As she walked, it occurred to her that by providing the Order with ogologo-ndu, she was helping a possibly evil community flourish. Should she refuse to provide more?

She stomped along, clutching the little flagon so hard it crushed her hand. She winced and loosened her grip. The pain served to settle her nerves a little. The Order House couldn't be far from here. She just needed to calm down. Those men were probably just trying to make themselves sound biggity, After talking herself into an ease, she rounded a curve in the path and saw lights ahead of her. Irene breathed a sigh of relief. At last. She could hand over the burlup to Ward and head home. This time, she'd pay attention and use the main path to the gate. She wanted to get home fast and hoped she wouldn't run into those two nasty men on the way.

The lights of the Order House illuminated the clearing just ahead. The house bustled with activity. There were people standing on the porch talking and others were leaving, heading off along narrow paths into the darkness. Irene hesitated, not sure where she was going to find Ward in the crowd. Someone must have spotted her and was waving in her direction. Squinting, she thought it could be Horace.

He jumped over the porch railing and landed lightly, then sauntered over to where she was standing, out of the light. "Irene! What brings you here tonight? Not that I mind. It's always good to see you."

It was Horace. His bright presence allayed her worries a little. He was amiable and easy to be around. She liked him in spite of his status as a member of the Order.

"I got something for Ward. He around?"

Horace raised his eyebrows, a look of concern crossing his face. "Ward? Is he ill? I didn't know he was ill, he seemed fine at dinner. Oh. Are you here with more of his potion already?"

Irene shook her head, not directly answering his question. She knew Ward wanted to keep their contract a secret. "So he around? Can you go and get him for me?"

Horace still looked surprised and more than a little curious. "Certainly, I can fetch him for you. Would you like to step inside while I find him?"

"Nah, I'd rather stay out here."

Ward didn't keep her waiting long. He hurried out of the house and down the stairs. Taking her arm, he walked her further into the dark. His fingers pressed painfully into her flesh. "Why did you come now? There are people everywhere at this hour. I told you I didn't want anyone knowing of our transactions. My people are asking too many questions."

Irene pulled her arm out of his grip and raised her chin. She stared down her nose at him, their eyes at the same level. "You keep your hands to yourself, mister. I's not one of your meek followers you can treat any way you like." Her tone was level but with steel below.

He dropped his eyes first. "I apologise, Irene. I forgot myself."

Irene regarded him in silence. This man needed to watch himself or he'd find himself on the wrong end of a hex. Ward cleared his throat.

Good. He nervous. He better know not to mess with me again.

He tried again. "It won't happen again. Now, do you have my potion? I was expecting you yesterday with a new batch."

She glared at him, not bothering to explain the delay, and held a hand out for her payment. He presented a sack of clinking coins. Irene accepted the sack, opening it to check the contents.

"Not here! Don't open that here." He moved to shield her from the onlookers on the porch.

She regarded him coolly. "You want my burlup, I going to check you ain't shorting me first." The coins glinted back at her and she quickly dug a finger in to make sure there were only metal coins in the bag. Satisfied, she closed the sack and handed the flagon to Ward.

"Finally. Thank you, Irene. I'll need the same again in a week."

She shook her head. "A week? Nope. I don't got ingredients for another batch yet. You going to have to wait. I'll let you know when I's making more."

He spluttered in anger. "But, but, that's unacceptable. I need more next week. When do you think you'll get your ingredients?"

Irene raised a shoulder. "Hard to say. I'll let you know." With that, she turned on a heel and strode off into the darkness. Let him wait. Perhaps he'd learn some respect.

* * *

The walk home in the dark seemed to take forever but the bag of gold felt good and heavy hanging from her hand. Irene smiled to herself. She would go into Driggs Hill soon and talk to the elders about buying a piece of land further inland. Her family would have to clear the land but they could use the wood to build new houses out there. She hummed to herself as she stepped along the road. Lanterns were lit in her yard when she entered and she heard voices raised in song. She may have missed supper but it sounded like her sisters and their families were having a sing. Her smile deepened to a grin, hearing Alec and Joe's voices raised in song. It was good to have her men home. She shook off the lingering concern about the Order, deciding to enjoy herself with her family. They were all sitting around a big, welcoming fire but when Johnny spotted her, he jumped up and came running to her. The boy threw his arms around her and squeezed. "Aunty Irene! You back! I saved you some supper. Aunty Mae made pigeon peas and rice and they were so spicy. Just the way you like, right?"

Irene hugged him back and dropped a kiss on his head. "You a good boy, Johnny. Thank you for saving me supper."

She approached the fire, hobbled by the little boy clutching her around the waist. Grins lit up the faces of her family as she joined them. Alec blew her a kiss and Irene sank to the ground next to him with a groan. He rubbed her back and Irene groaned again as her muscles eased. Johnny broke away to fetch her a bowl. She smiled her thanks at the boy when he returned. She took a bite. The peas and rice were as spicy as promised and filled her stomach with welcome heat. The group around the fire continued their songs and her oldest nieces got up to dance.

Irene didn't notice Mae until her sister lowered herself with a grunt next to her. "Irene, you been gone a long time and you got a heavy sack there. I's guessing you at de big house selling more of our ogologo-ndu to those white folk."

Irene shot a sideways look at her sister. It sounded like Mae had something on her mind. Irene suppressed a sigh. "You know I getting that last batch of burlup ready for Ward and his folk."

Mae shook her head slowly. "It just ain't right, selling it to them, Irene. De ogologo-ndu belongs to our people. It helps our elders stay strong and wise."

Irene exhaled impatiently. Mae was always going on about the elders. What had they ever done for them but sit under that tree all day? "Mae, you see this sack? I got enough gold now to buy us that land we been wanting. You want to come with me up to Driggs Hill tomorrow to buy it from de elders?"

Mae's eyes grew round. "For real? We going to buy that land? Oh, Irene, that is grand news. But I thought Alec and Joe were leaving in the morning? Don't you want to be there, Alec? And Henry is still out on de water."

Irene gave her a quelling look. Wait for their husbands to do a business transaction? Why would she do that? She was in charge of this family.

Alec smiled a lazy smile and stroked Irene's arm. "You know I trust Irene to do what's best for de family, Mae."

Irene shot a look at him, a smile hovering around her lips. She shrugged at her sister. "You don't have to come, Mae. I can go by myself."

Mae shook her head, her chins waggling. Irene knew her sister hated to be left out and would rather miss a week's meals than be left behind tomorrow. Mae's forehead creased in a frown. "So we got enough for de land? Does that mean you not gonna sell ogologo-ndu to those white folk anymore?"

Irene paused. She hadn't planned on cutting off Ward's supply but now that they had enough money for the land, she supposed she could. "I think we got enough gold but what if de elders want more than I think they do for that land? We need to have some left over in case we need it."

Mae scowled in silence. She darted a look over to Alice who rose and joined them. "Y'all have been talking up a storm over here. What happening?"

"Irene got enough money from selling ogologo-ndu to buy us a plot of land."

Alice's face lit up and she turned to Irene with a broad grin. "Irene, that some fine news. So why you two looking so glum?"

"She still wants to sell burlup to de white folk instead of giving it all to de elders."

Mae's tone seemed to accuse Irene of wrongdoing. Irene glared in response.

Alice's forehead creased with confusion. "But why, Irene? We got enough money now, right?"

"Maybe. What if de elders want more than I think? What if something happens and we need more money? And de chillun, we could send de young ones to school if we had some extra."

Her sisters looked unconvinced, frowning. Alice spoke up first. "Irene, I just don't think we ought to be helping those people. They don't seem like good folk. They don't treat their chillun right and they be disrespectful to you."

Irene narrowed her eyes. What disrespect was Alice talking about? She straightened her back and stared at her youngest sister. "I don't allow no disrespect. You know that, Alice."

Her sister stared right back at her. "You have to run back and forth at all hours taking them de burlup. They should be coming to you."

Irene crossed her arms and scowled. "I don't want that Ward anywhere near my family. I take de burlup to him and that keeps him away from here. If he comes here, he could start poking around trying to find out our secrets."

Mae sighed loudly and scratched a mosquito bite on her neck. "I got to agree with Alice. He nasty business. His type shouldn't be getting ogologondu. How long you been giving it to him now? And our mama before that?"

Irene's patience was wearing thin. She didn't like the man either but his gold spent like anyone else's and she wanted to be sure they had enough for everything the family needed. "You two stop fretting. I know what I doing."

The women fell silent. She hoped she was right. Irene glanced around the fire at her family, love for them squeezing her heart. After all this time dealing with Ward, she didn't want to bring trouble to her family now. She looked at Alec, a question on her face. He risked his life for this. It seemed only fair that he should have a say. He sat up and put his arm around her shoulders, pulling her close.

His breath was warm against her ear. "You got to do what's right, Reenie. You know I trust you."

She swallowed and nodded. They all trusted her to do what was right.

CHAPTER TWENTY-TWO

Irene clung to Alec in the dark before dawn. It was time for him to leave on the sponging trip and an uncharacteristic fear gripped her. Irene felt the weight of leading the family. The loss of Daniel was still raw. The accusing eyes of Daniel's wife, belly big with his baby, followed her everywhere. Irene's heart was heavy. She fought tears every day since the news. Now she had to stay strong without Alec's support. The burlup brought good money into the family's coffers but it wasn't worth the life of her son. She didn't know how she was going to reconcile that in herself. And even if she didn't sell the burlup to Ward, she still needed to provide it to the settlement's elders.

Alec murmured in her ear. "Sweet, I have to go. De tide be turning soon and Joe is already on de boat waiting to cast off."

Irene took a deep breath and stepped back. She nodded her head briskly, trying to shake off her neediness. She could do this. "I know, Alec. You got to go. You just be safe out there. No risks. I know you don't really want to do this, especially so soon after..." She gulped back a sob, then cleared her throat. "I—just be careful, you hear? You and Joe come back safe to me." Her chest tightened and she bit her lip, willing herself to be calm. Alec didn't need to know how upset she was.

Alec clasped her shoulders and kissed her gently on the forehead. "I will. We'll both be careful. Don't worry. And when we back, maybe we can stay a while and help clear our land?"

Irene stepped close and pressed her forehead against his. She rubbed her hands up and down his strong back. "Yeah, I like that idea. I going to de elders about de land today. If all goes well, we'll have our own land when you and Joe get back."

"That sounds good. I'll see you soon, my Reenie."

With that, he released her and strode off towards the harbour, his footsteps crunching across the yard. Irene took a deep, calming breath. It was going to be alright. Alec and Joe would be back soon and they would all have a plot of land to work. Maybe she could buy the right kind of sponge from other fishermen and her men could retire from the sea. Alec and Joe just needed to come back safe from this trip.

**

Elsie blinked at the glare of sun streaking across her cot. Her belly told her it was time for breakfast. Mama must have gone up to the Order House even earlier than usual today. Elsie and Reggie didn't see her nor their father except at meals. Mama seemed tired. She must be working hard. The warm air drifted across Elsie's face, bringing the scent of sweet flowers and ripe fruit. She climbed out of bed and went to the doorway. A purple and green hummingbird flew past before darting out of sight into the branches of a tall tree.

I suppose I'd better wash before going to breakfast.

She dragged fingers through her tangled hair, grimacing. She kept forgetting to braid it before bed.

Ugh. I definitely need to comb my hair before Mama sees me.

She plopped down onto a rock sitting next to the hut and tugged at the knots. Her scalp burned with pain and tears sprang to her eyes. She pulled harder, working through the tangles. Reggie appeared, yawning. He watched her for a moment, then wandered over to the fire pit and sat down. He poked at the dying fire with a twig until a tiny flame spurted into life at the end of the piece of wood. Elsie retrieved her hairbrush from the hut and attacked her hair, determined to smooth it enough to braid. She started when Horace spoke next to her. She hadn't heard him approach.

"Good morning, Elsie, good morning, Reggie."

His tone was uncharacteristically serious and Elsie glanced up at his face. He looked sad. She pulled her own mouth into a matching grimace. "Horace, you look sad. What's wrong?"

He shook his head and dropped a hand on her shoulder. "I'm leaving. I wanted to say goodbye."

She screwed up her forehead and cocked her head to one side. "Leaving? Where are you going?"

"Home. To England. I'm leaving on the mail boat this morning."

Elsie digested that. He had never talked about his home but she knew he was English by the way he spoke. She felt a surge of homesickness. Their visit to the Bahamas had been exciting but it didn't feel like home. She pictured her kindly grandparents in their comfortable house and Nanny, making sure they had everything she needed. It seemed like a million miles away.

"I wish I could go back to England too." Her voice was small and she couldn't control the wobble.

Horace nodded, his eyes heavy and sad. Elsie wondered where the twinkle had gone. "I understand. It's hard for you here, isn't it? But you're a brave, resourceful little girl and you'll do well. And think of all the adventures you'll have to tell your friends about when you go home."

"I know. But why are you leaving? You don't look like you're going home. You look sad."

He crouched down next to her and met her eyes. "My parents need me. My father is ill. So I have to leave. I'm sad because I'm going to miss you."

Elsie enveloped him in a sudden hug and sniffed back tears. Her voice was muffled. "I'll miss you too, Horace. You're a good friend."

He squeezed her and then released his hold, standing up. His smile didn't meet his eyes, bright with tears. He tramped across to Reggie, still poking at the embers. "Goodbye, old man. Be well."

Horace reached down and shook Reggie's hand. Elsie saw Reggie's lip quiver. "Goodbye? But...where are you going?"

"I'm leaving. Going home. You take care of yourself." Horace dropped Reggie's hand and clasped his shoulder.

The little boy's eyes filled with tears. "But I don't want you to leave!" Reggie wailed.

Horace bit his lip and nodded. "I'm sorry. I have to go. Take care, children."

He turned and ambled away. Reggie joined Elsie and they held hands, watching Horace walk down the path to the main gate. The path turned and he moved out of sight. Elsie sighed. "I wish he didn't have to go. Come on, we'd better get ready or all the breakfast will be gone."

Reggie pulled a face. "It's probably that slimy, mushy stuff again."

"I know. It would be nice to have proper food. I want scones and jam. I'd even eat a kipper."

Reggie groaned. "Oh Elsie, why'd you say that? Now I want scones."

As they stood there dreaming of food, Stephen marched by with three Order members the children didn't know. Elsie drew Reggie back into the hut. She avoided Stephen as much as she could. He found fault and issued punishments on a daily basis. The men continued past their hut, Stephen glaring at the children as he passed. The men were headed in the same direction that Horace had just taken. Maybe they were going to collect supplies from the mail boat.

Once they were out of sight, Elsie continued brushing her hair, then braided it. Locks of hair tickled her face where she'd missed catching it in the braid and the braid itself felt lumpy and uneven. She didn't mind since her hair was out of the way and wouldn't get so tangled. Reggie was back poking at the fire. He was going to get burned if he kept playing about. Elsie spotted one of the gourd bowls at his side. "Do we have any water left in that bowl to wash with?"

He glanced down at the bowl. "Yeah. It's got leaves in."

Elsie made a face. It would do. She didn't feel like walking to the well for more. She walked over and squatted next to the bowl. She splashed water on her face and hands, then poked Reggie. "Your turn. And hurry up. Breakfast time. I just heard the bell."

Reggie dipped a finger in the water and flicked it at her. She shoved him, knocking the bowl over. The water splashed into the fire, putting out the smouldering ashes. Reggie pouted at her. "Aw, look what you made me do."

"Not my fault, you started it."

The children glared at each other and a fight looked imminent but loud voices coming back up the path caught their attention.

"Let go of me! You have no right to detain me!" It sounded like Horace, but angry and afraid, not like the Horace they knew.

Exchanging a meaningful look, the children darted into the bushes and crouched down, out of sight. Peeking through leaves, Elsie saw Horace, surrounded by Stephen and the other members. Two of them held Horace by the arms as they marched him back along the path, towards the Order House. He struggled to get free, but the larger men had a tight grip on him. Elsie heard Stephen's deep voice. "Ward needs to speak to you before you leave, Horace. He is concerned about your behaviour."

"I already spoke to Ward and told him that I think he's a charlatan and a conniving tyrant. Get your hands off me."

"I don't think so, Horace. We can't have you spreading lies about the Order."

Elsie felt a shudder of fear go through her. Stephen's face looked ugly and scary. He sounded calm but very dangerous. She huddled down smaller, wanting desperately to make sure he didn't spot her. Horace struggled free and dashed towards the gate but his assailants were faster and tackled him to the ground. He cried out when they piled on top of him. Stephen approached more slowly and Elsie craned her neck to see what was happening. Stephen grabbed Horace's hair and pulled his face off the ground. "You're not leaving, Horace. Ward sent us to get you and that means you're staying."

The men got to their feet, hauling Horace up. This time, all four of them had a grip on him. Horace's face was red and he looked scared. "You can't keep me here. My family will wonder about me. They're expecting me in England."

Stephen sneered. "I'm sure Ward will make sure your family knows that you are staying with us willingly."

Horace looked defeated. He dropped his head and stumbled along, held up by the men. The group disappeared up the path. Elsie crept out of the bushes and peered after them, careful to stay hidden. Reggie tiptoed up behind her. "Where are they taking Horace?"

Elsie saw the men take a turn up ahead, away from the Order House. "I don't know. They're not going to the big house. C'mon, let's follow them."

The two followed slowly, taking cover in the bushes that lined the paths to stay out of sight. The men dragged Horace into a clearing. There was no hut, just a little shed leaning up against a silk-cotton tree. They threw Horace into the shed and chained the door closed. The men turned back to the path. Elsie and Reggie ran the other direction, not stopping until they reached the porch of the Order House. Adults glared at them when they tore up the steps and stood there panting. Neither spoke. Their concern about their friend 's fate was not something they could talk about here. Besides Horace, Elsie didn't know who they could trust. They went into breakfast, as silent and subdued as the other Order children.

CHAPTER TWENTY-THREE

The lanterns around the yard illuminated the paths but the bushes remained in deep shadow. Elsie and Reggie crept through them, avoiding the light.

"How can we get Horace out of that shed?" Reggie spoke in Elsie's ear, startling her.

"Shh. I brought this hoe. I think we can break the chain with it."

There was a long pause before he spoke again.

"D'ya think he's all right in there? It was hot today."

Elsie's heart sank. She hadn't thought about the heat. Poor Horace was probably really thirsty and she hadn't thought to bring some water. She shrugged off the thought. They would get him something to drink once they got him out of that shed. She stopped to poke her head out of the bushes to get her bearings. The bright lights of the Order House were to her right, so they were headed in the correct direction. Elsie caught the sound of murmuring voices along the path and retreated to the safety of the bushes. She grabbed Reggie's arm and shushed him. They froze, waiting for the people coming along the path to pass by. Rustling from the children's passage through the bushes would be sure to attract notice.

Several people walked by the children's hiding place, carrying lanterns and coils of rope. Elsie's heart started pounding. Where were they heading? Towards the shed where Horace was locked up?

The children followed as stealthily as they could. The adults didn't seem to notice that they were being followed. Elsie caught a few words as the adults spoke to each other. Something about Lug Hole and midnight. Then she heard Horace's name and had to suppress a moan. The people were going to let Horace out of his prison but why?

Elsie was torn. She and Reggie wouldn't be able to rescue Horace from the shed now but she couldn't just give up. The children reached the edge of the clearing where the shed sat. They stopped, remaining hidden from the adults who were now at the door to the shed. In the circle of light cast by a lantern, Elsie could see Stephen unlocking the door to the shed. She wanted to growl at the sight of his malicious face or maybe even throw a rock at him.

Stephen got the door open and reached inside the tiny building. He dragged Horace out by the arm. Horace stumbled and fell to the ground, limp. He looked dreadful. His hair was plastered to his head and he had dark circles under his eyes. Elsie berated herself for not coming earlier with water, even if they wouldn't have been able to help him escape in the daylight. Stephen kicked at Horace's prone body but Horace just groaned. Two of the other men bound his arms and legs with the rope they carried, then lifted his drooping body to their shoulders.

Reggie gasped and Elsie clamped a hand across his mouth to stifle the sound. The night was alive with the noises of insects buzzing and chittering. The adults didn't look around. They probably hadn't heard Reggie. She took her hand off his mouth and released a breath she hadn't realised she was holding.

They were moving away, carrying Horace. Elsie couldn't tell if Horace was awake but he didn't seem to be moving. She watched as they passed her hiding place, letting them get further along the path before beckoning to Reggie to follow. The lanterns the Order members held made it easy to track them in the darkness. The group turned along paths unfamiliar to the children. Elsie wondered where they were going. She thought they would be headed to the Order House but this wasn't the right way. The boundary wall, glowing white in the moonlight, appeared ahead of them. The group of adults paused while one of them opened a gate. Elsie didn't know there was more than one gate in the boundary wall. She'd just climbed the wall when she needed to get over. Elsie grabbed Reggie's arm and pulled him into the shelter of a mango tree. They would be hard to spot if one of the adults should happen to glance back. The group moved through the gate, carrying Horace's limp form. Elsie saw Stephen glance behind him before he passed through the gate, shutting it behind them.

"How can we get through the gate without them seeing?" Reggie whispered in Elsie's ear.

"We go over the wall. There's a sea grape tree right over there." She pointed to a tree growing next to the boundary wall. Those trees were easy climbers with lots of low, thick branches.

The children snuck down the path towards the gate, then veered off towards the sea grape tree. Elsie swung herself onto a branch, then stood on it. She peeped over the wall into the forest. Lantern lights glowed between the trees, not far off. Elsie reached down to give Reggie a hand up. They stood together and watched the lights moving away. Elsie scrambled onto the top of the wall from the branch and sat there for a moment, legs dangling over the edge. She couldn't see the ground below her in the dark. It would be risky to just jump off so she reached for the branch of a tree on the other side of the wall. It wasn't as thick or smooth as the sea grape and its bark grated at her skin. She leaned forward, putting some weight on the branch. It bowed but Elsie thought it would hold. She slid off the wall, holding the branch and hoping it wouldn't break. The branch bent under her weight and she felt with her feet for the ground. Too high still. Taking a chance, she let go of the branch and dropped to the forest floor, twisting her knee on a mess of downed branches. The branch flung back into place with too loud a noise for her comfort. Wincing in pain, she looked up at Reggie, sitting on the wall.

"C'mon, I'll catch you." She pitched her voice softly in case it carried to the adults in the forest. Reggie turned onto his belly and lowered himself part of the way down the wall, then dropped into her waiting arms. His weight was more than she could handle and they both fell over onto the ground.

"You okay?"

He nodded and stood, brushing dead leaves and muck off his hands. Elsie's knee was throbbing but she didn't mention it. It could bear her weight so she ignored the pain. "Come on, we need to catch up with them."

Reggie stood, unmoving, biting his lip. "What are we going to do when we catch up with them?"

Elsie was taken aback. What were they going to do? Two little kids up against six adults didn't stand much of a chance. "I don't know, Reggie, but if we're going to help Horace, we need to follow them."

Reggie shrugged. "It's really dark out here. What if there are snakes?"

Elsie felt her patience snap. "Don't be such a baby, Reggie. You want to go back? Go home then. See if I care. I'm following them."

"Okay, okay. I'm coming."

Elsie looked for the glow of the lanterns. The adults had progressed far into the forest. Picking their way to the trail leading out of the gate, the children tried to move as quietly as they could. It was probably not necessary. The insects were even louder out in the wilderness and animals crunched through the undergrowth. Elsie wondered what they were. Rats, maybe? More of those giant lizards?

The trail through the trees was lit by moonlight, the pale sand glowing. The children drew closer to the group of adults. Elsie realised that they could be spotted if one of the adults looked back, so she paused, and drew Reggie into the undergrowth. Water dripped on the back of her neck, startling her into a little shriek. She put her hands over her mouth, too late.

"What was that?"

A man's voice drifted up the trail.

"Probably an animal. Maybe an owl caught itself dinner."

Stephen. That was definitely Stephen up there.

Reggie and Elsie stood frozen in place, hoping no one would come to investigate. They were in luck. The adults moved off, apparently convinced that they had heard a wild animal's demise. Cautiously, the children followed, ducking into bushes as they moved, trying to stay out of sight.

Elsie's knee was stiff and painful by the time the group stopped. Elsie thought they were at the blue hole Johnny had called Lug Hole on the day she had met him. The children's view of the scene was obstructed by trees and bushes but they didn't dare walk along the trail to get closer. Elsie looked around for a good climbing tree. They were standing amongst mostly skinny pines with high spindly branches but she spotted a good climbing tree a little way into the undergrowth. Crooking her finger at Reggie to follow, she picked her way through the brush to the climbing tree. It wasn't as easy to climb as the sea grape tree but they hauled themselves into its branches high above the forest floor. Elsie looked down. She stood on a branch higher than her father was tall. A momentary wave of dizziness rushed over her and she grabbed the tree trunk for stability. Reggie stood on a branch a little lower and looked like he was scanning the area. She craned her neck and spotted the cliff overlooking Lug Hole. She tapped Reggie on the shoulder and pointed. The adults were gathered on the edge of the cliff, a bundle that could only be Horace on the ground at their feet.

"What are they doing down there?"

"I don't know. I think I hear something. Shh."

Voices rose into the night, not quite a song but different from speaking. It sounded like they were speaking in rhythm, the same words over and over. The male voices were deep and grating as they chanted their strange words. Candles flared into life surrounding the prone figure of Horace. He looked like he was straining against the ropes and the children heard him cry out. His voice echoed into the night. "Let me go, you lunatics!"

A dark figure leaned over him and his voice was suddenly muffled.

Elsie and Reggie looked at each other.

"Elsie. What are they going to do?" Reggie sounded small and scared.

Elsie shook her head. Why had Stephen brought Horace here of all places? She remembered Johnny's story about the monster who lived in the blue holes. Was it real? She had seen bubbles in the water that day but that didn't prove anything. "I don't know, Reggie. Shh. they'll hear us."

The children clung to the tree, shivering despite the warm night. The chanting went on and on. Elsie started to get sleepy standing in the tree and her knee ached. Reggie yawned. Maybe they were just going to let Horace go after they did their ritual. He had stopped struggling a while ago and just lay there. Elsie hoped he was all right. Maybe he was just tired.

The chanting got louder and the voices sounded harsher, almost angry now. Elsie shook herself to attention and peered down at the scene on the cliff. They were picking Horace up now. Were they finished? Were they going to carry him all the way back to the Order yard now?

She sucked in a breath and put a hand to her mouth. They were swinging Horace back and forwards over the edge of the cliff, then with one last heave, launched him into the air over the water. Elsie jerked as his body plummeted into the water, sending sprays of water high into the air. She moaned against her hand, trying to be silent. The lake water looked like it was boiling and she was sure she saw something long and snakelike thrashing around down there. Horace didn't resurface. The chanting stopped abruptly and Stephen intoned, "We pray that you accept our sacrifice, O Great and Powerful One."

The water calmed and became a shiny mirror reflecting the moonlight. Reggie turned to Elsie, eyes wide. Tears streamed down his face and his mouth quivered. She looked back at him, her face feeling wooden with shock. She squinted over at the blue hole, hoping to see some sign of Horace but the water was still and empty. The Order members trudged back along the trail, not noticing the children clinging to the tree above their head. Their lantern light disappeared into the forest. Legs shaking, Elsie climbed down from the tree, wincing from the pain in her injured knee. Reggie joined her. Neither spoke as they approached the edge of the cliff and looked down into the dark water.

"Why did they do that, Elsie?"

Elsie's shock boiled into anger. "Because they are evil, nasty people. I'm going to get them for this. They may think they got away with it but they don't know that we saw the whole thing. We're going to tell someone about it and that horrible Stephen is going to be punished." Her voice rose into a shriek.

Reggie nodded, his eyes puffy with tears. Elsie put her arm around her brother's shoulders and led him away from the water. Neither looked back.

***

A noise at the door of the dark hut woke Clara with a start. She saw two small figures slinking into the shack, framed by moonlight. Sitting up in bed, she called out to them. "Where have you two been all night?"

Both children started and Elsie let out a little squeal. "Mama! You're awake."

Reggie flung himself onto her bed and into her arms, crying.

"Reginald, what are you doing? Get off me. Elsinoe, explain yourself. It's past midnight and you two should have been in bed hours ago, not sneaking around outside."

Elsie stood in front of Clara, hands twisting in front of her. Clara could barely see the child's face in the dim light inside the hut but the child's face was twisted with fear. "I'm sorry we woke you, Mama. We saw something terrible..."

At that, Reggie burst into loud sobs. "There was a monster in the water and it ate Horace!"

Clara sat up in bed, pushing the wailing boy off her. She was far too tired for her children's escapades and fantasies. "Children, you must cease bothering me with ridiculous fantasies. I'm exhausted and I need to sleep. Now be quiet and go to bed. We'll discuss this infraction in the morning."

Elsie didn't move. Clara could see the glint of tears rolling down the girl's face. "But, Mama—"

"No, Elsinoe, I don't want to hear about your little fantasy games."

"It wasn't a game, it was real. We saw it. There was a monster in the water and they threw Horace in and—"

Clara rubbed her face wearily and held up a hand, interrupting Elsie. "Stop. What I think you saw is your friend Johnny. I think you were mucking about in the forest with him tonight and you didn't realise the time. Then you decided to make up this ridiculous story so I wouldn't know that you had disobeyed me by seeing him."

Elsie's mouth dropped open and she shook her head vehemently. "No, no, that's not it. We saw them throw Horace into the water—"

"Elsinoe, enough. Horace left this morning for Nassau. How could you possibly have seen him tonight?"

"But, he didn't leave. He was going to but then they took him away."

Clara shook her head, willing her daughter into silence. "No more stories. I mean it. Go to bed, both of you."

Reggie whimpered as he dragged himself to his cot, then flopped into it. Elsie stood there for a moment longer, then sighed and turned away to go to her own bed.

Clara shook her head before lying back down. She turned onto her side and put a foot out of her covers, trying to cool herself in the muggy heat. Her children were running wild and she didn't know how to manage them. Perhaps she needed to ask their father for help again. Not an appealing idea but monsters eating people? What outlandish fantasies the children were creating. They needed to be reined in before they were completely out of control. But what would Theo do? Beat them into submission? Lock them up until they settled down? He was so distant and had taken no hand in raising them. Why would he start now? Unsatisfied with her solution, Clara beat her pillow into a more comfortable shape and tried to sleep. She tried to ignore the muffled sobs from the children's cots, not willing to comfort their imagined upset. But had they really seen something to terrify them? Elsinoe rarely cried when scolded but she lay in her cot stifling real tears. What had they seen out there? Exhaustion washed across her. The morning would be here soon enough and she would be expected to serve Ward all day without a break. The children thought they had seen a monster. They had no idea what a real monster was. She shuddered inwardly at the thought and closed her eyes, willing sleep to come.

CHAPTER TWENTY-FOUR

The morning sun woke Clara long before she was ready, shining in the glass-less window, and heat filled the little hut. She rose and dressed hurriedly, leaving off her corset as Ward had instructed. Clara winced at the linen camisole rubbing her nipples. The absence of the corset's grip wasn't as freeing as it once was. She buttoned her blouse with shaking fingers. The children slept, their faces tear-stained and ruddy. They needed more sleep after last night's upset, but if she left them, they wouldn't eat this morning.

"Elsinoe. Reginald. Time to wake up. We don't want to miss breakfast."

Elsie yawned and stretched, mumbling a response. She turned over on her little cot. Clara reached down and stroked the child's head, damp under her fingers. Her hair was dirty and matted. It was so hard to keep clean here with no running water or bathing facilities. Why did Theo think this was acceptable? Clara's jaw clenched but she kept her tone soft. "Wake up, children. You know they won't wait for us and we'll miss breakfast."

Elsie sat up, blinking, her expression soft from sleep, then her face froze. Her eyes grew distant and filled with tears. She bit her lip and nodded. "Yes, Mama, I know. Thank you for waking us." She crawled out of the cot, still in yesterday's clothes. Clara handed her a wet cloth to wipe her face, grimy with tears and dirt.

"Would you like me to brush your hair? I'll be gentle, I promise."

Elsie threw a confused look at her. Clara hadn't offered to brush her hair for weeks. "Yes, please, Mama."

Clara picked up the hairbrush and started to untangle her daughter's hair. She tried to be gentle but the mats were dense. She tugged too hard and Elsie yelped. "I'm sorry, I'm so sorry." Clara's voice wavered and tears welled up in her eyes.

"It's alright, Mama, there are a lot of knots."

Clara sniffed back her tears and kept untangling. "There certainly are. Perhaps we should remember that and brush your hair more often."

She could hear the smile in Elsie's voice. "I like that idea, Mama."

Clara worked in silence on the child's knotted hair, soothed by the simple task. Caring for her children wasn't as onerous as she'd once thought. She finished and plaited the smooth hair into a braid. "There we are. Time to get you two dressed in something clean so we can go to breakfast."

She dug through the children's little travel chest but almost everything was grubby and covered in sand. She held up a travelling dress and shook her head. Too heavy for this climate. Why didn't they think to enquire about appropriate clothing before leaving England? Oh yes, because they were rushed by Theo's demands. She pulled out a dress that wasn't too dirty and stood in the door to shake the sand out

"Here you are. Hurry, please. I just heard the gong." That gave them fifteen minutes to get to the Order House.

Reggie sat up and rubbed his eyes. His usual cheery smile for his mother was missing. He said nothing as he climbed out of bed and changed clothes. Clara caressed his hair, smoothing it down. "Good morning, Reginald."

He threw his arms around her legs and squeezed. Clara patted his head and pushed him away. "No time for that, let's get you ready."

Reggie sniffled, his face downcast, still silent. He submitted to having his clothes changed.

Finally dressed, they hurried along the path to the Order House, and made it to the dining room in time to receive plates of fruit and the ever-present gruel. Tea was nowhere to be seen although Clara could swear she smelled steeping Assam somewhere. The children toyed with their food, their cheeks thin and pale. Clara hadn't noticed before how dreadful they looked, with dark circles under their eyes. She was no longer convinced about their late-night adventure. She had been so harsh with them last night. Had they really seen a murder? Clara poured them both glasses of some yellow-orange juice.

"Have some juice, children. And eat up. You need your nourishment."

Elsie sighed and ate a spoonful of gruel. Clara scanned the room. She hadn't paid attention to the other children of the Order in the bustling dining room but they too looked wan and undernourished, eating without enthusiasm or energy. Only the adults spoke and only to each other. They barely seemed to notice the children. Clara winced, remembering her own identical behaviour on every morning since arriving. If the parents of these children weren't caring for them, who was?

"Children, I know you've been asked to help with the garden but please be sure to take rests during the day." Clara wasn't sure who was in charge of the gardening but they were asking too much of mere children.

Elsie spoke into her food, not meeting Clara's eyes. "Stephen doesn't like it when we stop working. We get demerits and then they take away lunch privileges."

No lunch as a punishment? No wonder the children were so thin. They worked at manual labour in the heat all day without food.

"That's preposterous. How can they expect you to work so much and not eat?"

Reggie dropped his spoon into his empty bowl with a clatter and slurped up his juice. "Johnny helps us find food sometime. We go fishing."

Clara brushed her hand across his head. "Fishing? Be careful. You could get hurt."

He shrugged. "It's okay. Aunty Irene takes care of us. Any more food?"

Clara scanned the table. The gruel pot was empty as was the fruit platter. "No, there's nothing left."

Reggie sighed, sounding older than the little boy who'd arrived on Andros a few short months ago. Clara's heart sank. The children were growing up here but not how she'd expected. A gong sounded and everyone rose to their feet. It was time for the adults to go to Assembly. The children shuffled out of the room, heading to the fields. Clara watched her children leave, holding hands, something they'd rarely done at home. At least they were growing closer in this foreign land.

CHAPTER TWENTY-FIVE

Irene worked fast, hoping to get the sweet potatoes dug out before the sun got too high. The air already felt like warm molasses. She glanced around, wondering where the rest of her family was this morning. She intended to head up to the elders' house in Driggs Hill later and Mae wanted to go with her. Irene shrugged and dug harder, pulling a giant tuber out of the sandy soil. That one would be good roasted in the coals, just the way Daniel liked. The thought pierced her like a knife. Her sweet boy was gone. He wouldn't be eating sweet potatoes ever again. She blinked back tears and threw the tuber into her basket. She sent out a silent prayer for Alec and Joe's safety.

A cloud passed across the sun and Irene glanced up at the change in light.

More clouds followed it. She predicted an early afternoon storm from the look of those clouds. She surveyed her crop of sweet potatoes and decided to bring them into the yard. It wouldn't go far to feed her family but it was what they had. She could stretch it if she made it into fou fou. The other sweet potatoes would last better in the ground, especially if they got a good soak from the rain. She scooped the harvested tubers into a basket and heaved the load up onto her hip. She carried her hoe over her shoulder and sauntered back to the courtyard. Johnny was there, munching on a handful of guineps and talking to the white children. They looked serious, almost scared. Their clothing was dirty and the girl's hair was a tangled mess.

Irene frowned, remembering the talk about these children she'd had with Alice and Mae. Her sisters had complained that the children's parents weren't treating them right and now here they were in her yard, looking miserable and neglected. Johnny caught sight of her and scampered over. "Aunty Irene, Reggie and Elsie saw something bad and they need our help. No one will help them down at the big house."

Reggie and Elsie looked at her, hope written on their faces.

Irene moved closer and frowned down at the children. "What happening down there? Why you need my help? Did someone get hurt?"

"Not hurt, killed, Aunty Irene!" Elsie burst out. Irene drew back. Killed? That was something for the elders to worry about, not her. And if someone had been killed, she might have to take this bad news to the elders instead of buying land today.

"Someone got killed? What happened, chile? Who got killed?"

Elsie's lip wobbled and her eyes filled with tears. "Horace. They killed Horace. And no one will believe us."

The little girl sobbed, her tears loosened.

Irene felt a lump settle into her stomach. Horace was dead? "Calm down, chile. Tell me more. Who killed him? What happened?"

Elsie shook her head, unable to speak through her tears. Reggie held her hand. He looked pale and drawn. Looking up at Irene, he volunteered more information. "There were some men and they carried Horace into the forest and threw him in the water and then the monster ate him."

Irene's blood ran cold. The monster? He could only be speaking of the monster that was said to live in the blue holes, the Lusca. A story she told the young'uns to keep them away from Lug Hole.

Johnny took her hand. "Aunty Irene, what we gonna do?"

She looked down at her nephew. His brown eyes were wide with fright. She shook her head. "Do? What we gonna do? There not'ing we can do. If de men gave Horace to de... monster in de water..." She broke off her thought, not wanting to scare the children more than they already were. The Lusca was said to crave human flesh and would grow stronger with every offering. Could it really be true?

Elsie quieted her tears and started speaking again. "What happens, Aunty Irene? What happens if the monster ate Horace?"

Irene snorted, needing to lighten the mood. The children were overwrought. "Well, you get a bigger monster, that what. But you chillun know de Lusca nothing but an ole storee, right? Just like the Chickcharnie. They not real."

Reggie stamped his foot and scowled at Irene. "But we saw it, Aunty Irene, we saw the monster!"

Irene studied the little boy. His cheeks were flushed red and his eyes were over bright. He looked exhausted. "You said it was dark? Maybe it was just de tide what took Horace. De tide in some of those holes is awful fierce." Irene knew that the inland blue holes didn't have the same tides as the ones right off shore but it was possible. She didn't know what had happened last night but it was best to calm the children's fears.

They nodded, doubtful looks still on their faces.

Elsie piped up. "But even if there was no monster, those men killed Horace by throwing him in the water all tied up. They need to be punished, Aunty Irene."

Irene brushed a hand across the child's tangled hair and looked down at her with a heavy heart. "Who saw them do that? A couple chillun? And where Horace's body? Chile, I sorry. Nobody gonna believe you."

Mae meandered into the courtyard and over to the huddled group. She scrutinised their miserable expressions. "What's going on? You look like someone died or something."

Reggie and Elsie burst into tears and Mae drew back in surprise.

Irene fixed Mae with a glare. "The chillun say they saw men kill that Horace last night."

"Who killed him? Was it white folk or islanders?"

"I think it was people from the Order." Elsie's voice was thick with tears.

Mae shrugged. "Huh. De elders don't have nothing to do with the white folk. They only make rules for us islanders. You gotta go to your own folk for justice, chile."

Elsie's shoulders slumped. "But they won't believe us. We tried to tell Mama but she just hushed us. She said we were making up stories."

Irene placed her hand on Elsie's shoulder. "I sorry, girl. We can't do nothing for you."

Elsie nodded and taking Reggie's hand, turned and walked away. Irene watched them go. This was bad trouble indeed and not just for the white folks down island. She needed to let the elders know what Elsie and Reggie had seen. The men she had overheard in the Order's yard had killed Horace, she was sure of it. But why did they think they should sacrifice to the Lusca? What made them think those ol' storees were true?

＊＊＊

The men lounging in the shade of the cotton tree eyed Irene and Mae as the women approached. The elders didn't smile. She held her head higher and stared back. The little square in the centre of Driggs Hill was quiet and empty except for the dark men clad in pale linen suits, the elders of the settlement. The sun beat down and Irene wished she had brought her straw hat. Her feet burned on the sunlit sand near the tree but she didn't flinch, not wanting to show weakness in front of these men. The shade of the enormous tree cooled her instantly when she entered it. She stopped, shoulders back, and shifted the box of gold in her arms, waiting for one of the men to speak first. She may not agree with everything the elders said but she knew to show respect for their positions.

The senior of the elders, Irving McFee, sat cross-legged, back braced against one of the tree's buttresses. His skin was as dark as Irene's. He was also African-born and had been an elder for many years, although he looked to be a man in his forties. He cleared his throat and spat on the ground.

"Good day to you, Mrs. Bain...and Mrs. Adderley. What brings you out here in this heat?"

Irene darted a warning look at Mae to stay quiet, as they had agreed. "Good day to you, elders. We bring you news and a request."

"And a flagon of ogologo-ndu?"

Irene dropped her gaze and shook her head. "No, I don't have any ogologo-ndu, elder Irving. You heard about my Daniel. I was waiting for my menfolk to return with de ingredients I need for de burlup when de sea took him. Alec and Joe went back out just a few days ago."

"We were sorry to hear about Daniel. That was a terrible loss for both your family as well as our community. So there is no ogologo-ndu for us?"

"Not yet."

An ominous silence descended. All three men glared at her. She shifted from one foot to another. The weight of the box of gold coins seemed to grow too heavy for her arms.

Irving sighed. He put his hand to his forehead. It was trembling, Irene noticed, a side-effect of the ogologo-ndu. "Irene, you yourself know what will happen to me if I don't have that medicine every day. I am 95 years old. You want this settlement to lose its senior elder because you can't make enough ogologo-ndu to keep me going?"

Irene shook her head again.

"So what happened? I thought you preparing a batch?" He paused and narrowed his eyes at her. "Don't tell me you sold all the burlup you made to those white people down island."

Mae, unable to keep silent, burst out, "That exactly what she did, elder Irving. I told her not to but she went and sold it all to that Ward down there in de big yard. He giving our burlup to more of his people now so he needed more."

"Mae!" Irene's voice was sharp.

Mae lapsed into silence, muttering an apology.

"I will be getting you more ogologo-ndu soon, elders, before you run out, I promise." Irene winced inwardly, hearing herself grovel.

"You've never let me down, Irene, nor your mama before you. You be sure you don't let your avarice endanger our lives."

Guilt gnawed at Irene at the possibility that her own elders could suffer for her greed. The amount of the potion Ward demanded grew every year but this was the first time she had run out before giving her elders their share. She nodded in agreement.

Mae spoke up again, despite her promise to stay quiet. "We make sure you get your burlup. No worries." She bit her lip when Irene shot another glare at her. This wasn't going the way Irene had planned. She thought it was time to divert attention away from her own shortcomings on to the doings of the white folk.

"Elders, we got news that we thought you should know about. One of those white men died in Lug Hole last week. He was thrown in."

Irene watched the men's faces tense with fear. They all knew the mythology surrounding death in Lug Hole.

"He was thrown in? Who did it? Did you yourself see this?" Irving's voice came out high and reedy, betraying his true age.

"Couple of chillun from that yard followed a bunch of white men and saw them throw one of their own people into Lug Hole. De chillun say they saw a monster eat the man."

One of the elders barked a short laugh. It was Alan, a short, plump man who had disliked Irene ever since they were both children. "A couple of chillun claim they saw a monster eat someone? Ridiculous. You know that's nonsense, Irene. There's no monster in Lug Hole; that just a story you tell to scare de chillun."

Irene glared at him in silence.

No monster? Parrot ass think he know everyt'ing.

The men muttered to each other, too low for Irene to make out their words, their heads bent together. Irving straightened and levelled a gaze at Irene. "The white folk aren't under our power, you know that, Irene. We can't do nothing about this problem, except report it to their folks over in Nassau. But you say just a couple of chillun saw this murder? No one over in Nassau will listen to the word of a chile. And we talk 'bout mythological monsters, that will make them laugh."

Irene huffed. Why did they have to give up so easily? It was like they were scared of offending the British, even though they didn't care what happened on Andros. Lusca or not, someone had been murdered and these men just sat there and shrugged. "I know that, but we got to stop them from killin'

The Cultist's Wife

folks. We can't let them sacrifice people to ..." she stopped, unwilling to say the word aloud. Lusca. Even saying the name of the Lusca was said to give her power and Irene didn't want to take any chances.

The men shook their heads in unison. Irving shifted on his haunches, looking like he was sitting on a sharp pebble. "I just told you, Irene, we can't control those people. They live in their yard under their own rules. We start interfering with the white folk, the British will think they can interfere with island affairs. I will not allow that. We worked hard to get the British off our island. I's not going to let them back in."

"None of us want that, elder Irving. I just wish someone had said no to Ward back when he wanted to buy that land. That man, he too biggety. He like a little king in that yard of his."

Irving shrugged and shook his head, his mouth drooping. "You helped make him that way, Irene. If you weren't supplying them with ogologo-ndu, they wouldn't be living so long. Maybe Ward would be dead already."

Irene gritted her teeth. "This my fault now? I expect you want me to stop selling de burlup to them? I give you all you need. I's making a living off de rest. I don't see the harm in that."

Irving shook his head, a pitying look on his face. "You don't see the harm, Irene? You sure 'bout that? You just told me 'bout an evil act perpetuated by those people but granting them longer lives isn't harmful?"

"I never heard them doing anyt'ing like that in all the years they been living on this island. And a person's got to make a living. I don't want my family just scratching by."

Irving sat staring at her, not responding to her. She shifted from one foot to another. She hated how he made her feel so young and foolish.

"You got somet'ing else today? You said you have a request."

Irene felt her gut clench. She shouldn't have questioned Ward's purchase of his land when she wanted the same. This might be the wrong time to make her request, but she was here with her gold.

"Ah, yeah, I was hoping to talk 'bout some land. You know that piece of land east of here, got a spring on it, not too far from the road? I was thinking that I could buy it. Me and my family could clear some of de coppet, build ourselves houses."

Alan spoke up, a perpetual sneer on his face. "You complain about us selling that white man some land and now you want to buy your own? With money you earned from selling OUR potion to them? That's rich, Irene."

Irene ground her teeth to stop herself from retorting. She knew insulting Alan would not end well for her. She raised her chin and looked down her nose at him. The third elder, Jason, sat, his legs stretched out in front of him, his eyebrows quirked as he studied her. He remained silent, as always. Irene couldn't remember ever hearing him speak aloud. His appraisal complete, he bent his head to Irving's ear and whispered something.

Irving nodded in response. "I don't believe that we are prepared to sell land at this time, Mrs. Bain. We must consider the future of Driggs Hill and plan appropriate development."

Damn fool, always trying to sound educated. Who does he think he's fooling? He doesn't want to sell to me because of de ogologo-ndu. This has not'ing to do with de future of Driggs Hill.

Irene shot a glance at Mae. She bowed her head as if Irving was speaking with the voice of the ancestors.

That's who he's fooling. My damn fool sister.

"And when do you think you might be ready to sell land, elder Irving?" Irene tried for polite and respectful but couldn't quite keep her bitterness out of her tone.

The old man sighed and scratched his head. "I can't say at present. We'll need to ponder the matter carefully. Maybe next year."

Irene suppressed her scream of frustration.

Next year? I have to wait for a real house for another year?

She cast down her eyes and bobbed her head in acknowledgment, not trusting herself to speak. She cast a sideways glance at Mae, who looked confused. She probably hadn't followed the undertone of the conversation.

"We can't buy our land now, elder Irving? But, but, we got de money. We got it right here." Her tone was querulous, like a confused child.

"No, Mrs. Adderley, as I told Mrs. Bain, we will not be granting land purchases at present."

Mae's mouth hung open. Irene felt a twinge of remorse. She had presented the land purchase to her family as a simple matter now that they had the money. She hadn't anticipated the elders' sudden recalcitrance.

"Good day to you, elders. Come, Mae." Irene pulled her sister's arm to steer her away. She needed to get away and think about what was going on. Were the elders truly punishing her for selling the burlup to Ward? They wanted her to stop supplying him with it, that was clear. And did they want to keep control over the coppet for some reason? What about Horace's murder? Were they really going to pretend it didn't happen?

She strode down the road home, her anger propelling her faster. Mae puffed along at her side. She needed more gold to convince the elders to sell the land. Irene didn't see a reason to stop selling the burlup to Ward. He probably didn't even know about the murder, if it really did happen. She had only the word of a couple of frightened English children.

CHAPTER TWENTY-SIX

Lieutenant MacLachlan strode through the little village of Driggs Hill, stirring up sand from the ground. There was not even gravel on this path, grandly called the Queen's Road. The villagers watched him pass by, gaping at what they probably thought was the outlandish outfit of a white man. He wore the full dress uniform of the Queen's Own Cameron Highlanders, including a fine white ostrich plume-topped helmet. The outfit wasn't designed for the tropics, being mostly wool, but it was certainly cooler than the frock coat and trousers worn by the Ambassador, his superior here in the Bahamas. MacLachlan wasn't concerned about the gaping islanders. He was on a mission to investigate the disappearance of Earl Egerton's son and heir, the Honourable Horace Egerton. The young man had been living on this remote island for the past year and had got mixed up in some sort of outlandish cult. The Ambassador had received a letter from Earl Egerton inquiring as to the whereabouts of his son. After an exchange of letters, Mr. Egerton had agreed to the journey from Andros Island to Nassau. The Ambassador had been expecting Mr. Egerton's arrival on the mail boat a week ago, but he had never appeared in Nassau. Considering the political awkwardness of somehow losing an Earl's heir, the Ambassador had sent MacLachlan to investigate the man's whereabouts.

But where to start? All MacLachlan had to go on was the name of the group Mr. Egerton had been associated with: the Order of Andronicus. South Andros Island was big and mostly untamed. This order could be hiding anywhere.

MacLachlan hailed one of the villagers squatting next to his house, bracing against long strands of sisal he was twisting into a rope. MacLachlan reasoned that a local should know if there was a group of white people on an island populated almost entirely by people of African descent.

"Good morning, sir, might I trouble ye?"

The dark-skinned man looked up from his labour with a surprised look on his face. "You talking to me, mister?"

MacLachlan stepped closer, his bulk shading the man from the sunshine. "Yes, I need some help locating someone. Do ye think ye can help?"

He smiled, knowing most people found his countenance hard to resist. Apparently not this man. The islander dropped his eyes back to the sisal in his hands. "Nope."

MacLachlan was taken aback. Sweat trickled from under his helmet as he stood staring down at the man. "I beg your pardon? I just need a little information. I'm looking for someone in the Order of Andronicus."

At the name, the man started and glared up at MacLachlan. "Yeah, I's not surprised. White man like you, dere not'ing here for you 'cept those whiteys down island."

"Down island, ye say? South then? How far is it?"

The man didn't respond, just twisted the rough rope around and around.

Sighing, MacLachlan realised that he would get no more information from the rope maker. He scanned the small settlement, wondering which building housed the elders of the community. They all looked the same. Sighing, he turned back to the rope maker. "I'm sorry to bother ye again, but perhaps ye could direct me to the elders' house?"

The man looked over at the Lieutenant. "There ain't no house for de elders. They just sit under dat cotton tree over dere all day."

He pointed to a giant silk-cotton tree, its curved buttresses providing shelter for the trio of men sitting in the tree's shade.

MacLachlan thanked the man and strode over to the towering tree. The dark-skinned men lounging there didn't look old enough to warrant the honorific "elder." They scrutinised MacLachlan as he approached, but said nothing.

"Good morning to ye, gentlemen. Have I the honour of speaking to the elders of Driggs Hill?"

One of them broke the silence, staring at MacLachlan's kilt. "Huh, dat be a fine outfit you have, feather and all, but why you be wearing a skirt?"

The Scotsman felt his colour rise and his temper caused him to speak more sharply than the Ambassador would have preferred. "Tis no skirt, 'tis a kilt, and I wear it proudly as I am a true Scot."

The men seated in front of him looked amused and exchanged glances. MacLachlan breathed to get his temper under control. A different man nodded at MacLachlan. His voice was deep and sonorous. "We are the elders here on South Andros. Who is asking?"

The man seated in front of him didn't look older than thirty but his voice held the gravity of many years. MacLachlan sketched a quick bow. "Lieutenant MacLachlan of the Queen's Own Cameron Highlanders, at your service, sir."

The man smiled mildly but his tone remained serious. "And what are you doing on Andros, Lieutenant?"

MacLachlan relaxed a little. Finally someone who seemed to be taking his presence seriously. "The Governor sent me here to inquire after a missing person, a British subject said to be residing near Driggs Hill."

The seated men shifted and again exchanged looks. The speaker, he seemed to be the head elder, regarded the Lieutenant for a long moment. "We don't have a lot of British subjects residing here on Andros Island."

"No, sir, but I was informed that a small group of British and American people had settled near Driggs Hill. I'm looking for the Order of Andronicus. Do ye know where I can find them?"

At the mention of the Order, the men's expressions changed from amused to a watchful disdain. One spat on the ground. "They weren't welcome here, you understand? But they came to our island, throwing gold around and some big-eyed islander decided to sell them that land. We are not responsible for their doings, you see?"

MacLachlan nodded. The Order sounded like more trouble than he had anticipated. Perhaps he should have brought reinforcements. "Have they been causing trouble, sir?"

His question was met with a glare from the head elder. "We don't get involved in their business. As long as they stay in their own yard, we don't concern ourselves with them."

"Very good, sir. If ye could direct me to their location, I will sort out the matter myself."

The elders gave them explicit instructions to the Order's yard. It would be a fair hike in the heat of the day but trees shaded at least part of the long road running along the shore. The shallow aquamarine water glinted under the noon day sun and a feeling of languor crept over MacLachlan. He would have loved to sink onto the pure white beach and watch the waves lapping at the shore. He shook off his urge to laziness and continued down the road, looking for the turn off into the coppice the elders had mentioned. He spotted the trail as he drew level to it. The path through the woods was dark and he shivered a little. It reminded him of the fairy forests back in Scotland. He scolded himself for his sudden fancy and marched into the trees. He was on official business, not mooning about on a tropical island like some great ninny. The Order's boundary wall, built of white coral limestone, shone through the dense undergrowth. The sandy path followed the wall until it turned in towards a wooden gate. He paused. Something didn't feel right. He shook his head at his fancies and pushed through the opening in the wall. The way through the yard meandered through tall trees and full bushes. Ripe fruit dangled overhead. He had heard that the Order was self-sufficient and from the looks of their compound, they grew all their own fruit. Birds chattered and chirped in the foliage but MacLachlan could hear no sounds of human presence. He continued walking and came to a crossroad. How large was this compound? It seemed more like an entire estate. He peered down the path to his left but the curving way left him unable to see very far. The path to his right was the same. MacLachlan shrugged and continued straight on. He reached a clearing containing five little huts made of thin pine logs and thatched with palm leaves. Clothing hung on lines behind the huts and a fire pit was burning, but he didn't see any other signs of people. He moved on and after several twists and turns, came into a large clearing dominated by a grand Bahamian palace of a house. It was conch-pink with brilliant white shutters and a wide wraparound porch. A pair of white women clad in faded clothing trimmed the hibiscus bushes around the base of the porch. MacLachlan could hear voices floating out of the open windows of the house. He approached the women and greeted them with a shallow bow. "Good day, ladies. I wonder if ye could help me."

The two looked at him as if he were a ravenous wolf. They turned and ran into the house without making a sound. MacLachlan stood there for a moment, flummoxed. What had he done to terrify the women into fleeing? Was it him or were they hiding something? Heart thumping, MacLachlan mounted the steps to the porch and approached the open door. He peered inside. People moved through the foyer without even glancing at him. They seemed to move as if in a daze. Emboldened by the lack of response to his presence, he stepped inside and looked around. The interior was sparse with few decorations but scrupulously clean. There was a sweeping staircase in front of the door and doors leading off in every direction. He hesitated, not sure where to try first. A door opened to his right and a blonde woman stepped out. He looked closely and realised that the drawn woman in the dingy, stained gown was Clara Cooke. Shock rooted him to the floor. She had been the epitome of glamour and elegance when he had seen her a few months ago at the Governor's dinner party. What on Earth had happened to her? Why was she here?

He stepped forward, catching her attention. "Clara? I mean, Mrs. Cooke?"

She stared back at him as if she were in a dream. He could barely hear her whispered words. "Lieutenant MacLachlan? Is it really you? Why are you here?"

She darted a look back over her shoulder at the door. Her expression when she turned back to him was full of fear and shame.

"Yes, 'tis I, madam. But what are you doing in this place? Where is your husband?"

Clara looked down at her clothing and rubbed at a smear of something dark on her blouse. She lifted her gaze but didn't meet MacLachlan's eye. She fluttered her hand in the air. "He's around somewhere. You shouldn't be here, Lieutenant MacLachlan. You ought to leave now before…"

Her voice trailed off and she stared across the foyer past him. MacLachlan glanced over his shoulder and saw a tall, slender man pacing towards him. A toothy smile stretched across the stranger's face that didn't quite reach his eyes. "May I help you, sir? I am the…steward of this establishment."

MacLachlan was confused. He made it sound like some sort of hotel. So what was Clara's role here? Her bedraggled state made her look more like a servant than a guest. "My name is Lieutenant MacLachlan. I serve as the aide-de-camp to His Excellency, the Royal Governor. I'm here to investigate a missing person's report."

The so-called steward gestured towards the door behind Clara. "Why don't we continue this discussion in my office? Clara, fetch beverages."

Clara bowed her head. "Yes, Ward, right away."

She scurried off towards the back of the house. MacLachlan watched her go, even more unsettled.

The man she called Ward ushered MacLachlan into a small plain room overlooking the front garden. He sat behind a desk, waving MacLachlan into the opposite chair. It was wicker and creaked alarmingly when he settled his stocky frame into it. Ward fixed him with his gaze. "Now what is this about a missing person, Lieutenant MacLachlan?"

Before the Lieutenant could answer, someone knocked on the door. Ward called for the person to enter. A statuesque red-haired woman sauntered into the room. Ward gestured at MacLachlan. "Ah, Lydia. We have a visitor. This is Lieutenant MacLachlan. Apparently the Governor sent him to us in search of a missing person."

Lydia regarded MacLachlan as if he were an insect she was considering squashing. She lifted her eyebrows at Ward. "How fascinating." Her drawl betrayed her Southern heritage. "Oh and look, here's your little servant fetching drinks for us. Apparently she forgot to bring enough cups for all of us."

Clara had entered, balancing a tray of cups and a pitcher. She halted and stared at Lydia in dismay. "I apologise. I'll fetch another right away."

She placed the tray on the desk and dashed out. MacLachlan sat without speaking, trying to process the bizarre situation. A servant? Clara Cooke had become a servant? He had been under the impression that she came from a monied family but perhaps that had been a façade? MacLachlan noticed that Lydia and Ward were glaring at each other but he didn't have the foggiest notion why. He cleared his throat. "Now about my investigation. I am endeavouring to ascertain the whereabouts of the Honourable Horace Egerton. His father, the Earl Egerton, is quite ill and had summoned his son home to England some time ago. Mr. Egerton had indicated to the Governor that he would be returning to Nassau on one of the mail boats last week sometime. He has not appeared."

Lydia shrugged and perched on the edge of Ward's desk. "The Honourable who? I don't recall anyone of that name here at the Order House."

Ward frowned, a crease appearing between his eyebrows. "Horace Egerton, you say? Horace. That name sounds familiar. Lydia, could Horace be one of the Mean?"

Lydia looked bored. She stared at her fingernails. "I have no idea. I don't keep track of the Mean. Ask Stephen."

Ward got to his feet. "We'll have to fetch someone else to ask. Please wait here. Lydia, come."

They both exited the office, brushing by Clara as if she weren't there. She stood in the doorway, holding a cup and biting her lip. MacLachlan rose and moved towards her but she turned on her heel and ran out of sight. Something very odd was going on here and he wished he knew what it was. He hoped Clara wasn't in danger from these severe people. They seemed to delight in degrading her but to all appearances, she had submitted to their demands without a fight. He sat puzzling the situation before noticing that the sunlight had changed. He glanced out of the window and saw that it was quite a bit later than he had realised. His throat was parched so he poured himself a drink from the pitcher Clara had brought in. It was some sort of juice mixture with an herbal aftertaste. Grimacing a bit at the odd taste, he finished the cup.

The door swung open to reveal Ward and another man. The new man wore baggy linen clothing covered in dirt. He glowered at MacLachlan. Ward smiled with more than a hint of reptile in his expression. "Lieutenant, this is Stephen. He is in charge of the people who work our land. He may know of this Horace person."

MacLachlan stood to shake hands but Stephen didn't seem to notice the Scotsman's outstretched hand.

"Haven't seen Horace for days. He said he was leaving." The man's tone was gruff.

Ward's face twitched in a smile and he eyed MacLachlan. "Are you sure our Horace is the same as the man you're looking for? We don't use last names here so I'm afraid I don't know if we are talking about the same person."

MacLachlan's head was muddled and his body felt heavy. He shook his head to clear it. The heat and, he realised, the lack of food seemed to be catching up with him. "Aye, we're quite positive. Mr. Egerton mentioned the Order of Andronicus by name in his letters. This IS the Order of Andronicus, is it not?"

Ward nodded. He glanced at Stephen. "You may go, Stephen. Thank you for your assistance." Ward spread his hands wide. "I'm sorry we are unable to help you. It appears that this man left the Order some days ago. But you say he never appeared in Nassau. Such a shame. The Bahamas can be a treacherous place. Storms at sea, venomous animals, dangerous sink holes. Who can tell what his fate was?"

MacLachlan narrowed his eyes at Ward. It sounded like he was assuming that Horace Egerton was dead, rather than missing. Did he know more than he was admitting? "Aye. Full of treachery to be sure. Thank ye for your trouble, Ward. I'll be on my way."

Ward showed MacLachlan to the porch of the Order House and was still standing there, watching when the Lieutenant glanced back over his shoulder. The path back to the gate was in deep shadow. He stomped along, trying not to stumble in his fatigue. He would need to find somewhere to spend the night on the island but the Order didn't seem to welcome guests. He rounded a corner and spotted the little clump of huts he'd seen on the way in. Two children crouched in front of one of the fire pits and MacLachlan caught an English accent.

"Reggie, you're not doing it right. Move over and let me."

The girl speaking was shabbily dressed with tangled hair but her accent marked her as upper-class English. She shoved the boy next to her. He fell over and started wailing but stopped abruptly when he caught MacLachlan's eye. "Are you a Scotsman?" The grubby little face was full of curiosity and enthusiasm.

MacLachlan smiled back at him. "Aye, I am. And ye are English, are ye not?"

The little girl stood and stared at MacLachlan. "We are from England but we're living here now. Why are you here?" Her tone was serious and more mature than he expected given that she only appeared to be about eight or nine.

He blinked to clear away the wooziness that crashed across him. His voice slurred. "I'm looking for someone. He's gone missing."

To his surprise, the children's faces drooped and their eyes shone with tears. The girl's voice was a whisper. "Who are you looking for?" She looked like she wasn't sure if she wanted to know the answer to her question.

"I'm looking for a man named Horace Egerton. Have you seen him?"

A cry escaped the girl's lips. "Horace?" She glanced about frantically, then beckoned to MacLachlan. "Come with me."

The children led MacLachlan down a different path than he had taken earlier. He tried to gauge his location from the Order House but the tall trees and thick foliage baffled his efforts. He seemed to be seeing double and he blinked to clear his vision. They reached a gate set in the limestone wall but this one let out into a different part of the forest from where he had entered the compound. The girl closed the gate carefully behind them. "We saw them take Horace away. They carried him down that trail to Lug Hole. It's a really deep lake. And then they threw him into the water. He was tied up and couldn't swim."

MacLachlan looked down with astonishment at the girl. Her eyes were big and bright with tears.

"He was killed? Who did this?"

Her shoulders slumped. "One of them was Stephen. He's horrible. We didn't know the other ones."

He took a deep breath, trying to banish the fatigue. "I'm going to go and take a look at Lug Hole. I need evidence of this awful deed."

He strode off into the forest, leaving the children behind.

CHAPTER TWENTY-SEVEN

Elsie stepped into the warm, clear water of the ocean, careful to hold her skirt high. The sand caressed her toes with its softness. Reggie paddled a few feet from her, his eyes glued to the ocean floor, looking for seashells. She spotted a conch shell a little ways away and made her way to it. She waded out a good distance from the shore but the water only reached her knees. Elsie reached down for the shell, failing to keep her sleeve out of the water. She grabbed the conch and raised it out of the water, only to drop it with a shriek when she saw that a creature still inhabited it. A cloud of disturbed sand momentarily shielded the shell from view and Elsie backed away, her sleeve dripping wet.

"Elsie, I found a crab! Come and see!"

She glanced back over her shoulder and saw Reggie flourishing a wriggling, snapping crab. "Reggie, put that down, you're going to get pinched."

She headed towards him, the water dragging at her legs and slowing her down. He pouted defiantly at her, still dangling the crab. "I caught it. Johnny says they're good to eat."

Elsie put her hands on her hips and gave him a look. "And how exactly are you going to eat it?"

His face grew even more defiant. "I'm gonna ask Aunty Alice. She'll cook it for me."

Elsie rolled her eyes. Yes, he probably could convince Johnny's mother to cook a crab for him. Especially if Reggie called her Aunty and batted his long eyelashes at her. "Come on then. We don't have a bucket to put that crab in so we'd better go to her now."

The children sauntered along the beach, Elsie retrieving her discarded shoes and socks as they passed by the bush where they hung. Reggie scampered across the sand in front of Elsie and dodged around a whitish clump of debris. He called back to her, "Watch out for the jellyfish!"

Elsie approached the clump and examined it, planning to avoid its tentacles. With a start, she realised that it wasn't a beached jellyfish after all but a sodden feather, full and curled. "Hey, Reggie, come look. It looks like one of the fancy feathers on Mama's hat."

The boy approached, holding the crab with two fingers away from his body. "Huh." He leaned down and poked at the feather with his bare foot. "Look at the metal thing. It's a thistle. That feather was on the Scotsman's hat."

Elsie stared at her brother, dread stealing into her heart. "The lieutenant who was asking about Horace the other day?"

He nodded. Elsie scanned the beach for any other clues but didn't see anything out of the ordinary. She gestured at the feather. "So how did this get here? He was going into the coppet, not the beach. Maybe he left on a boat and lost his feather then."

"With the thistle on it? Nah."

A pale figure moved at the treeline, catching Elsie's attention. She squinted against the bright sun, trying to make out who it was. A chill coursed through her. It looked like the lieutenant but she could see through him. She shivered. The figure pointed at the ocean behind her. She turned and the dark water of an offshore blue hole snagged her eye. Johnny had told her that those holes were connected to the ones inland, like Lug Hole. "Reggie, maybe he lost his hat at Lug Hole and then it washed up out of that blue hole." She pointed out to the water, willing herself not to look back.

Reggie's eyes grew wide, looking from the blue hole to Elsie and back. "Lug Hole? What...?"

Elsie felt nauseous. "I think he's dead. Maybe someone followed him out to Lug Hole and...and...killed him." Her voice dropped to a whisper. Elsie didn't want to believe it but she had seen his ghost. And after what had happened to Horace, she was afraid that the Order had got rid of the Lieutenant too. Reggie dropped his crab and drew closer to Elsie. The crab scuttled away.

Reggie shook his head, his mouth trembling. "Elsie, I'm scared. There are bad people here."

She put her arm around his shoulder and squeezed tight. "I know, Reggie. I know."

The hot noonday sun did nothing to warm the chill creeping through her body. Reggie pressed his face against her neck and mumbled against her skin. "I want to go home."

Elsie patted his hair, feeling the sand encrusting it. "Me too."

They stood there embracing for a moment, then Reggie popped his head up, his eyes bright and eager. "Let's run away. We can get on a boat and go back to England."

"All the way to England? We'd get caught for sure. And we'd need money for the boat tickets. We don't have money."

Reggie's face fell. He was silent for a moment before brightening up again. "Maybe Aunty Alice could give us some?"

Elsie raised an eyebrow at him. "What makes you think she has money? And even if she did, why would she lend it to us?"

"She says Irene is going to buy land and build new houses for them all soon. So maybe she has extra."

Elsie was tempted but she remembered her mother's face as they left England, stoic but with tear-filled eyes. "No, Reggie, we're not going to borrow money to run away. We can't leave Mama here. We have to convince her to leave too."

Reggie pushed away from Elsie and shoved his foot into the sand, wiggling his toes. His face reddened. "We never see her. If we leave, she wouldn't even know. Or care."

Elsie was struck silent. It was the truth but she couldn't bring herself to agree with him. It seemed too disloyal to Mama. "She's our mother. We can't leave her here."

Reggie made a rude noise and kicked at the sand, spraying it into the air. He wouldn't meet her eyes. Elsie reached out to touch his shoulder but he shook her hand off. He mumbled something.

"What? What did you say?"

He raised his tear-stained face. "We're gonna get killed like Horace and the lieutenant."

Elsie shook her head, struggling to stay calm. "No, Reggie, don't say that. Mama and Papa won't let them hurt us."

Reggie scrunched his mouth up and rubbed a grubby hand across his face. "I'm hungry. I'm going to Aunty Alice's house."

He turned on his heel and stomped away. Elsie winced down at the mangled feather and glanced at the trees but the figure had disappeared. Danger lurked around them. Even her little brother could feel it.

CHAPTER TWENTY-EIGHT

Clara straightened from scrubbing the wooden assembly room floor and tried to rub away the soreness at the base of her spine. Sweat pooled under her breasts. She sighed, her voice echoing in the empty, darkened room. The latest of Ward's exercises in physical degradation had once again left her sore and filthy after the intoxication of the session had worn off. Once again, she remembered very little but an image of a bloodied syringe and tubing on Ward's desk remained. What had he used that for? Was he an addict? He didn't act like the people who were addicted to cocaine that she'd met at Madame B's London salons. But if he were a cocaine addict, that might explain why he needed so much money.

Theo sauntered into the room, his arm curved around Lydia's waist and thoughts of Ward's possible addiction were banished. Theo and Lydia were laughing, seeming oblivious to everything but each other. Clara froze, transfixed and watched Theo lean into Lydia, kissing her hungrily. Everything seemed to slow down and the kissing couple snapped into focus. Clara gasped as it clicked into place. They weren't merely partners for cleansing sessions. They were lovers. Palsies of rage shook Clara's body and with a suddenness that surprised her, she barked out, "Theophilus!"

She saw him start, and felt a brief surge of satisfaction. He peered across the room, meeting Clara's eyes without shame. Lydia smirked and drawled with her low throaty voice. "Why Clara, whatever are you doing there, skulking about in the darkness? Spying on your betters?"

Clara trembled, both anger and fear warring within her. The anger won the skirmish. "That's my husband you're shamelessly philandering with. Your so-called cleansing sessions? I think you have some explaining to do. I don't believe Ward would approve of this immoral behaviour."

Lydia shrugged. Theo stood silently at her side, his face impassive. Typical. He had always been so passive, disconnected.

Lydia cocked her head to one side. "Dear Clara, what makes you believe that Ward isn't aware of our relationship? Theo and I have been lovers for five years."

Clara flinched. Five years? So Theophilus had been having this affair the entire time he had been in the Bahamas. She burned red-hot with her outrage at the thought. "Five years. I see. You didn't tarry long before taking up with another woman, did you, Theophilus?" Clara's voice was full of venom.

Theo crossed his arms and stared across the room at her. "Truly, Clara? You're really this upset? You never loved me. You married me for my pedigree. Why should you care if I'm in love with someone else?" He drew Lydia closer to him.

Clara spluttered, trying to form a rebuttal. It was true. She had never loved him but they were married. How dare he be so casual with their marriage vows? "You are my husband. Of course I care."

A chuckle broke from Lydia's mouth. "If you cared so much, you would have joined your husband sooner. Five years, Clara. You let him stay here for five years without you."

Clara's eyes snapped to her rival. "I didn't ask for your opinion, hussy."

Lydia's peal of laughter stirred the flames of Clara's anger higher. "Hussy? What an old-fashioned term. Like you. I'm afraid his proper Victorian wife bored Theo. He needed a modern woman, someone with more warmth than the Arctic, you see."

The words spurred Clara forward and she rushed across the room, growling her hatred. Theo stepped in front of Lydia and held up a hand. "Stop right there, Clara."

She ignored him and tried to dodge around him, hands outstretched and curled into claws. He grabbed her, pulling her against him and pinning her arms to her side. Lydia backed away, out of reach.

"Let me go, Theophilus!" Clara shrieked, squirming. Theo loosened his grip but held onto her upper arms, his fingers digging painfully into the tender flesh there. She glared at him, her face hot and wet with tears. "I hate you, you bastard! Let me go!"

"Clara, calm down." She tried to pull her arms free but he had her in too firm a grip so she kicked at his ankle. He winced and released one arm to slap her across the face. Clara gasped. He took hold of her arm again, glaring at her. "I told you to calm down. You're hysterical."

"Hysterical? Hysterical? You're having an affair!" Her voice rose to a shriek.

He shook her, looking more irritated than upset. "Lower your voice, Clara. You're drawing attention to yourself."

She glanced away from him and saw a group of Exalted standing on the threshold of the room, gazing curiously at the scene. The horror of social embarrassment stifled the scream rising in her throat. Clara took a shuddering breath and raised her head, her voice dropped to a whisper. "Fine. I'll be quiet. Here's how it is. Theophilus, you must do your duty and give up this so-called love of yours. No more lengthy private cleansing sessions. I will forgive this trespass since you were distant from the family for so long."

She wouldn't be humiliated by this affair a moment longer. He needed to be a real husband to her. No matter if she was happiest when he was thousands of miles from her.

Theo's eyebrows shot up and his mouth dropped open. He barked a short laugh. "You'll forgive my trespass if I give up Lydia? You must be joking. I am not giving up Lydia, Clara. Why would I even contemplate that? So I can go back to a miserable life with you?"

Clara's mouth dropped open. Did he have no sense of loyalty?

"You see, dearest Clara, Theo wants to be with me, not with you in some loveless marriage," Lydia said.

Clara shot her a look full of hatred. "Hussy. Jezebel. Harlot," Clara hissed.

Lydia shook her head slowly, mocking Clara's anger. "Is that any way to speak to an Exalted, Clara? How can you possibly hope to be Exalted yourself if you cling to the animality of jealousy and rage?"

Clara paused. All her spiritual work seemed to have unravelled with the discovery of Theo's affair. Was he really that important to her? Had he ever been? Confusion overwhelmed her and she felt tears well up. Biting back a sob, she pulled away from Theo's grip and dashed towards the door. She pushed her way through the crowd pouring into the room for the Assembly, head down to hide her tears. She didn't look back at Theo and Lydia.

***

"Mama, what's wrong? Why are you crying? Are you ill?"

Clara lay curled up on her bed. Elsie was standing in the doorway of the hovel they inhabited, tangled hair in her eyes. Clara dashed a hand across her wet cheeks and glowered at her daughter. She tried to respond but tears strangled her voice. Shaking her head, she gestured for Elsie to leave. The child frowned, hesitating.

"Go away, Elsinoe," Clara choked out. Elsie spun around and ran from the hut.

Clara scratched at a mosquito bite on her ankle and stared at the dirt under her broken fingernails. How had she sunk so low, to be grubby and cowering in a bug-infested hut in the middle of nowhere? The child's interruption had stopped her tears of anger and hurt but she still burned with her husband's betrayal. She wanted to scream, hit him, kill Lydia, but instead she sat here crying over his affair.

Realising that Theophilus was in love with Lydia brought back feelings she had tried to squash in her quest for spiritual growth. She had never been in love, not like Theophilus was with Lydia. She had considered love a distraction. She sighed and swatted at a mosquito buzzing around her ear. The heat inside the hut was intense. Exhaustion pinned her to the bed. Why should she care about Theophilus and Lydia? She didn't need Theophilus. If she had been honest with herself, she hadn't ever really needed him. She had enjoyed her life and her friends and their marriage hadn't changed that. He had his mushrooms and rotting plants, she had her esoteric studies. When she arrived in the Bahamas, Clara had been surprised at his involvement in the Order. She remembered him as a rational man with no patience for spirituality but now she saw that he must have been drawn into the Order by Lydia.

She sat up, empty and trembling. Should she somehow convince Theophilus to leave Lydia and come home? Or was her marriage over? What about her spiritual work here? She could return to England and resume her life there but would that be giving up? There was no guarantee of happiness back home, not to mention society's shunning if she were to divorce her husband. What was she to do with the children? What if Theophilus wouldn't let her take them back to England? She couldn't very well leave them on this island with him.

Taking a deep breath, she smoothed her hair back. She could continue her studies wherever she was. She didn't need Ward's guidance. She needed to go home but the social ruin if they were to divorce was not something she was willing to endure. There had to be a way for her to convince Theophilus to leave. They might not be an exemplary couple, and there was no guarantee of warmth growing between them in England, but at least they would be together as a proper family, without the scandal of his adulterous affair. He had always followed what society expected of him so he must certainly not wish to be the cause of a scandal.

A figure appeared at the door, dimming the light in the hut. It was Theophilus. Clara drew in a shaky breath. Now was the time to explain her reasoning, to make him see why it was imperative for him to return with her to England. "Theophilus. I think we need to talk."

He didn't move from the doorway. His face was in shadow. "Clara, I don't understand your behaviour. It's very unlike you to be so melodramatic. I expected you to be more rational."

Clara clasped her hands, hoping to quell the shaking. "I apologise for my outburst. The discovery of your indiscretion shocked me. I suppose it was naive of me not to expect that you would find relief in another woman's arms after being apart for five years."

Theophilus shook his head. "Clara, I don't think you understand. What Lydia and I share is deeper than physical pleasure. The Order has changed me, it has taught me that she and I are spiritual soulmates. The life you and I shared in England was a shallow mockery of what I have with Lydia. I intend to live here with Lydia, my partner. I'm not going back to England."

Hot tears trickled down Clara's face, burning her already damp skin. She suppressed a sob. Soulmates? This was no simple affair. None of her arguments would make a difference to him. Her marriage really was over. There would be no pretending that everything was fine. "What am I to do then?"

Theophilus leaned on the doorway and sighed. "I thought you were interested in exploring the philosophies of the Order? Don't you want to work towards becoming Exalted?"

"Stay here? Knowing that you and Lydia are…" She couldn't say it out loud. Her husband was in love with another woman. She didn't understand why it bothered her so deeply when she had never been in love with him.

"Control your reactionary behaviour and you can earn your Exaltation. Ward speaks very highly of you. He may Exalt you very soon. Isn't that what you want?"

Clara tugged at a loose thread in her cuff and watched as the lace unravelled from the sleeve. Was this what she wanted? Could she suffer the indignity of seeing Lydia with her husband? She'd worked so hard to be an enlightened woman. She couldn't give that up. She raised her chin and stared at Theophilus. "Very well. I'll stay. I've made progress with Ward's help. I can bear this humiliation for a bit longer."

CHAPTER TWENTY-NINE

Irene sat on the beach but the gentle shushing of the waves on the sand failed to clear her mind. She wanted Ward's gold but after hearing about Horace's fate at the hands of the Order, selling them the ogologo-ndu felt like a bad idea. The elders had made it clear that they were not happy about it either. After thinking about it, she was pretty sure that was why they wouldn't sell her land.

The children might have been mistaken about what they saw. They were children and children made up funny stories. Still, she asked around the settlement and no one had seen Horace leave on the mailboat. He had disappeared. Maybe he was in seclusion. Who knew what strange rituals those people got up to? Or he could have run afoul of any number of things out in the coppet. Snakes, sinkholes, even poisonous plants could be lethal. But then the children had told Alice a second story. Someone had come from Nassau to investigate Horace's disappearance and now he was missing too.

The sunlight glinted off the bright water but clouds loomed on the horizon. Irene ran her hands through the sand, letting it trickle between her fingers. She knew she was just trying to fool herself. The white folk had done something terrible to Horace and probably this other man too. The real question was, what was she going to do about it? She had no control over them except for the burlup they needed. She could fix them but that kind of power always came with a price. Irene wasn't sure she wanted to pay that price. Sighing deeply, she dragged herself to her feet, brushing sand off her skirt. She would go and tell Ward that she would no longer give him the burlup. He had been taking it for a long time, since her mother was the wise woman around here. She wasn't sure how a sudden stop in the medicine would affect him or the others who received it but that wasn't her concern. They weren't her people. She glanced up at the sky. The clouds were moving fast. The rain would begin before she got home from talking to Ward. She pulled her straw hat down over her ears and trudged down the road, her cloak slung over her arm.

Rain dripped through the leaves above her head as she turned down the path to Ward's yard. She slung her cloak around her. The heavy, sweet scent of flowers mingled with rotting fruit. She breathed in deeply, enjoying the fragrance of her island. Her island, her home, not this foreign intruder's home. She straightened her aching back, weary from her long day.

The yard looked empty as she strode towards the big house. The rain came down hard but it didn't bother her. Her hat kept most of the water off her head and her cloak kept the rest of her dry. A boy crouched in the shelter of a flowering yellow bells bush, shivering and drenched. Ward didn't like her to go up to the big house so she called out to the boy. "Chile, come here. You know where Ward is?"

The scrawny boy slowly rose and shrugged his shoulders. His pale eyes were wide and unblinking.

Irene wondered if he was simple. "You go find him for me. Tell him Mrs. Bain wants him."

He slunk away without a word. Irene wasn't sure that he would do as she asked so she sighed and followed the child. They reached the clearing around the big house and Irene stepped into the shade of an alligator pear tree. The boy darted a look back at her, then scurried towards the big house. She hoped Ward wouldn't take long. The rain cascaded down and soaked through her cloak to her shoulders. She peered through the downpour at a tall man approaching. As he drew closer, Irene recognized Ward. He joined her in the shelter of the trees, his wet linen shirt clinging to his skin and his hair plastered to his skull.

Ward smiled at her with tight lips, eyes glittering like a crocodile in the swamp. "Mrs. Bain. I wasn't expecting you so soon but as always, I welcome more of your potion."

The woman shook her head, lips pursed. "That ain't why I came. I won't be bringing you no more of my burlup."

His smile faltered a little. "No more? Well, you are early for a new batch. I wasn't expecting it until later this week."

Irene lifted her chin, looking down her nose at him. "No more at all. You won't be getting no more burlup from me."

Ward choked out a laugh. "Whatever do you mean, my good woman? Are you raising the price? I'm sure we can negotiate if you feel the need for a higher price."

"I ain't looking for more gold from you. Just not interested in selling you my burlup no more." Irene's hands trembled and she took a deep breath to settle her nerves.

The fake smile dropped off his face. "I don't understand the problem. I've been buying the potion from your family for decades. Why have you suddenly decided to stop selling it to me? What has changed? This is unacceptable. Without the potion, my ageing process will start again and I cannot allow that." His tone was clipped and harsh.

Irene shrugged, trying to appear nonchalant while inwardly she quailed from his anger. "That ain't my concern, mister."

He stepped closer, his face ugly, twisted with rage. "Not your concern?" he hissed. "I'll make it your concern. That little nephew of yours has been spending a lot of time in my yard. It would be a shame if something unfortunate happened to him. We have a lot of sharp farming tools laying about. A little boy could cut himself badly, maybe even bleed to death before help could reach him."

Irene felt her heart thud and skip a beat at his words. She grew dizzy. Blinking hard, she sucked in a breath. "Don't you dare threaten my family."

Ward laughed and grasped her shoulder, squeezing hard. "Threaten? I don't threaten people, Mrs. Bain. That would imply that I don't follow through on my words."

She tried to pull away from his hand but he held her tight, hurting her with his grip. He locked eyes with her. She gritted her teeth.

He leaned in closer. "So about the potion?"

Against her will, Irene found herself nodding and agreeing to bring more burlup. She didn't know how else to keep this snake and his threats away from her family. The rain stopped and the sunlight reflected off the water droplets all around her, dazzling her eyes.

Ward bared his teeth in a hard smile. "Excellent. I will expect you next week. Goodbye, Mrs. Bain. Give my regards to little Johnny."

Ward released her shoulder and stalked away. Blood coursed back into her shoulder, bringing pain with it. She rubbed the ache, biting her lip in anger. She couldn't believe she'd backed down and agreed to his demands but she needed to keep her family safe. Irene slipped away into the trees and headed home. She grimaced. Ward may have thought he'd outwitted her. She would bring some burlup to Ward next week but it wouldn't do what he expected. She didn't have any ogologo-ndu sponge left.

CHAPTER THIRTY

A crowd of other Means pressed against Clara as she stood at the back of the assembly room. Their unwashed smell, dirt and vegetal, stifled her. She tried not to breathe deeply. Voices from the stage droned on, incomprehensible among the murmurs and breathing and shuffling surrounding her. Clara strained to see over the shoulders of the people in front of her, cursing her lack of height. She caught a glimpse of Ward from in between two people but they shifted, leaving her facing their dull, dirty shirts. She huffed with impatience. How would she hear her name when they announced her elevation to the Exalted? Being Exalted would make her situation here bearable until she could convince Theo to leave. She contemplated wriggling between the people blocking her view but decided that would be too undignified. Despite his best efforts, Ward had not managed to strip away all of her pride.

A change in the tone of the speaker caught her ear, then the audience applauded. The Mean around her shifted, moving as one towards the door. Clara struggled against the movement of the crowd, trying to stay in the room. What was going on? She hadn't heard her name or been lifted out of this mass of lowly servants. What had happened to her elevation?

She ducked to the side of the exit, letting the rest of the Order stream out of the door. Clara searched the emptying room for Ward, but he was gone. With a sinking feeling, she spotted Lydia drawing level with her, smirking as always. Theo was absent, a not uncommon occurrence. Clara rarely even glimpsed her husband, especially since the revelation of his affair. "Ah, Clara. Ward won't require your services for the rest of the day. Perhaps you should take the time to wash your clothing." She wrinkled her nose as if assaulted by a bad smell.

Clara's face burned. The filth on her body was constant, thanks to Ward's demands. He seemed to delight in degrading her. "Yes, of course. But what happened to the elevation ceremony?"

Clara hated to beg Lydia for information but everyone else was gone. Lydia trilled a laugh. "Did you miss it? It's all over. Ward has gone to celebrate with the new Exalted and I'm going to join them too."

"The new Exalted? But…"

Clara couldn't complete her question, dreading the response. Lydia painted a look of mock sympathy across her face. "Oh, poor Clara. Were you expecting to be Exalted? Why, you've barely started here in the Order. You've been here all of a month? Six weeks? I suppose you're used to being given everything you want. That's not how it works here. You must earn your elevation."

The burning in Clara's face spread through her body, transforming from shame to anger. She was to be denied elevation, after weeks of drudgery and humiliation at Ward's hands. She convulsed with revulsion at the thought of what she had endured, all in the pursuit of releasing her physical constraints. Was it all a sham? "I've worked hard for Ward for three months. I've done everything he has asked of me."

Lydia crossed her arms and tilted her head to the side, her eyes drooping in apparent boredom. "That doesn't matter. Ward will never elevate you, no matter how hard you work."

Clara grimaced. Ward had implied that her service to him would result in her elevation, hadn't he? "Why do you say that?"

The other woman quirked an eyebrow at Clara and giggled. "Silly goose, Ward loves having you, a proper English lady, serve him. You're so compliant. He tells me that nothing is too low or degrading for you. Why would he elevate you and lose such a biddable little slave?"

Clara choked, outrage and shame filling her. "Are you saying he lied to me? All he wanted was some kind of slave girl?"

Lydia's laughter echoed in the empty room. "Yes, exactly. You figured it out! He doesn't care about your lofty philosophies and studies. How positively delicious. You had no idea? All those nasty little...chores...he made you do had nothing to do with elevation. They were just for his entertainment. The filthy games you played with him were purely to titillate an old man too jaded for normal women."

Clara felt bile rise in her throat, hot and acidic. Sweat trickled down her back. She shivered, trying to block out images of Ward and his "tests." "Why are you telling me this?" Her voice, cracking and low, betrayed her misery.

Lydia dropped her smirk and leaned in close, her hazel eyes hard. "To make you leave."

"Leave? But Theophilus insisted I come here. Why?"

Lydia straightened and flicked her hair over her shoulder. "We needed you for your money, of course. And the children. We needed the children."

Clara's stomach churned. Of course Theophilus wanted more money, money that went straight to Ward. But the children? "What do you need the children for?" Her voice croaked as she spoke.

Lydia shrugged. "We have our uses for them. As Ward found his uses for you." She sauntered from the room, without a backward glance.

Clara wrapped her arms around herself, her shivers deepening. All of this had been a pretence so that Ward could satisfy his perversity. She shook her head, astounded that she had been taken in so thoroughly. Now that Lydia had spoken, the truth was blindingly obvious. The charade of attaining spiritual elevation through physical degradation at Ward's hands was over. She would leave Andros Island immediately, Theo be damned. Whatever danger he was in, she would have no part in helping him out of it. He had made his decision by bringing her here and then abandoning her to the whims of a pervert. As he had indicated, their marriage was over. She was going back to England and taking her children with her. Clara wasn't going to allow them to become some kind of servant or whatever else the Order had planned for them.

* * *

Mosquitoes swarmed around Elsie's face. She swatted at them with a grubby hand sticky with fruit juice. The sunset stained the sky red over the trees of the yard. She finished the mango in her hand and approached the hut. Light spilled from the doorway and Elsie could see movement inside. She moved closer warily and spied her mother, dressed in a brilliant white dress, banded with navy blue. One of her travelling dresses. She was even wearing a corset again.

Why is Mama dressed for travel? She didn't tell me we were going anywhere.

Elsie glanced behind her, trying to spot Reggie in the gathering dusk. Her brother squatted next to their fire, poking at the embers with a long twig. She waved at him to get his attention, but he didn't respond. Elsie shook her head and edged closer to the hut. The little house overflowed with open steamer trunks, clothing and household goods scattered on the floor. Clara stood contemplating a little silver travel kettle, then tossed it aside, the lid clattering to the floor. She reached for another item and caught Elsie's eye. Elsie winced, wishing she had ducked out of sight before her mother had spotted her.

She looks angry. I wonder what happened. She'll probably tell me to clean up this mess.

"Elsinoe! Come in here at once. You need to pack your belongings. Only the essentials, pack only what you can carry. Where's Reginald?" She peered around Elsie and raised her voice. "Reginald! Come here at once!"

Elsie shuffled into the hut, not waiting to be told a second time. Her mother was in a strange mood. She never raised her voice to Reggie. The girl looked around at the chaos, not sure where to begin. She turned her face towards her mother. "Mama? Where are we going?"

Clara paused in her sorting and frowned at Elsie. "Stop dallying, Elsinoe.

You need to pack quickly. We are going home to England and I don't want to miss the mailboat to Nassau."

Elsie gasped, her heart thudding with sudden excitement. She beamed. "We're going home? Really?"

Reggie sauntered in and caught Elsie's words. "Home? We're going home? Hooray!"

Clara huffed, impatience cast across her face. "Yes, we are going home so I need you two to pack your belongings. Quickly."

She shoved a pair of leather satchels at the children and waved her hands in dismissal. The leather was musty and stained with mould. Elsie wrinkled her nose at the smell. Clara bustled about and slid a pile of her neatly folded clothes into a valise. Reggie haphazardly shoved a toy, a book, and a single shoe into his satchel while Elsie struggled to insert her art case into hers. Clara caught sight of the children's activity. "What are you two doing? No, no, no, give me those. You don't need all of that. Just clothes. You can bring three toys each." She tipped the contents out and packed the satchels herself.

"But, Mama, what about my art case? I can't leave that behind." Elsie's lip wobbled as she saw her beloved art case thrown onto the floor, pencils spilling out.

"It's too big to take. You need clothing for the journey. Now, now, don't be sad, I'll buy you a new art case when we reach England."

Elsie nodded, her eyes fixed on the case. She tried to swallow her tears. Reggie pouted, his arms crossed, and stamped a foot. "Mama, why can't we take all of our things? I don't want to leave my toys behind. Why are we in such a hurry? Can I go and say goodbye to Johnny?"

"Reginald, please. I need you to stop asking so many questions and stop whining." Clara's voice was harsh, her mouth pursed. Reggie started to sob. Clara sighed and brushed his hair off his forehead. "Oh come now, darling, no need to cry. We need to get you washed up and dressed in your travel outfits. I've put them out."

She gestured towards the bed. Elsie stifled a sigh. She hated that itchy plaid dress and she knew Reggie thought that he was too old for sailor suits. She stole a look at him. He had stopped crying and was glaring at the detested suit.

"Don't stand there, you need to wash yourselves." Clara shooed them out of the hut, then stood over them as the children splashed cold water on their faces. She sighed, then grabbed a rough towel and scrubbed their hands and faces. She lead them back to the hut at a fast clip. Elsie's mind was spinning and she paid little attention as her mother pulled off her grubby clothes and dropped them to the floor. Clara dragged the heavy dress over Elsie's head. The wool of the dress itched under her arms. Clara hastily stripped Reggie and re-dressed him. He glowered at Elsie from under his cap, silently daring her to make fun of him. She grinned and he stuck out his tongue in return. Clara pinned her hat into her piled-up hair and drew on her long white gloves. She gathered her reticule and valise and cast a look of disdain around the hut. "Come, children, let's be away."

Reggie and Elsie obeyed, slinging their satchels over their shoulders and following her out.

Clara headed up the path towards the Big House. "I need to inform your father that we are leaving Andros Island."

They picked their way carefully along the dark pathway. The sun had set abruptly, as it always did on the island and no one had lit torches along the way yet. The balmy air caressed Elsie's skin, its soft floral scents tickling her nose. She loved this time of day on Andros. The temperature was comfortable, the biting bugs disappeared, and the air smelled good. The lights of the Big House reached them through the foliage and Elsie could see Order members gathering on the veranda, waiting for their turn to enter for the evening meal. Her tummy grumbled at the thought of food but she guessed that Clara wouldn't stop to eat. Clara strode up to the house, swinging her valise. Her head was high and she seemed more confident than Elsie had ever seen her. She stopped at the foot of the stairs up to the front door and surveyed the people milling about.

"Stephen! I need you to go and find Theophilus. Now."

Elsie gaped at her mother. Had she actually ordered Stephen to fetch someone? She had been so meek since joining the Order a few months ago. Stephen frowned down at Clara. He too seemed confused. Clara didn't wait for a response. "Did you hear me? Go now. I have something important to tell him and it can't wait for you to engage that dull brain of yours."

He shook his head, eyebrows creased, mouth open. She shooed him with her hand. Stephen finally shrugged and sauntered into the house. Clara tapped her foot and dropped her valise to the ground. Elsie and Reggie exchanged glances but kept quiet. Order members pushed past them to mount the steps and enter the house, casting curious looks back but no one spoke to them. A few moments passed before Theo appeared on the veranda. Ward, Lydia, and Stephen stepped up behind him.

Theo scowled down at his family. "What's going on, Clara?"

Clara lifted her chin. Elsie stared up at her mother. In her white dress, she seemed to almost glow. "I grow weary of this place and the Order of Andronicus. The children and I are going home. We leave on the next mailboat to Nassau." She lifted a delicate shoulder then let it drop. "I thought you ought to know."

Ward raised an eyebrow. His face was stoic but his posture was tense. "You're leaving? Clara, how can you abandon your studies this way? We have only begun to delve into the mysteries. If you leave now, all of your progress will be undone."

Clara laughed, a hard, brittle laugh. Elsie heard her mother laugh like that when she really disliked someone but was being polite. "I don't believe that I will be devastated to abandon the chores involved in being your personal slave. Your power over me is finished. I won't be degraded by you again."

Elsie watched as Ward's face darkened with anger. His fist clenched at his side. She waited, expecting him to shout or storm down the stairs at his mother. He stood there, rigid as a statue, staring at her. "You are a vain and stupid woman, Clara Cooke. You will never find the enlightenment you seek." His voice was low and full of venom.

Theo cleared his throat, his face red and sweating. Elsie waited for him to beg Clara to stay, or offer to come with them. "Clara, go if you must. Obviously this is not the right place for you."

He wasn't coming with them? Why did he want to stay? Elsie couldn't understand. She thought that her father would want to stay with his family after their long time apart. Her eyes filled with tears. She had thought him too busy to spend time with them while they had been staying with the Order, but now she saw that he just didn't care.

Ward waved a hand at Clara. "Get out then. Once you are gone, you will never be welcome back. But the children aren't going with you."

Elsie and Clara gasped in unison. Reggie grabbed Elsie's arm hard.

"Don't be ridiculous, Ward. Of course I'm taking my children with me. Theophilus, I am quite sure that you are not interested in keeping the children here with you."

Ward smiled the smile of a predator and Elsie shivered. Theo gawked at Ward, a look of confusion across his face.

Elsie turned to Clara. "Mama? You aren't going to leave us here, are you?"

Clara cast a look down at Elsie before glaring back at the men on the veranda. "Don't be ridiculous, Elsinoe. Of course I won't leave you two here. What a preposterous notion. Come children, it is time for us to depart. We don't want to miss the mailboat. I do not intend to spend another moment with these people."

She reached down for her valise and Elsie saw Stephen and another Order member approaching. They took hold of Clara's arms. From behind, Elsie felt hands grab her around the waist and yank her off her feet.. She shrieked, and heard her mother and brother screaming. Her vision blurred as she was spun around but she could see the glowing white of her mother's dress, receding. "Mama! No, come back, Mama!"

Her voice was shrill then she felt a hand clamp down over her mouth, silencing her. She wriggled, trying to get loose, and kicked her captor's shins. With a cry, the person dropped her and Elsie looked up to see it was Lydia. Elsie jumped to her feet and scurried down the path, following the white of her mother's dress. "Mama, Mama, wait for me!

As she drew closer, she could see two burly men marching Clara down the path, her arms in their strong grip. She was struggling and protesting.

Without warning, Elsie was tackled from behind and fell prone onto the ground. Lydia hissed in her ear. "Hold still, you little beast, or I will beat you black-and-blue."

The sounds of Clara's protests faded out as she was dragged farther and farther away.

"Mama..." Elsie sobbed, gritty sand rough against her cheek.

Lydia held her down until Elsie stopped struggling, then hauled her to her feet. "Quiet down. Your mother has left you. You're staying here with your father now so you'd better behave."

Elsie dragged a hand across her running nose and sniffed. She cast a look down the empty path and spotted Reggie curled up on the ground, snivelling.

Stephen loomed over him. Elsie walked over, then crouched down next to her brother and patted his shoulder. "It'll be alright, Reggie. Don't worry. Mama will come back for us soon. She wouldn't leave us here with...them," she whispered, stealing a look up at the adults. Theo was talking to Ward and Lydia in an undertone, seeming to ignore the children. He looked upset, his face flushed.

His voice rose and Elsie could hear him now. "What am I supposed to do with them now? This ruins everything!"

Ward hushed him and spoke quietly in his ear. Theo nodded, grimacing, then shrugged. He approached Elsie and Reggie, his mouth twisted in a frown. "Come on, you two. Bring your bags."

"Where are we going, Papa?" Elsie got to her feet, helping Reggie.

"To your new hut. You can't stay by yourself. You'll be living with the other children." He sounded more determined than he ever had.

Live with the other Order children, the ones who barely speak?

Elsie shuddered but decided not to argue with her father. She didn't want to anger him. She followed him silently, holding Reggie's hand as they made their way through the compound to the children's hut.

* * *

Clara trudged along the dark path towards the Queen's Road, leaves batting her in the face. Her arms were sore from the men's grip when they had marched her out of the Order's yard. She still shook with anger and fear and her legs wobbled under her. The moon cast light between the bushes towering on either side of her. She pulled out her pocket watch, its face glowing with reflected moonlight. She still had time to catch the mailboat to Nassau. She could go and fetch help from the Embassy there. Perhaps Lieutenant MacLachlan would be willing to assist her. It struck her that she hadn't seen Lieutenant MacLachlan leave the compound that day a few weeks ago.

I wonder why he was here. I didn't think the British Embassy staff came to Andros. Will the Ambassador even listen to me? Or help me?

Theophilus had all the rights as the children's father under British law. Her shoulders slumped with the realisation and nausea crept into her belly.

No, I won't get help from the British government. I'll have to stay on Andros and get the children back myself. Theophilus doesn't truly want them. He won't care if they're not around. I'll have to sneak them away somehow.

Having made that decision, she realised that she needed somewhere to stay on the island. Clara hadn't left the Order's compound since arriving on Andros so had no idea what facilities might be available. She peeked into her satchel. She still had a good amount of gold sovereigns. Theophilus hadn't managed to get them all. She grinned at that thought.

That's the last money he'll get from me. I won't send it to him to squander on Lydia and the Order. He can come to England if he wants more.

Revitalised by her mental defiance, Clara lifted her head and marched onto the empty Queen's Road. She hesitated, trying to get her bearings. She could see water glinting in the moonlight through tall palm trees and a white sand beach in front of her. Searching her memory, she recalled walking with the ocean to her left on their arrival. She turned, the water to her right and trudged along the road.. Her valise seemed to grow heavier as she continued her trek but she was grateful to have it. At least she had some clean clothing and toiletries, along with her favourite books. Stephen had shoved it at her at the gate., then stood sneering until she had departed. She had been surprised that he had bothered to give it to her.

Clara passed a gathering of small thatched huts, similar to the ones in the Order's compound. People, dark-skinned islanders, sat around a fire in a little courtyard, talking in low voices. They must have spotted her because there was a hush as they watched her walk by. She was tempted to call out and ask for directions to a guesthouse but they didn't seem approachable.

Her high-heeled white boots pinched her toes as she walked. Clara sighed. She should have worn something more practical. At least the temperature had dropped and was more bearable now.

How far is Drigg's Hill? I don't remember it being this far.

The road reflected white under the moonlight. Palm trees waved in the breeze and ocean waves crashed on the beach nearby. She could see no side roads or buildings.

I can't have taken a wrong turn. And Drigg's Hill is at the tip of the island. So where is it?

Clara felt fear squeeze her heart. She was wandering alone and possibly lost in a foreign land, no husband or father to protect her. A small whimper escaped her lips. Clara shook herself, pushing back the helplessness threatening to overwhelm her. She had to take care of herself. She had no choice. Putting one foot in front of the other, consciously moving forward, Clara continued.

The moon had dropped lower into the sky. She had been walking for what felt like hours when she spotted an enormous tree in a square, surrounded by small wooden houses. Certain that she had at last reached Drigg's Hill, she scanned the buildings for signs advertising accommodation. They all appeared to be residences, windows darkened, except for one. Its wooden walls were painted with adverts for bait and provisions. A general store. Its proximity to the little harbour beyond the square pointed to its importance to the fishermen. The rest of the settlement seemed to be fast asleep. Clara spotted a white man exiting the little general store, hauling a basket over to the mailboat.

Clara teetered towards him, as quickly as her boots would allow. "Hello there! Are you the mailboat captain?"

The man hesitated, scrutinising her. "Yeah. You looking for passage to Nassau?"

Clara shook her head. "No. I mean, not yet. Not tonight but soon. I actually stopped you to ask for directions to the nearest accommodations."

He barked a laugh. "Accommodations? You'll find something thataway about 50 miles."

He pointed out to sea. She felt the blood drain from her face. Nowhere to stay here? "Oh, I see. I don't need to stay at a fashionable hotel. Don't you stay on the island somewhere?"

He laughed again, shaking his head. "I sleep on my boat. There ain't nothing here, lady."

Clara's face dropped and her eyes filled with tears. "Nowhere to stay? But what am I going to do?"

He shrugged, adjusting the basket in his arms. She could see crab claws poking out, seeming to wave at her. "Go back to where you came from and stay there til you're ready to leave the island. I's here again in a week."

Clara's voice wobbled, her tears thick in her throat. "I can't. I can't go back there. But I need to stay on Andros. I can't leave yet."

She looked up at him, hoping he could solve her problem.

He shook his head. "Sorry, lady. Sounds like you're in a bit of a jam. I's heading out soon. I can take you to Nassau tonight."

"Is there really no one here in this settlement who will put me up? I can pay."

"Most folks here don't have much room in their houses for an extra body, lady. Look around. Do you see any fancy houses?"

Clara did as she was told, scanning the square. A wave of exhaustion hit her and she swayed on her feet.

"Hey now, don't be fainting on me." The captain sighed, seeming to relent. "Why don't you try Irene? She's the healer for this little town and she's got a kind heart. Her husband and boy are off on the water so she might have a spare spot."

Irene? The odd name sounded familiar to Clara. Where had she heard that name? At this point, she didn't care so nodded her agreement. The captain pointed her in the direction of Irene's yard. Clara thanked him and tottered away from the harbour, wincing at her aching feet.

The small huddle of huts sat on the edge of the settlement and Clara heard voices singing as she approached. It didn't sound like familiar music. She peeked over the gate and saw a dozen islanders, a family, gathered around a bonfire. A stab of envy entered her when she took in the congenial scene. She was struck by how different it was from the usual social affairs she attended, full of stiff, well-dressed people trying to impress each other.

They all look so happy. I suppose they don't need much money to enjoy themselves.

No one seemed to notice her standing there, looking like a lost lamb.

Clara steeled her nerves. "Pardon me? Hello? Is this Irene's place?"

The voices hushed and she felt the weight of a dozen pairs of eyes.

A slender woman, maturity lined across her face, called back to Clara. "This is where Irene lives. And who is looking for her?"

Clara shifted the weight of her valise and licked her suddenly dry lips. "I...that is...the captain of the mailboat mentioned that Irene might be able to help me."

The woman stood and sauntered towards her, reminding Clara of a stalking leopard. "I's Irene. What kind of help you need from me? You got a sickness?"

Clara stuttered, somehow nervous in front of the island woman, regal despite the faded dress hanging off her frame. "N-no, ma'am, I'm not ill. I—"

"I's not a ma'am. You call me Irene. No sickness? Then why you here so late at night? You in some trouble?"

Clara tried to meet the woman's piercing dark eyes. Trouble? At the thought of the day's ordeals, her self-restraint snapped and she burst into tears. "I'm sorry, I'm so sorry."

***

Irene tsked and patted the weeping white woman's arm, the white fabric of the woman's sleeve soft under Irene's hand. This stranger was obviously not a pauper, but she supposed even rich people had their problems. "Don't fuss so, woman. Come into de yard and sit yourself down. You exhausted and I's betting in need of food."

Mae approached, her ample frame slowing her down. She never could resist a dramatic situation. "We got ourselves a stray, Irene?" She addressed the stranger. "Come in, boo, sit down and rest. You look hungry. You want a bite to eat?"

Without waiting for an answer, Mae ambled into one of the huts. The white woman, her fine white gown smudged and no doubt going to get even dirtier, lowered herself shakily to a log next to the fire. Irene caught looks from her silent family gathered around the fire. They were all curious, no doubt wondering who she was.

The white woman made an attempt to smile. "Thank you, Irene. I appreciate your kindness in allowing me to enter your yard."

Irene cocked her head to the side and raised an eyebrow. "That not a worry. Why you wandering about after dark looking for my help? Your husband beat you?"

"Nothing like that. Well, not exactly a beating. I mean—I just need somewhere to stay for a few days. The captain of the mailboat said you might have room."

Irene flattened her mouth. Another white person begging her for help. "You from that big yard down the road, folks that call themselves the Order? They threw you out?"

The white woman shook her head. "They didn't throw me out. I left. I would have been on that mailboat back to Nassau but Ward wouldn't let me take my children. I need to stay on Andros until I can convince him to return my children to me."

Irene clucked her disapproval. Ward again. The man was becoming a source of trouble, that was for sure.

Mae returned with a steaming bowl of fragrant conch stew, left over from dinner. She handed it to the white woman, shaking her head sympathetically. "Keeping a muma from her babies. What kind of people they down there?"

Irene shot a look at her sister. She knew perfectly well what kind of people they were.

Why couldn't Mae ever keep quiet?

The white woman begged Irene with her eyes. "Please, Irene, I need someplace to stay. I can pay you."

Irene stared at her impassively. This woman was going to bring trouble to her yard, she could feel it. "I like my privacy. My men folk gone to sea and it nice and quiet in my house."

Mae, apparently without Irene's worries, broke in. "You can stay with me. My husband at sea too and I get lonely all by myself. I's Mae, Irene's sister."

The white woman sagged with obvious relief. "Thank you, Mae. My name is Clara. It won't be for long, just until I can get my children back. I'll pay for my accommodation. Would a sovereign per night be sufficient?"

Mae's eyes rounded. "A sovereign? That be fine. You can stay as long as you like."

Irene huffed. She stared at Clara while responding to Mae. "She ain't staying here long, Mae. And Clara, I hope you not bringing trouble to my yard. I don't want no angry husbands showing up at my gate."

Clara's face fell. "Don't worry, Irene. He won't come looking for me. He doesn't care that much."

CHAPTER THIRTY-ONE

The door latch slid into place with a loud click. Chinks in the siding let some light into the room but Elsie could barely see the interior of the children's hut. Humps on the floor could only be the other inhabitants of the hut, children, snuffling and moaning in their sleep. Reggie gripped her arm still. He hadn't let her go since Stephen had marched them here after dinner. The walk through the dark compound had seemed much longer than she remembered from the hut they had stayed in last night. She tried to place herself within the Order's yard but couldn't figure it out. Somewhere near the north end maybe?

Someone spoke in the darkness, the voice of a young American boy. "So they finally moved you in here with the rest of us. What happened, did your mother get tired of having you underfoot too? Children are not "conducive to spiritual elevation," you know. They have to get rid of us somehow. Guess it was time for you."

Elsie squinted in the darkness, looking for the speaker. A boy, his pale face appearing out of a mound of blankets near one of the walls, watched them. Reggie spoke up. "Our mother left, but she's coming back for us. We're not staying here long."

The pale boy laughed, a bitter, mirthless laugh. "Yeah, that's what they all say. Don't hold your breath, ya goop."

"A what? A goop? Is that an American word?"

The boy sniggered in response then coughed until he gasped for air.

Elsie waited until he caught his breath. This boy seemed to know something. It would be better to stay polite and get some answers rather than argue. "How long have you been here?"

He sniffled and coughed again. "I dunno. A year or so. It's hard to tell with the weather not changing much. We got here right after Independence Day. My folks thought that was a good sign or something. I dunno what month it is now."

Elsie thought for a moment, trying to tally up the days. With a start, she realised that it was mid-July. Almost her birthday. Was she going to turn nine locked up in this hut without either of her parents? "It's July. I think it's the thirteenth or fourteenth. Where are your parents now?"

The boy was silent. Elsie thought he might have fallen asleep but then his voice startled her with its harshness. "Up at the Big House. I never see them any more. They're busy elevating themselves or something. All the Order wants me for is free labour and blood. Pretty soon I'll be too weak to work, then all I'll be good for is blood. Like those ones over there."

Elsie's stomach lurched at his words. She sat down, her legs shaking too hard for her to keep standing. "What...what are you talking about? I've seen you in the field working—"

Reggie interjected, sounding scared and little. "Blood? Are they gonna kill us?"

The boy laughed again. "Eventually, I suppose. They come to take our blood and some kids get real weak. They go to sleep, then the adults take them away. Those kids don't come back."

Elsie bit her lip hard, trying not to cry. "Why do they do that...take children's blood?"

The boy didn't respond. Elsie could hear his laboured breathing and Reggie's stifled sobs. The air in the hut, warm and unmoving, weighed on her. Elsie sank to the ground, exhausted. Reggie sat next to her, slumping against her side. A tree frog croaked just outside, its loud creaky call filling the small room.

The boy spoke again. "I dunno why they take our blood. They never say."

Reggie burrowed his face into Elsie's shoulder, his sobs muffled. The wetness of his tears soaked her wool sleeve.

She whispered in his ear. "Don't worry, Reggie. We're going to get out of here."

He raised his face, a stripe of light illuminating it, puffy with crying. "How? We're locked in."

Elsie bit her lip and scanned the room. She didn't see a way out besides the locked door. The hut had no windows and the gaps in the wall were narrow, too narrow to slip through. "I don't know. I'll figure it out. Maybe we can sneak away when we're supposed to be working."

He nodded. The tree frog's song cut off abruptly and footsteps crunched outside. Elsie tensed. The latch slid back and moonlight streamed into the room. Reggie and Elsie shrunk back against the wall, staying in the shadows. A man, silhouetted in the doorway, stepped inside. He raised a lantern, shining it in the other children's pale, blinking faces. He stepped into the hut, followed by two other men. Elsie didn't know them but their faces, eerie in the lantern light, looked familiar. Order members that she had seen at meals. One carried a white china bowl, the other a wicked-looking knife, glinting in the moonlight. None of them spoke but moved quickly, kneeling at the side of one of the sleeping children. With what looked like practised efficiency, one of the man wrapped a narrow piece of fabric around the child's upper arm and slashed her skin. She moaned, not quite conscious, and her blood spilled into the waiting china bowl. Elsie swallowed back bile and pressed a hand against her mouth, trying to stay silent. Reggie had his face buried in her shoulder again. The blood letting was over quickly, the girl's arm bandaged with a clean, white strip of cloth. The men exited the hut, still silent, and the door latch slid back into place. Elsie trembled and tears streamed down her face.

We need to get out of here. We can't wait for Mama to help us.

The little girl who had been bled moaned a little in her sleep. The American boy hadn't spoken since the men had left. Elsie didn't know what time it was but it must've been getting late. Her body felt heavy with fatigue but her mind was racing and she couldn't rest. She needed to figure out an escape plan. If they left from the fields, Stephen might see and follow them. It would have to be at night but how were they going to get out of the locked hut? Maybe if she saw Johnny, she could ask him to sneak into the compound at night and unlock the door. Yes, Johnny would help. Satisfied with her plan, she let sleep steal over her.

CHAPTER THIRTY-TWO

Elsie stared at the ocean but saw nothing of the clear, sparkling water or waving fronds of seaweed. Her mother's face, white and tight-lipped, appeared in her mind's eye. Clara's words echoed in Elsie's head, Of course I won't leave you, but she had left. Elsie mourned as if her mother were dead. She and Reggie were alone now, defenceless against whatever the cultists wanted to do to them. Their father had proven himself worthless, caring only about what Lydia wanted. Ever since Mama had left, Elsie and Reggie had spent nights locked up with the other children of the Order in the children's hut. Elsie still wanted to ask Johnny to let them out when they were locked up at night but where would they go? She and Reggie were supposed to be working in the yard this morning but had snuck away after breakfast, before Stephen could round them up. He would be angry when they returned. Elsie shivered under the hot sun and choked back a surge of tears.

Mama. How could you leave us?

A shout brought her back to the beach. Reggie and Johnny dashed towards her, carrying a bucket between them. The water sloshed out as they ran. "We've got fish for dinner! Look what we caught! Do you think Mama will like it?"

Elsie shook her head, scowling. "Mama left, remember? She's gone. She left us."

Reggie's mouth drooped into a pout. "But she'll be back. You said she would. I fished so she'd have a nice dinner. Better than that yucky stuff at the Big House. Will she be back today?"

Elsie couldn't contain her bitterness. "She's gone, Reggie. Don't you understand? She doesn't care about us so she just left us here. She left us!" Her voice rose to a shout.

Reggie flinched. Johnny stepped back a pace, spilling water onto the sand. Her brother shook his head. "But...she's our mother. She'll be back. You said so." Reggie sounded on the verge of crying. Elsie felt the weight of responsibility sink onto her. She had to take care of herself and Reggie all the time. It wasn't fair.

At that thought, Elsie snapped. She shoved her brother down, sand flying as he impacted. "Shut up, Reggie! You don't know anything!"

She turned on her heel and pounded away across the shore, her brother's sobs echoing in her ears. She kept moving, fighting off the guilt that threatened to make her go back and comfort him. Once out of earshot, she slowed to a walk.

Now what do I do? Go back to the yard? Stephen will make me work if I go back there.

She scanned the seashore and realised she was near Irene's yard. Maybe Irene could help. With a sense of hope, Elsie quickened her steps. She didn't have to go far. Elsie found Irene in the field near her house, hoeing weeds with her sisters and nieces. The woman's straw hat hid her face as she bent over. Elsie hesitated. Would Irene be angry with Elsie for coming to her with her problem? She knew Irene didn't like the Order but she seemed to like Elsie and Reggie. Elsie sighed. She had no choice. She knew no other adults she could trust.

Elsie reached the low stone wall around Irene's field and stopped. "Aunty Irene! Hello!"

The woman looked up, squinting in her direction.

"It's me, Elsie. Remember me, Johnny's friend?"

Irene picked her way through the plants towards Elsie. She wasn't frowning exactly but she didn't look happy to see the girl. "I know who you are. What you want with me, chile? You bringing trouble to me again?"

Elsie started. She did seem to always be in trouble when she came to see Irene. "I'm sorry, Aunty Irene, but you're the only adult who will help me."

Irene sighed heavily and crossed her arms. "What now, girl? I pray no one dead this time."

Elsie bit her lip. Sweat trickled down the back of her neck. She looked away, the palm trees ringing the field reminding her again of how far from home she was. "I'm sorry to bother you. No one died. It's just that—" She paused and gulped down tears. "It's just that Mama left us. She went away and I don't know what to do."

Irene let out a sound somewhere between a growl and a groan. "She left you? Chile, don't she always leave you every day to go up to de Big House? You tired of that now?"

Elsie's face was wet with the tears she couldn't hold back. Her words came out in a rush. "No, she left days and days ago. She told the Order she was done with them and she left and she tried to take us but they wouldn't let her and now she's gone and they lock us up every night with the other kids and I'm scared what they're gonna do to me and Reggie."

She drew a shuddering breath and clenched her fists, willing her tears to stop but they kept trickling down her face.

Irene tutted her disapproval. "That a shame, a mother leaving her babies like that. And your daddy no-good, true-true?"

Elsie nodded, wiping away her tears. "It wasn't Mama's fault, she tried to take us with her but they wouldn't let her. They dragged her out of the yard and wouldn't let us go with her."

Irene crossed her arms and fixed a piercing gaze on Elsie. "And you not seen her since?"

Elsie shook her head. "No, Irene. I think she took the mailboat back to Nassau."

"Hmph. What you expecting me to do for you, chile?"

Elsie paused. She had no idea how to get out of this mess but had hoped that Irene would. "Do? I don't know, Aunty Irene, I'm just a child. I don't know what to do. I thought you could help."

Irene stared at her, sadness filling her eyes. "True-true, you just a chile with trouble on your head, but you not my own chile. I can't help. Those your people, not my own. I can't take on that trouble."

Elsie sucked in a breath and dropped her voice low. "But Aunty Irene, I'm afraid they're going to kill us."

Irene paused, searching the girl's face. "You afraid, I can see. They not going to kill you. Listen up, you keep your eyes and ears open and be ready to move fast. I think you be leaving Andros soon."

Elsie gasped. "We are? How do you know that? Can you see into the future like Mama?"

Irene gave Elsie an odd look. She quirked her mouth in a half smile. "Cunning be better than strong, chile. Go on back to your yard now. Don't worry."

Elsie nodded and turned away. It was no use trying to convince Irene to do anything but give advice. Don't worry? They would be leaving Andros soon? She hoped Irene was right. She gestured to Reggie. They'd better get back to the yard before they were missed.

CHAPTER THIRTY-THREE

The children of the Order shuffled into the hut after dinner, unnaturally silent as they had been every day since Elsie and Reggie had been housed with them. Stephen shut and latched the door without a word. His footsteps faded away as he left them all locked into the small hut for the night. Elsie resisted the urge to shout at the other children or shake them out of their stupor. Now that she knew the reason for their dullness, she knew it would do no good. The other children sank down into the nests of covers on the ground before Reggie and Elsie could find a spot to lay down. They looked at each other and shrugged. They shuffled over to the wall of the hut and Elsie sank to a clear spot on the ground. "I guess we should try to get some sleep, Reggie."

The boy shook his head. "Not yet."

Puzzled, Elsie opened her mouth to question him but heard scratching on the door of the hut and Johnny's voice, low and urgent. "Elsie? Reggie? You in there?"

Elsie's heart leaped. Johnny was here. He could let them out. She hoped Stephen was far enough away to not hear him. She pushed herself to her feet, and put her mouth to a crack in the wall. "Yes, we're in here. Can you unlock the door?"

In answer, the door latch rattled and the door opened a crack. Johnny's face peeked in, his eyes wide. "You'd best hurry. I think I heard someone heading this way."

With a surge, Elsie, dragging Reggie behind her, pushed past Johnny and through the door. It was dark outside but the moon was full, shedding light on the hut. She could see light from a lantern through the bushes, moving towards them, and froze. She turned to Johnny, eyes wild with fear.

He spoke in a rush. "I'll head towards them. They don't want me. They'll let me go if they catch me. You two head into the coppet and get to our yard from there. Don't get lost."

"Into the coppet? At night? What if we run into the Chickcharney?"

"Just go. These people won't find you out there. But be careful. Stay away from Lug Hole."

Elsie nodded and grabbed Reggie's arm, racing for the boundary wall. She risked a look back and saw Johnny speeding down the path towards the approaching light. She wondered how he had found them. She had never had a chance to ask him for help. Hopefully she'd be able to ask him later. Elsie tore towards the wall, dragging Reggie stumbling along behind her. The night song of birds and insects intensified around her, almost drowning out the sound of her panting breath. The soft ground threatened to turn her ankle, her feet clad in patent leather boots not designed for running. Elsie and Reggie darted around a dense wall of shrubs, hoping to stay out of sight. Angry shouts from behind warned them to keep going. Elsie darted looks around her, trying to find a low spot in the limestone wall. Her heart pounded in her chest. She discovered a crumbled section, low enough to climb over. Elsie pushed her brother over the rocks and scrambled up after him. She risked a glance back and saw lantern light, madly dancing through the bushes. They were coming towards Elsie and Reggie. Elsie tumbled to the ground on the other side of the wall, twigs and dry leaves crunching and cracking as she landed.

"Over there! I heard something over there!"

The men had heard her noisy landing.

The children dragged themselves away from the wall, struggling through a maze of downed branches. Their progress was slow, too slow. The men were going to catch up with them. Elsie stifled a moan. She grasped Reggie's hand. Thorny branches tore at her skin. She struggled to catch her breath in the humid air. "Keep moving. We've got to move faster, Reg."

The boy mumbled his assent and stumbled faster over the rough ground. Elsie's arm jerked as he tripped but she hauled him upright before he could fall. She pushed aside a low-hanging branch, revealing a small clearing, bright in the moonlight. The litter of branches and leaves was absent here. A faint trail appeared on the opposite side, leading deeper into the coppet. Picking up speed, the children tore across the ground and ducked under a branch to enter the dark trail. Bushes pressed against them, forming a tunnel of vegetation. The children kept their heads low as they raced along the winding path. The coppet was alive with the sounds of crickets and frogs. The calls of the children's pursuers faded.

Panting with the exertion, Elsie slowed her pace to a walk. "We left them behind. But they're faster than we are. We have to keep moving."

The trees, wrapped in twining vines, loomed tall around them, blocking the light from the moon. Elsie shivered. Her legs shook from the race through the coppet but she kept a tight hold on Reggie and forced herself to keep walking.

"I don't feel good, Elsie. I'm gonna..."

Elsie stopped and peered at her brother in the dim light of the coppet. He clutched his chest, gasping for air, then staggered and fell to his knees. He vomited onto the ground.

"Oh, no, Reg. You can't be ill now. We have to get away from here."

The little boy wiped his mouth, catching his breath with a wheeze. "I know. I'm alright now. I couldn't breathe from running. Then I had to be ill. I think...I think I feel better."

She helped him to his feet, worry wrinkling her forehead. She rubbed his back and sighed. "There's a good boy. I wish I had some water for you. Can you keep moving? Maybe we'll find a stream to drink from."

They traipsed over the uneven ground. Elsie's feet ached from running in her boots. She could feel blisters forming on her little toes. They followed a faint trail through the thick undergrowth. Then the trees thinned out and the moon glinted through their branches. Elsie could see the coppet stretching off in the distance in every direction.

How long will we need to keep walking? Which way to Irene's compound from here?

As if reading her thoughts, Reggie spoke. "Elsie, where are we? Can you find Aunty Alice's house? She'll hide us from those bad people."

"Hmm, yeah, that's a good idea, Reg. We'll head there."

Elsie had no idea where that was exactly but she thought she could find it. They just needed to keep walking in the right direction.

Reggie tugged on her sleeve. "Let's climb a tall tree and look 'round."

Elsie surveyed the tall thin pine trees interspersed through the thick undergrowth. The lowest branches were much higher than her head. "We can't climb those trees. Let me think. The moon is over there. I think it's setting. That means that way is west? Or is it east? Oh bother, I can't remember."

Reggie pondered the moon, low in the sky, his face solemn. "I don't wanna be lost."

"We aren't lost, Reggie. I can find Drigg's Hill. We just need to follow the moon. Just keep the moon behind you. I'm quite sure we're headed west. Let's trot along and we'll reach Aunty Alice's in an hour or so. "

The sounds of the coppet echoed around them as they trotted deeper into the wilderness.

***

Irene watched Clara pace around the fire and noted the worry creasing the younger woman's smooth face. Clara hadn't touched her supper. The sun had set a while ago and the moon was high in its place, but Johnny still wasn't back from the Order's yard. The plan to help Clara's children escape from the children's hut had been Johnny's. Irene hadn't been convinced that it was a good one. He had been passionate about helping his friends, so they'd conceded. The family sat around the fire, hushed, waiting, their usual singing and storytelling abandoned.

Alice darted anxious looks at the gate of the compound. "Irene, shouldn't Johnny be back with Reggie and Elsie by now? It's not that far down there, is it?"

Irene waved a hand towards her sister, pretending a nonchalance she didn't feel. "It's a fair walk, and they chillun. It might be a bit yet."

Clara halted, turning her eyes towards Irene. "Irene, what if they are caught trying to escape? The Order might lock all the children up and then what will we do?"

Irene pursed her lips, glowering at Clara. "Those people had best not lock up my nephew or I will be wexed. And that Ward knows he would be in a world of trouble were I to become wexed with him."

Alice turned from the gate. She cast a wide-eyed look at Irene. "Locked up? They not going to lock up my boy? Irene, you told me there would be nothing to worry about and now this white woman talking about them locking up my child? I knew I shouldn't have listened to his crazy plan."

Irene sighed and shook her head. "Alice, there no need to worry. Those people wouldn't dare harm a hair on that boy's head. They know they would have me to deal with."

Alice wrapped her arms around her waist and paced in front of the gate. Irene sauntered up to join her vigil. She knew her nephew would be able to get out of any trouble he got himself into but Alice raised worry to a vocation. Alice glanced at Irene, then back out at the road. The sky lit up and flashed, then thunder rumbled. Rain tumbled from the sky and drenched the women waiting at the gate. They bowed their heads against the downpour.

Alice hissed with irritation. "Oh, look at this rain. Now my boy's going to get soaked."

Irene squinted into the darkness. Was that a child racing down the road towards them? "Alice, look, is that Johnny?"

"Yes, it is, he back! Johnny! Boo, what happened?" Alice dragged the panting boy into her arms and smothered him against her chest.

He struggled free. "Muma! Don't!"

Irene took hold of his arm and turned him to face her. "What happened, Johnny? Where be Elsie and Reggie? Did you get them out of that hut?"

Johnny nodded, his face solemn. "Yeah. But a bunch of those men came and we had to split up."

Clara approached, her white dress soaked from the rain and clinging to her. Her face was a mask of fear. "Johnny, where are my children?"

Johnny looked at the women gathered around him. His tone was low. "I don't know where they now. I told them to run into de coppet to get away from de men. I thought those men would chase me instead but they let me go. They went after Elsie and Reggie. I hid for a bit near de hut but I didn't see them come back."

Alice caressed the boy's head and smiled at him. "You did good getting them out of that hut, boo. It wasn't your fault de chillun didn't come back with you."

Irene cocked her head to one side and frowned. Her tone was sharp. "You sent them into the coppet? At night? What you thinking, boy? You know how close that yard is to Lug Hole."

Irene glanced at Clara. She was even paler than usual. Rain streamed down her face and plastered tendrils of hair to her cheek. "Clara, don't go fainting on me. That will not do a bit of good."

Clara blinked slowly and nodded. She took a deep breath. "Please, Johnny, how can I find my children? What is this coppet? I need…I need to go and find them."

* * *

How long was an hour when you're traipsing around the woods at night? Elsie glanced back over her shoulder at the moon. Clouds drifted across the sky. The moon looked lower in the sky. She wasn't sure how fast the moon set but her feet told her she'd been walking for a long time. Had it been an hour? Two? She pushed through the muggy air, wishing she could stop and rest.

Reggie poked her in the arm. "Elsie, do you think there are snakes around here?"

Elsie started. She hated snakes. "What? Why do you ask that?"

Her brother's face was calm. "I felt something on my foot."

She let out a little shriek. "Oh no, don't say that, you know I hate snakes!"

He shrugged, unconcerned. Animals didn't bother him. "Maybe an iguana. Too small for Mr. Sharp."

If we keep moving, the animals will probably leave us alone. And the Chickcharney. We're not doing any harm out here. I'm sure it'll leave us alone too.

She shuddered. She tried to push out the thought of snakes and other horrible creatures from her mind.

"Oh right, yes, let's keep walking then. Hey, Reg, how do you think Johnny found us in that hut?"

Elsie looked back at Reggie. He grinned at her. She noticed that his cheeks weren't as plump as when they left England. He had lost weight on Andros. "I told him old Stephen was gonna lock us in with the other kids. Then I told him where the hut was. But the bad men came. I hope Johnny's okay."

"He'll be fine. Irene would be awfully angry if those men did anything to Johnny."

An animal's shriek tore through the air and both children gasped. Elsie's heart pounded, threatening to jump out of her chest. She peered into the dark forest, trying to locate the sound. "Probably an owl." Her voice trembled. *Not the Chickcharnie. Please let that be just an owl.*

Reggie was right behind her, eyes wide. "Yeah. An owl. A loud one."

The shriek sounded again, closer, spurring the children to pick up their pace. Owl or no owl, Elsie didn't want to be near that sound. The children moved further into the coppet and the air pressed against them, warm and heavy. The undergrowth thinned out again and the children picked up their pace, not hampered by clambering over downed branches. The scent of rotten fruit and decomposing leaves deepened. With a groan, Elsie realised that the moon was hidden by the dense canopy of trees over their heads.

Now how will we find our way out of here? We could be lost for days out here in the coppet.

"Reg, I think we'd better climb one of those big trees and see if we can figure out where we are."

The children scampered up a mahogany tree, its smooth bark and wide branches making it an easy climb. On an ordinary day, Elsie would have loved climbing this tree but it was late and her legs were tired from their race through the coppet. She reached a branch halfway up and had an overwhelming urge to close her eyes and sleep, nestled in the crook of the tree. She shook her head to clear the fuzziness and continued her climb. She could hear Reggie gasping on a lower branch, trying to catch his breath.

The snap of a twig on the ground far below banished her fatigue. She froze and swallowed. Was someone down below? Had the men caught up to them? Reggie was silent. She could see him huddled, unmoving, against the tree trunk. He must have heard the noise too. Elsie squinted at the ground, trying to make out what was down there. Was that movement? The children were far up into the tree, concealed by thick foliage from the ground. At least Elsie hoped they were hidden.

If we stay still, whoever...or whatever is down there won't know we're here.

Reggie turned his face up to her. He was pale, with dark shadows around his eyes. His face looked like a skull. Elsie shuddered at the resemblance. She put a finger to her mouth to signal for him to stay silent. He nodded. She wrapped her arm around the tree trunk and laid her face against it, trying to breathe quietly. Her legs trembled. Voices drifted up to her from the ground. Men's voices, muttering to each other. The cultists had caught up with them. Elsie's heart raced and she bit her lip to stop herself from crying out.

Please don't look up.

Elsie turned her face, forehead resting on the smooth wood. Tears trickled down her face. She thought they had left their pursuers behind. Her body trembled with fatigue.

I don't know how much longer we can run. They're going to catch us. Please don't look up.

The shriek came again, closer now. Was it really an owl? She didn't dare look. The voices grew louder, and one man shouted. The shriek repeated, this time directly below where Elsie and Reggie clung to the tree. Elsie whimpered. It sounded angry. Owls didn't sound angry. Yells and screams of fear from the men floated up. She peeked down. Shadowy, jerky movements interspersed with flashes of light from a lantern. A glimpse of a white wing, grasping fingers on its end. The shrieking of the beast and the screams of the men mingled in the hushed coppet. Something extinguished the lantern's light. Had someone dropped it? The cacophony moved away from the tree. The men must be fleeing their attacker.

They hadn't spotted us?

Elsie counted in her head, listening to the sounds below. By the time she reached thirty, she couldn't hear the yelling. She let out the breath she hadn't realised she'd been holding.

Stay still just a little longer. We've got to make sure they're gone. And hopefully whatever attacked them is gone too.

She peeked down at Reggie and gestured for him to stay where he was. The tree branch was broad and easy to perch on but she knew they couldn't stay up in the tree all night. Her strength would run out soon and Reggie was fading fast. They needed to find somewhere safe to rest. Somewhere far from that shrieking angry owl that could've been the Chickcharnie.

CHAPTER THIRTY-FOUR

Irene glanced up at the starry sky. The rain passed, as it always did at night, and a fresh breeze teased the flames on the torch bottles. The flames flickered and the stink of burning kerosene filled Irene's nose. "I don't want everybody coming; we don't need to make a ruckus out there in de coppet. Mae, you stay home and keep an eye out. Alice, Johnny, take a flamper each. Boy, watch yourself, don't get burnt. Clara, this bottle will get hot as de rag burns, but so long as you hold it away from yourself, you be fine."

She scanned the faces around her. Johnny was the only one who knew the coppet at all. She and Alice avoided it. The herbs they needed grew on the outskirts of the coppet, not the interior. And Clara? The Englishwoman stood there, tiny and slender, looking like a little girl in that fancy white dress of hers. Irene had her doubts about taking her into the coppet at night but Clara insisted on going. The moon would be setting soon so they wouldn't have its light for much longer. "Come on now, folks, we need to get moving. I don't want to stump around in the dark after that moon goes down."

The little band departed, voices hushed. Mae touched Clara's arm as she passed and Clara paused. "Be careful out there, Clara. Find your babies and bring them back safe."

Clara nodded and smiled. "Thank you, Mae. You've been so kind."

"Aww, it not'ing. Go on, they leaving you behind."

Alice stood next to Irene, an arm around Johnny. She whispered in his ear, not seeming to pay attention to the rest of the group.

Irene cast a look back over her shoulder at Clara. "Keep up now, Clara. I don't want to have to find you as well as your chillun."

"I'm sorry, Irene, I'm coming."

Clara scuttled up to the waiting group, hampered by her slim skirt and her satchel of gold coins. Irene sighed to herself. How was this woman going to be any use tramping around the coppet?

I just hope she don't set fire to herself.

The torch Clara held flickered wildly and Irene winced.

The road was still bright with the moonlight. All the inhabitants of the settlement were at home so the road was empty. The ocean glinted through the palm trees, the swooshing of the waves soothing Irene as it always did. She hoped they would be able to find the children quickly, before anyone... or anything else did.

Johnny came up beside her, slipping his hand into hers. "Aunty Irene, how we going to stay safe out there? Do you know spells to keep away de monsters?"

Clara's head swung around to face them. "Monsters? What monsters are you talking about?"

Irene frowned. She didn't need Clara panicking. "Don't any of you worry about monsters. De only thing you should worry about there is tripping over a branch and breaking your ankle."

Alice spoke up. "Whereabouts we headed? Johnny, where you think those chillun would run to?"

Johnny shrugged. "They ran out of the yard away from the ocean, so kinda to the east? I figure they circle round to get over to our yard. De coppet gets easy to walk through up near Lug Hole."

Irene shook her head. How many times had that boy been told to stay away from Lug Hole and here he was, telling them about the area around that cursed lake. "Sounds like you awful familiar with Lug Hole, Johnny."

Johnny had the good grace to look chagrined, hanging his head. "I don't get real near there, Aunty Irene, but de coppet nearby got lots of good fruit growing in it."

She harrumphed and strode on without responding. Despite his disobedience, his familiarity with the area might be able to help them find the children.

Clara walked closer to Irene, needing fast, mincing steps to catch up with the taller woman. "Is it very dangerous out there in the wilderness? Are the children in danger?'

Irene shrugged. She didn't want to lie to the woman but the truth might panic her. People loomed into view on the road, walking towards them. White people. Irene tensed. Who would be out at night?

Clara gasped, apparently also spotting the people. "Oh no, it's Stephen and his cronies. What are they doing out here?"

Irene quirked her mouth. "Maybe they out for a moonlight stroll. Going crabbing or something like. Just like us. Crabbing."

The men drew closer and Irene could see their expressions, tense and irritated.

Stephen called out to them. "Clara Cooke. You're still on Andros? What are you doing here?"

Clara lifted her chin. Her voice quavered her response. "My business is my own."

He laughed without humour and he sneered at her. "Are you out here looking for something?"

Irene spoke up, drawing out her Bahamian accent. "We be crabbing. Moon high, good time for crabbing, y'know."

Stephen spread his arms out in their direction. "Crabbing? Where are your nets and baskets? Or are you going to carry the crabs home in your skirts?"

The men guffawed at their leader's attempt at wit.

Alice hissed but kept her tongue.

Johnny spoke up. "Our crabbing gear out there already so we don't have to carry it all in de dark."

Irene was fed up with the conversation and pushed through the group of men. "Time's a'wasting. Let's get us some crabs."

Clara, Alice, and Johnny followed her. Stephen shot a hard look at them as they passed but let them through.

Irene waited until the men were out of sight before speaking. "They out looking for Elsie and Reggie."

Johnny snickered. "And Elsie and Reggie outsmarted them. I bet they found a good hiding spot out in the coppet."

Irene grimaced. "Just so long as they don't follow us. I don't want to lead them straight to de chillun. Keep an ear out for those men, folks."

※ ※ ※

Reggie leaned on Elsie as they stumbled through the undergrowth. He wheezed and sniffed. "Elsie, are we close? I can't walk more."

Elsie bit her lip and looked down at her little brother, his hair plastered to his head, his face pale. He'd lost his sailor hat but she would bet he didn't care.

"I don't know, Reggie, I thought we'd be there already."

His voice wobbled. "Are we lost?"

Elsie fought back her own tears. The trees loomed all around them, and seemed to go on forever. "Maybe. We need to find somewhere safe to rest until morning. Once it's light, we'll be able to see where we are."

She hoped she sounded more confident than she felt. She remembered the scary ole storees that Irene told her, all about dangerous creatures who lived out in the coppet, preying on people wandering around after dark.

Just stories, they're just stories. There's nothing that bad out here. Just big lizards with sharp teeth.

Reggie lurched to one side and cried out. His foot had dropped into a hidden hole in the undergrowth and he flailed for balance. "Elsie, help! I'm trapped!"

She grabbed for him and tugged. He came free with a jerk and fell onto her. The children collapsed to the mucky ground. Mud squelched under Elsie and bits of twigs poked her back. The stench of rotted vegetation wafted around her.

"Are you all right, Reg? Come on, we've got to get up. The ground is disgusting."

They clambered to their feet. Reggie burst into tears. "Elsie, I want to go home. I'm scared. I'm tired."

"I know, chukaboo, me too. Just a bit further. I think I see a clearing up ahead. We'll find some nice, dry rocks to sit on and rest."

The little boy snuffled a reply and trudged forward. He was limping and a trickle of blood ran down his leg. Elsie hope the cut wasn't too deep. She didn't have anything to bandage it with.

The coppet thinned out and the children walked onto a flat outcropping of rock. With a gasp, Elsie spotted the water below and realised where they were. "Reggie, that's Lug Hole!"

The boy jerked in surprise. "Lug Hole? You mean where..."

Elsie nodded, the realisation sickening her. "Yeah. Where they killed Horace. I think this is the spot they were standing when they threw him in. We were hiding in the trees on the other side."

"But Elsie, that means the monster is...right there."

Reggie pointed down at the dark water. Bubbles rose from its endless depths. The water transitioned from calm to turbulent as they watched in horror. "The monster. It's here."

Elsie froze, unable to move. Reggie blubbered, an incoherent jumble of words. He stepped back from the edge of the cliff. Elsie stared at the bubbling, roiling movement of the water itself. Was the monster right below the surface of the water or was it still rising from the depths? Would it be able to reach her, standing on the rock above Lug Hole? She shivered despite the warm air, squinting down at the water. No sign of the monster's tentacles yet. Reggie yanked on her hand. "Elsie, come back. You're too close."

She gasped and pulled her gaze from the water. "Right. Coming." She stumbled back from the cliff, her hand clinging to Reggie's, until they reached the treeline. She pulled him into a tight hug. "Thank you. I was stuck there." He nodded and patted her arm with his grimy hand.

A whirlpool swirled in the centre of the lake, then the water's movement calmed bit by bit until it became smooth and tranquil again. The children watched in silence.

Reggie sniffed and wiped his nose with the back of his hand. "Did it go away?"

"I don't know. But I didn't see any tentacles or fins or anything."

"It might be just waiting. Maybe we're too far." Reggie squinted at the cliff and took another step backwards.

"It didn't come out of the water and grab Horace. Maybe it wasn't a monster. Maybe it was just the tide or something."

"I dunno. My feet hurt. Let's sit on that rock. It's far enough from the cliff."

A wave of exhaustion hit Elsie. They limped over to the pitted limestone rock and sank onto it. Reggie scratched his leg and examined the blood gathered under his fingernails with a look of surprise. He rubbed his eyes, smearing dirt across his already grubby face. The water glinted in the moonlight. The moon was down to the treeline, and they'd lose its light soon. The stars were bright in the warm tropical night so it wouldn't be dark even after the moon set. Elsie watched the moon and wished to be somewhere safer than in the middle of the wilderness on a rock high above a deep lake that might have a monster in it.

***

An owl hooted nearby, hunting for prey in the thick coppet. Clara jumped at the noise. Irene sighed. The woman was afraid of her own shadow, not just the ones cast by denizens of the wilderness. She wondered again why Clara had insisted on coming to search for her children. From what the children had told her about Clara's treatment, the Englishwoman didn't seem to care much about them. Searching the coppet at night for lost children seemed out of character for her. She certainly wasn't dressed for it, and Irene had to bite her tongue as she heard Clara stumble for about the hundredth time. Clara looked determined but miserable. Irene guessed that this did not appear to be high on her preferred activities for an evening. Irene stifled a chuckle, silently berating herself for laughing at the woman's expense.

Clara finally spoke up, out of breath. "Irene, I beg your pardon, but where are we going exactly?"

Irene shrugged. "Johnny is taking us to de places where he played with Elsie and Reggie. Maybe they ended up in one of those spots."

"Oh. That makes sense. How many more spots are we going to look at?"

Irene glanced over at Johnny. Despite the lateness of the hour, he looked wide awake, excited. The flames from their torch bottles burned high in the still air under the canopy. The tang of burning kerosene tickled her throat. "Johnny, where to next?"

Her nephew twisted his mouth in disgust. "I thought for sure they'd be here. We climb this big old tree all the time. See how big de branches are? They could have rested here and waited for us."

Alice clicked her tongue and raised her flamper higher. "Looks like de brush has been trampled right around here by more than a few kids."

Johnny opened his eyes wide and pointed at the ground. "Yes, Muma, they did come here! And I bet those men did too. Aw, they trampled on my favourite flowers."

Irene frowned and looked around in the undergrowth of the dark coppet. The mahogany tree soared high above her head, its lower trunk entwined with a flowering vine. She sniffed at the rich scent of vanilla wafting from its crushed flowers "I don't see not'ing odd. Except maybe those tracks." She pointed to large bird tracks. "They're kinda big. Chickcharney been here. But I don't think those men found Elsie and Reggie. No sign of a struggle. Let's move on, folks. Where else can we look, Johnny?"

He stole a sideways glance at her, looking furtive. "We ain't been to Lug Hole yet."

Alice groaned and grabbed her son's arm. "Lug Hole? Why would we go there? Boo, don't tell me you play out at Lug Hole. I thought you told me you didn't get near it."

Johnny dropped his head, seemingly to escape the adults' accusing gazes. He nodded. "Not much but we been out there a time or two."

Irene exhaled with a whoosh. "Boy, we told you how many times not to go out there? It not safe. The cliffs are steep and that water deeper than you know."

Johnny didn't raise his head. "We didn't get in the water or not'ing. Just looked around. The Lusca didn't come."

Alice hissed and leaned into Johnny, forcing him to look at her. "Don't say that name out here, especially at night. That's when she strongest."

The owl hooted again, startling the searchers. Clara's voice quavered as she spoke up. "I see them. There's water nearby. Dark water. Not the ocean. Trees all around. Bright rock."

They all stared at her. Patience wearing thin, Irene took a deep breath. "How do you know? You having the Sight?"

Clara stood gazing into the coppet, her eyes unfocused. "Yes. I can see them. They're next to the water. It's very dark."

"Could be Lug Hole. We don't much go out there. The ole storees say there all manner of creatures living in Lug Hole. One creature in particular." She exchanged glances with Alice.

Alice shook her head. "Vision or no, we don't go to Lug Hole. It too dangerous."

Clara shook her head and blinked, turning to Irene. "Ole storees? Is that what you call your people's folklore? The stories you tell your children?"

Irene twisted her mouth in response and shrugged.

Johnny piped up. "Aunty Irene tells us all the ole storees and what to watch for out here in the coppet. Mr. Sharp, de Chickcharney, de Little Red Men, de Lu—" He cut off at his mother's stern look.

Clara scanned the faces around here. "So are these real creatures or are they just stories? We tell our children fairy tales about golden geese and sleeping princesses, but they're fantasies, not real."

Irene harrumphed. "Stories can be truths or lessons."

Clara wiped sweat from her forehead and peered into the dark forest. "My children are lost somewhere out here and now you tell me there might be some kind of monster? We're wasting time, standing around chatting. Let's get moving. Which way to Lug Hole from here, Johnny?"

Irene hid her smile. So she did care for those children. Johnny pointed out the way and they continued their trek.

CHAPTER THIRTY-FIVE

The moon set, leaving them with only the light of their torch bottles and starlight to see by. The wick of Clara's bottle sputtered and the flame died. She bit her lip and willed herself not to shriek at the encroaching darkness. She thought her little toes were broken, they felt so crushed in her pointed boots. "How much further?" She hoped her voice wouldn't betray her concern but suspected what Irene must think of her. The woman had been choking back sighs and scoldings ever since they'd left her family's yard.

Irene looked back over her shoulder at Clara, then at her nephew forging ahead of the group. "Johnny, we near yet?"

"I think so. See that clearing up ahead? I think that it."

The trees parted, revealing a flat expanse of rock. Dark water glinted below. Alice slowed her stride and paused. She hunched her shoulders high. Clara peeped at her and was surprised by the look of fear on the islander's face. Alice seemed to really believe there was something monstrous here. Clara looked ahead. The deep, round lake was still, the water calm and clear. It didn't look particularly ominous. She stepped around Alice, who had stopped. Clara searched the shore of the lake, hoping to see her children. She didn't know how much longer she could walk but knew she had to keep going until she found them.

Johnny spotted them first and yelled, "There they are! Over there! Elsie! Reggie!"

He charged across the cliff towards what looked like two stirring lumps of fabric on a rocky outcropping near the edge of the lake. It was them. Clara's heart skipped a beat and she moaned. "Oh, thank God." She trotted towards the children as quickly as her boots and aching feet would allow, calling out their names as she ran.

The children sat up, rubbing sleep out of their eyes. They blinked like owls at the people racing towards them. Clara reached them first and scooped them into her arms. Dimly, she realised that the other women hadn't kept up with her. Johnny stood back, trying to peer over the side of the cliff without getting close.

Clara's voice shook. "Darlings, are you all right? I was so worried. My poor loves, lost in the woods."

Elsie murmured something incoherent and pulled away, but Reggie burst into tears and clung to his mother. Clara tenderly wiped the tears from his cheeks and kissed his forehead.

"Reginald, darling, are you alright? You look exhausted and you're absolutely filthy." She reached a hand out to Elsie who sat next to her on the ground, blinking away sleep. "Elsinoe, my love, can you speak? Are you hurt?"

"No, mama, just tired. I thought...I thought you had left Andros."

Clara's mouth dropped open then she shut it again with a clack. She shook her head and her bedraggled curls dragged across her damp cheek. "You thought I had left the island? Without you? I would never have abandoned

The Cultist's Wife

you. I've been waiting at Drigg's Hill for an opportunity to save you from those horrible people."

She leaned forward and caressed Elsie's hair, smoothing down the tangles.

The girl stared at her, eyes wide. She took Clara's hand in hers. "You're really here? Oh, Mama, you're really here." Tears trickled down her face, leaving rivulets in the dirt encrusted there.

Clara nodded in response, her eyes full of unshed tears. "I told you I would come back for you, don't you remember?"

Reggie popped his head up, his eyes swollen and his face red with tears. "See, Elsie, told you Mama would come back for us. That's why I caught that fish."

Elsie and Clara turned their heads towards Reggie simultaneously. Clara was befuddled. "Fish? What fish?"

Alice called to them from the trees. Clara glanced in her direction. Irene and Alice hadn't come to the cliff's edge with Clara. Alice looked ill-at-ease and cast anxious looks at the water. "Johnny, you get back over here. And the rest of you ought to get away from that water. Now."

Her voice quavered, and Clara wondered again why the islander seemed so afraid. One glance at the lake told Clara what was frightening her.

The surface of Lug Hole was bubbling.

Clara slowly rose to her feet, transfixed by the water's movement. "Children. Can you stand? We need to move away from the cliff's edge. Something's happening down there."

Elsie and Reggie stood up, groaning, and Elsie peeked over the side. "Oh, it's those same bubbles and waves we saw earlier. In a bit, it'll turn into a whirlpool. We thought it was a monster but I think it has something to do with the tide."

Clara took hold of Elsie's arm and tried to drag her away from the cliff. "Elsinoe, please. Whatever is in that lake is frightening Alice very badly. We need to move away from it."

A tiny smile hovered around Elsie's mouth. "I know Alice is scared of Lug Hole. She thinks there's a monster living in there. But, Mama, look, there's nothing there except water. See, it's just a whirlpool. There's nothing to be afraid of."

Clara frowned, a crease appearing between her eyebrows. She took a closer look at the water. She didn't see anything that looked like a monster or even a large fish. The whirling water was empty. "Elsinoe, I believe you're correct. There doesn't appear to be a creature in the water."

Johnny huffed out a breath. "I been trying to tell Muma that for ages, but she won't ever listen to me. She and Aunty Irene just tell me to stay away from here."

Clara pursed her lips and eyed the little boy with a stern look. "Johnny, there may be no monster in this lake but it's certainly too dangerous to play here. Irene is right. The cliff is quite high, and the water appears to be deep. If that is indeed the tide, you could get sucked under water and drowned."

Johnny pouted. He peeked at his mother and aunt. They had moved closer, trepidation making Alice's body stiff.

Irene cast a look into the depths of Lug Hole. "See Alice, there nothing in that water. I know plenty of monsters. They just don't live down in that hole."

Clara felt the blood drain from her face. She knew of monsters also. Monsters that looked charming and handsome, then asked unspeakable things of you. She gulped down a lump of tears in her throat. "It's almost dawn. We ought to go back to Drigg's Hill. I want to get off this island as soon as I can."

A pale figure materialised on the edge of the cliff, frowning and pointing to something behind Clara.

Elsie gasped. "Horace? But you're dead."

She stepped towards the apparition but Clara restrained her. "No, don't go closer to the cliff. He's trying to warn us about something."

"You can see him too, Mama?"

Clara quirked her mouth. Despite all that Ward had put her through, her powers had grown. But the ghost grew more distressed as they stood watching him. Clara turned to where he was pointing and Stephen stepped out of the undergrowth. Clara's heart thudded. He must have followed them during their search for the children.

"I thought we chased you off, but you're back, causing trouble." His face contorted into a snarl. "You're not welcome here. But don't worry, Clara, I can help you get off the island. Through that hole." He lunged forward and grabbed Clara's arms. She screamed, her throat tight with fear. He drew her back against his body and dragged her towards the lake. Horace's ghost disappeared. Clara swayed in his grip, her legs weak, but Stephen held her tight. He inched them closer to the cliff's edge. Her heart pounded. She couldn't breathe. Her boot caught the edge and rocks crumbled into the water. She struggled against his powerful grip. Stephen was too strong. He was going to throw her into the water, and she couldn't stop it.

"Let my mama go!"

Clara looked down. Elsie yanked Stephen's arm, trying to break his grip on Clara. They teetered on the edge of the cliff. He grimaced and kicked out at Elsie. She squealed in pain but didn't let go. Clara kicked back and hit Stephen's knee with the heel of her boot. He grunted with pain and let go of Clara. She collapsed to her knees and grabbed Elsie, pulling her away from Stephen. He lost his balance and he plunged over the edge. He screamed for long seconds before hitting the water with a huge splash. Clara peered over the side and saw the familiar bubbles rise in the water. There was no sign of Stephen. He was gone, pulled under. She shuddered, blinking back tears, and gathered Elsie into her arms. "Are you hurt, dearest?" Elsie shook her head and snuggled against Clara. Reggie threw himself on Clara, whimpering.

Irene crouched down in front of them. "You alright? That Stephen almost tossed you in. I couldn't get here fast enough to help. Good thing you got your Elsie."

Bile rose in Clara's throat. She looked up at Irene. "I caused him to drown. I killed him."

Irene shook her head. "No, he did that to himself, Clara. You didn't toss him in. He tripped. Weren't no fault of yours." She straightened and reached a hand down to help Clara up. "We best be moving. You need to get off the island."

Alice spoke up, her voice shaky. "There's no mailboat today. We can hide you in our yard until the next one comes."

Irene shook her head. "No, I don't think they ought to stay." She frowned at Clara. "I can find you a boat down to Congo Town. You can wait there for the mail boat. Someone's gonna come looking for that man. Best if you were gone from Drigg's Hill today.'"

Clara clasped Irene's hand. The women exchanged wary looks. "Yes, I agree. We need to get as far away as we can this morning."

The little group shuffled out of the clearing. The light from their torch bottles sputtered and flickered but the flames continued to burn, weak against the approaching dawn.

CHAPTER THIRTY-SIX

Dawn in the coppet arrived with the chittering and squawking of birds. Johnny led the weary party out of the trees and onto the Queen's Road. Clara heaved a sigh of relief and muttered something, possibly a prayer. Irene felt like offering up a prayer of her own after the night's ordeal, but it was best to wait until she got home. Once she got these folks safe and off her island, she could spend some time in giving thanks.

The dark forest retreated behind them, broad round leaves waving goodbye from dangling branches. The group crawled along, adults hampered by drooping children. Reggie had fallen asleep in Alice's arms. Clara darted looks at the pair. The interaction amused Irene. Her sister seemed better at mothering than the little Englishwoman. Their life in England was probably a lot different than life on the islands. Irene had heard that the rich English people actually hired people to raise their children rather than do it themselves. After seeing Clara's manner to her children, she could believe that.

Johnny guided them out of the coppet and near Drigg's Hill. He and Alice stopped, ready to head to their yard. The boy's face drooped with sadness as he said goodbye to his friends. Irene realised with a start that he would never see them again. Alice lowered a sleepy Reggie to the ground. She wept as she brushed the hair out of his eyes. Irene was eager to get the foreigners off her island, but she hadn't considered how that would affect her family. They had all grown fond of Elsie and Reggie.

Alice and Johnny called goodbyes and the diminished group walked into Drigg's Hill. The settlement was quiet with no one else awake to see the sun rise over the water. The ocean glowed like an aquamarine, dazzling Irene's eyes. The white sand and grey rocks of the harbour were soft in the morning light. Irene relaxed a little, enjoying the beauty of her home.

Clara's voice broke into her reverie, an edge of panic to it. "You said there's no mailboat today, Irene. How are we going to get to Nassau?"

Irene pointed to one of the sponging boats tied to the dock. Its captain hauled up the mast and tied it, then the dingy white sail unfurled. "No mailboat today. Don't you worry. See that boat? I know the captain. That's my husband. I'll ask him to take you down to Congo Town. You can pick up the mailboat from there."

"Your husband? But won't it be an imposition?"

Irene laughed. "Offer him some gold and he'll do it."

They drew closer and the sponging boat captain scanned the approaching group. His face split with a grin. "Good morning, Reenie. I wasn't expecting you to meet me. Why you out at de harbour so early?"

"Welcome home, Alec. We just had a bit of an adventure. Can you do a little t'ing for my frens here? I need you to head down to Congo Town with de morning tide."

Alec cocked his head to one side and threw an appraising look at Clara and the children. "These your frens now, Reenie? I'd like to hear a bit more 'bout this adventure. Why not wait for de mailboat?"

Clara cleared her throat and stepped forward past Irene. "Captain, we need to leave immediately. I can pay you in gold. Please."

Alec guffawed. "You not de usual sort I ferry around. My boat is no fancy steamship."

Irene shook her head. She knew Clara didn't need anything grand. The woman was desperate to leave Andros and Irene was going to help her. "Alec, stop your teasing. De woman needs to get to Congo Town and she can pay you."

The man held up his hands in surrender. He tried to hide a smile, but Irene spotted it. She put her hands on her hips and glared.

Alec ducked his head. "Okay, okay, I'll take her and de chillun down to Congo Town. We can leave as soon as de tide turns. About a half hour. Gotta get these sponges unloaded first."

Irene's face softened. "I'll be glad when you're home later on." They exchanged warm smiles, familiar and comfortable.

Irene turned to the Cookes. The dull ache that grew in her chest surprised her. Alice and Johnny's sadness at saying goodbye didn't seem so strange after all. She would miss little Elsie coming to her with her troubles and she would miss tutting at Reggie and Johnny's antics and tending to their scrapes and bruises. She swallowed the lump in the throat. "Well, time for me to say goodbye. I hope you get home with no more troubles."

Reggie and Elsie wrapped their arms around her hips, squeezing tightly. They mumbled their farewells into her skirt then pulled away, their faces red and damp.

Clara held her hand out to shake Irene's. "Goodbye, Irene. Thank you so much for your assistance. I deeply appreciate everything you have done for myself and my children." She paused, scrutinising Irene's face as if she were trying to memorise it. "Be well."

Irene pursed her mouth and nodded. She pivoted and strode away, not looking back.

I should be glad to be getting rid of those folks. They've been nothing but trouble.

She felt their stares on the back of her neck until she reached a curve in the road, then heaved a sigh of relief and sadness.

I need some sleep, then I'll feel better.

Her yard was a few minutes' walk but her weary legs felt every second of it. When she rounded a bend, her yard came into view and she paused. A group of white people were gathered around her gate. Her body tensed. She couldn't see them clearly, but it had to be folks from the Order. They were probably looking for Elsie and Reggie still. Maybe had questions about that Stephen.

More trouble. I thought I was done with that, at least for today.

She stalked closer, glaring at the interlopers. She recognized Ward, standing amongst some of his people, and an older woman who reminded her of that Lydia. With a start, she realised that it actually was Lydia.

Irene called out. "Ward, what you and your folks doing at my gate? You not welcome here."

The sun rose above the trees and Irene could see that Ward's hair appeared more white than blond. New wrinkles cut across his face. The latest batch of burlup he had insisted on had contained no ogologo-ndu sponge. The cultists were ageing again. It had happened faster than Irene had expected.

Ward scowled. "Irene, we are here to collect some of our people. We were told that they were sheltering here. Bring them out and we'll leave peacefully."

Irene exhaled, hissing. "I don't know what you talking about. I's not sheltering anyone here but my own family, so you all can get out of here now."

Lydia sneered at Irene. The white woman's face had become deeply lined since Irene had seen her last. Grey streaks had appeared in her red hair. Irene wondered how old she really was. "She's lying, Ward. I know they're here. Where else could they be? We've searched everywhere else and that fellow who calls himself an elder told us to come here."

A man with Elsie's blue eyes stepped forward. "Please, we're here to collect my children. Their mother kidnapped them from our compound."

Irene cocked her head and frowned. So this was Clara's husband.

Ward tried his ingratiating smile on Irene, but she remembered his trick and steeled herself to resist. "Why would you want to be involved in our internal squabbles, Irene? Just send the Cooke children out and we'll be on our way."

In return, Irene bared her teeth in a mock smile. "I told you once and I'll tell you again, no one's here but my own family. Now as I see you this morning, it seems my burlup isn't working for you no more. I don't believe that I will be wasting it on you. That means you have no more business with me. You all need to get going."

Ward winced at her words. Lydia glowered her response.

He held up a hand. "I recognize that I rushed you on that last batch and so perhaps it didn't have its full potency. I am willing to wait for a more potent batch. I won't ask for our payment to be returned for the weak potion."

Irene raised her eyebrow. The man sure was bold. "Nothing wrong with that last batch. Elders did fine with it," she lied. "It just not working for you. I guess you been taking it too long. No sense in you wasting your gold and me wasting my burlup. Don't bother asking for more."

With that, she pushed past the sputtering Ward and sauntered into her yard.

Lydia held out a trembling hand towards Irene. "Please, I need that potion..."

Irene shook her head. "I told you, I's not wasting it on you. Now get out of here and don't let me catch you hanging around me or mine."

She slammed the rickety wooden gate and stared at the group until they drifted away. Irene heaved a sigh. Once she told the elders that she wasn't providing Ogologo-ndu to the white people, they would probably sell her the land she wanted, and her men could be home more. Her family would be safe from the sea. She allowed herself a smile before trudging off to her well-earned bed.

CHAPTER THIRTY-SEVEN

The rising sun breached the top of the trees behind Drigg's Hill, its rays promising a hot day. A brisk breeze off the ocean lifted wisps of Clara's hair. She took a shaky breath to calm herself. Soon they'd be gone from this place, leaving its nightmares behind. Her boots clattered on the wooden planks of the pier as she and the children headed to the boat that would take them away. Elsie stumbled and Clara grabbed at the girl to keep her from falling.

"I'm so tired, Mama."

Clara reached out a gentle hand to smooth the child's tangled hair. "I know, my darling. It's only a little further and we'll be on the boat. It'll take us a few hours to get to Congo Town and you can sleep the whole way."

Reggie tightened his sweaty grip on Clara's hand but said nothing. The boy was practically asleep on his feet.

The captain of their escape route popped up from below the deck of his boat as they approached. "You ready to board? Tide be turning in about five minutes or so."

Clara smiled, relief washing over her. Images of her home and her parents flashed through her mind. She would return to England changed, able to finally grasp at happiness, without Theophilus oppressing her and belittling her every move.

As if summoned by her thought, Theo's voice echoed across the harbour. "Clara! Stop!"

She jerked to a stop and turned, her body quaking. Theo paced towards her from the end of the pier, Ward and Lydia marching alongside him. As they drew closer, she could see their expressions more clearly. They looked like stern constables, coming to arrest her for her transgressions. The children drew closer to her, and she took a firm hold on their hands.

The group closed the distance and Theo approached, standing too close to Clara and looming over her. "Where do you think you're taking the children?" His voice was deep and menacing, matching his ferocious scowl.

Clara flinched, half-expecting him to strike her. She raised her chin and looked up at him, willing her voice not to shake. "I'm taking the children home."

He glowered down at her. "I didn't give you permission to take them away. They're staying here with me."

Elsie sobbed and threw her arms around Clara's waist, pressing her face against her. "Mama, please don't make us go back with him, please."

Reggie dropped Clara's hand and scooted behind her. His head pressed up against the small of her back. She was shackled in place with her children's bodies. Somehow the sensation was comforting.

Theo took hold of Elsie's arm but she tightened her grip on Clara. He growled, a frustrated exclamation. "The children must return to the compound with me. The law is on my side. You know that, Clara. No magistrate would allow an unfit, neglectful mother like you to retain control over these children."

Lydia spoke up, her sneering face a mass of new wrinkles. "Theo told me that you never wanted these children. Leave them here with their father and you'll be free. Free to live your life without the obligations of motherhood. Isn't that what you want? Freedom?"

Clara swayed on her feet, exhaustion humming through her body. Her children's arms encircled her, radiating heat. Freedom. All her life, she had wanted freedom but what did that really mean? Would she really be free if she cast off her children? What was truly tying her down? Her old life of esoteric study and occult society gatherings had been exactly what she wanted. Had her perceived bonds been her own creation? She closed her eyes for a moment and Theo must have taken the gesture as an assent. He and Ward rushed forward and snatched her children, pulling them off her body.

Elsie and Reggie shrieked in unison and Clara surged forward. "No!" She reached over Elsie's head and grabbed Theo's shirt with both hands. She tugged him close and looked up into his eyes. She bared her teeth at him with a hiss. "You. Will. Not. Take. My. Children."

Eyes wide in surprise from her vehemence, Theo let go of Elsie. The girl scuttled towards the boat, out of his reach. Clara turned to Ward and with a ferocity that shocked even her, slapped him across the cheek, the force jerking his head to one side. Ward tottered on his feet and moaned at the impact. She narrowed her eyes and spat out, "Release my son."

Reggie broke from the man's weakened grasp and scampered back to Elsie. Clara put her hands on her hips and drew a deep breath, thankful that her corset was loose. "Theophilus, you are a disgrace to fatherhood. You never bothered to make an attempt to parent our children. I don't know what you and these people believe will happen as a result of your perverse rituals and debauched lifestyle, but you will not do it at my children's expense. Elsinoe, Reginald, and I are getting on that boat and leaving now. I expect you to never contact me or my family again. We've had enough of your neglect and abuse. I may not have been a model mother but from this moment on, I will be a better parent than you ever were."

Theo scowled his response and wrapped his arm around Lydia's waist. Ward looked from Theo to Clara. His pursed mouth surrounded by white bristles reminded her of a sea anemone. He waved his hand in Clara's direction. "Theo? Are you simply giving up?" His voice wavered like an elderly man. "We can't let these children leave. We need them."

Theo shrugged helplessly. "Do we really? The blood experiments aren't working. You and Lydia are still ageing."

Blood experiments? In a flash, Clara realised why the Order was so intent on keeping her children. They weren't merely a source of free labour. They were a source of blood. Bile rose in her throat. She drew back, her lip curled. "You sicken me. You're even more depraved than I thought. Goodbye, Theophilus."

She turned on her heel and marched towards the sponging boat, catching her children's hands as she passed them. The trio clambered aboard, the stink of rotting sponge barely registering to Clara. She threw a glance over her shoulder. Theo and his supposed friends stood on the pier, watching her departure with cold, flat eyes.

She turned and smiled at the captain. He jerked his head towards the people on the dock. "All ready to go then?"

Clara held her head high. "Yes, thank you, Captain Alec. My business here is done."

She reached into her reticule and pulled out a gold coin. It glinted in the sunlight as she handed it to Alec and she looked back, catching Theo's gaze, still watching her departure. She smirked at him.

Alec cast off the lines and the boat drifted for a moment, rocked by gentle waves. He ducked into the cabin and with a sputter, the engine started up. Clara's heart surged as the boat pulled away from the dock, leaving Theo and his nightmares behind. Elsie and Reggie drew close and leaned against her.

"Mama? We left Papa behind. How can we be a proper family without him?" Elsie said.

Clara leaned down to kiss her daughter's head. "We don't need him in order to be a proper family, darling. We got along well enough without him for five years. We're free now. We'll be perfectly happy."

The boat sailed on, rocking and bobbing in the water. Reginald curled up against Clara's hip. Elsinoe clung to her on the opposite side. Embracing both her children, Clara said a silent goodbye to Irene and her family at Drigg's

Hill, thanking them in her thoughts for their help, and wishing for their good fortune as Andros Island disappeared over the aquamarine horizon.

FIN

Acknowledgements

My eternal thanks to Aaron who supported me along the seemingly endless journey to completing this book. His keen ear for story and steadfast support were essential, not to mention the copious cups of tea he brewed to keep me going.

A shoutout to my cheerleading squad, Dover Whitecliff, Margaret Sikes, and Charlotte Sikes. Sorry there's not more tentacles.

I would also like to acknowledge the contributions of my beta reader Ariisa Tynes, who helped with Bahamaian language and culture, and my proofreader Allison Behrens for catching all those niggly errors that I missed.

This book was inspired by my experiences as a young immigrant. The details and events are all fictional, but the feeling of losing home and entering a strange new world is true.

About the Author

BJ Sikes is a 5'6" ape descendant who is inordinately fond of a good strong cup of tea, Doc Marten boots, and fancy dress. I live with one large cat, two sweet teenagers, and one editor-author, plus an array of chickens in a place very unlike my homeland.. My fave genre is historical fantasy with a focus on women finding themselves.

After writing a dissertation on avocado root rot, I was drawn back to her first love, fiction. My debut novel, *the Archimedean Heart*, is the first book in the Roboticist of Versailles world, a French Belle Epoque that never was. *The Vitruvian Mask* is the second full novel set in that world. *The Cultist's Wife* is a departure from that story world but still features women trying to become independent.

Find me on social media at
Website: https://bjsikesauthor.com/
Goodreads: https://www.goodreads.com/bjsikesauthor
Instagram: https://www.instagram.com/bj_sikes_author/
Pinterest: @bjsikesauthor https://pin.it/7EMwHwD
Bookbub: https://www.bookbub.com/authors/bj-sikes